dependent

a novel

brenda
corey
dunne

For my husband: my life, my soul mate, my friend.
And
For the surviving spouses and family members
of those who lost their lives on duty
Rescue 305 (1998) and Tusker 914 (2006)

That Others May Live

(From Air Force Administrative Regulation, 025.33 (A), Definitions.)

For administrative purposes the title "Dependent" shall refer to:

i. The member's legal spouse* who resides with the member at the post for a minimum of eight(8) months in a twelve(12)-month period, but does not include such persons when they are living separately from the member for other than official Air Force reasons;

ii. The member's dependent child*;

iii. The member's special dependent as determined by the unit commanding officer*.

*see section 025.44 (B) for supportive documentation required.

CHAPTER 1
HOUSE #13

May 15, 2008

BUDDY IS BARKING.

The heat of the day has changed to cold rain, and Buddy is barking at the door.

There is a man at the door.

I won't see him. He won't be there if I don't look.

Don't look. Don't look. Don't.

Oh, God! Don't look at him!

The doorbell is ringing. I can see a shadow waiting outside the door. Buddy is barking, and I see the man standing there in the dark, cold rain. I know the man. I know that I don't want that man to come in. There are more men behind him, looking from behind and yet not looking—not wanting to see me standing here. The man looks at me and then looks down. His face is drawn and wet. I see the look on his face.

Don't look.

I see that he doesn't want to be here. The rain is hitting the kitchen window and the man is standing there, wet, asking to come in. I know he doesn't want to come in. Somewhere, within me the ache is beginning. The ache that I don't want to feel.

"No."

I will not open that door. Buddy barks again.

"Mrs. Michaels?" The wind tries to steal his voice away, like it tries to steal his hat. I hear it even though I don't want to.

"No." I whisper to the wind.

"Mrs. Michaels, may I come in?" He is trying to speak kindly. What that man has to say is not kind. I will not let him in.

Buddy barks once more and then whines expectantly. The man has a kind voice.

The man has a uniform on. His medals shine in the rain. There are other uniformed men behind him. The man is John's boss.

"Mrs. Michaels?"

My feet are walking toward the door. Each step is like stepping on shards of glass. Slowly and painfully I walk toward the man at the door. My mind whispers—*don't let him in!* I reach for the lock as Buddy whines beside me. I won't look at this man...but my eyes see without wanting to look. I can see a war on his face. I can see his face fighting for control. I know he is looking for the words to say what he doesn't want to say. I know that he is there to tell me what I don't want to hear. A hand that can't be mine reaches for the handle. My face is wooden. I won't let them in.

But I do.

The man comes in, and three more behind him. The wind, spiteful and wicked, pushes them through the door. They are dripping and dark. Their uniforms smell of wet wool and their shiny shoes are flecked with mud. Buddy wags his tail but stays beside me. He knows that something is not right. The men are not dangerous, but neither are they safe as they stand there, dripping on the tiles, looking at me with pain and compassion. I don't want them to be here.

Please, go away.

"Mrs. Michaels, may we come in and sit down?" Says John's dripping boss.

I look at him. I feel the war he feels. I do not want you to come in and sit down, I think. Go away. Scram! Leave!

I hear my voice say yes.

The man takes off his wet hat and wet coat. We stand there awkwardly as he looks for somewhere to put it, and the wet wool drips on the floor. "May I put my coat in the closet?" He asks.

I hear my voice say yes again. My mind screams *No!*

Somehow the men get their wet, dripping clothes into my quiet, dry closet. They slip their shoes off and leave them on the mat. The hot, accusing sun from this morning has gone, and now rain pelts the window, fighting to get in. Buddy stays by my side. My hand reaches down to touch his warm, golden fur. A protective growl vibrates deep within the warmth. I walk into our living room. A magazine sits on the couch. My wooden hand picks it up and places it on the coffee table. I sit without thinking, and the man sits across from me. The other men look around and, finding nowhere to sit, they stand.

John's Boss clears his throat. "Mrs. Michaels...Ellen...May I call you Ellen?"

No you may not call me Ellen. Please don't call me Ellen. Go away!

The voice that is not mine says yes.

"Ellen, I'm afraid I am the bearer of some bad news."

Don't say it. Don't.

I will my eyes to look at him. I will them to harden. I will not let this man take away my dignity. I will not let my eyes betray me. I look into his eyes, and I can see his eyes begging to make this easy. His eyes are asking me to do what I cannot. I know what he is going to say; it will not be easy. Go away, John's boss.

"Ellen, do you remember who I am?" He asks awkwardly. "My name is Evan Connors. I work with John."

You don't work with John, I think. John works for you. John does what you tell him to do. This will not be easy for you, John's boss. My hard eyes stare back at him.

"This is Colonel Joe McMann, Reverend Don Lawrence, and Major Bob Saunders. Col McMann is the Base Commander, Reverend Lawrence is the Base Chaplain, and Major Saunders works with John...with me." More awkwardness. Bob Saunders is one of John's best friends. Of course I know him. I look briefly at Bob. His eyes are strained and red. I look away from his eyes. The ache threatens to take me away. No!

"Ellen... there's been an accident."

No! No, no, NO!

Go away, John's boss!

I look at the carpet, away from his eyes. Don't say it. Don't! The rain hits the windows. Bob's feet are across from me. His socks are wet on the toes. I see him shift his weight on the carpet—left foot, right foot, left foot, right foot.

My lips press together in a fight for control. Oh, God. I know what John's boss is going to say, and I won't let him say it. I want this man to hurt for what he is going to say. My mind searches for a way to get away from this man's words.

"Is... he... alive?" My voice is dead, robotic. "Is John alive?" I look at this man's face, forcing him to say it.

"Ellen..." I can see how uncomfortable he is. His ears are red, and a bead of sweat—or is it rain?—sits on his forehead. Let him be uncomfortable. Every muscle in my body is fighting for control. My hands are clenched, the fingernails biting into my palms.

"Is..." The rain is pounding on the window behind me. "...He..." This cannot possibly be happening. "...Alive?" I will not let this man win.

I look up at his face and the question dissolves. I know.

"I'm sorry."

The ache swallows me. My life is gone.

CHAPTER 2
HOUSE #1

October, 1982

THE TRANSFER COMES IN THE door with a goofy grin on his face and a haircut that can mean only one thing: military kid. No local would cut his hair that short. Nor would they swagger quite so cockily. This kid has confidence to burn.

He hands the teacher the little slip of paper that explains his presence, and Mr. Brown nods, gesturing with a flick of his hand that the kid should sit. He scans the room, and I look down, hoping he won't come and sit next to me, because I want absolutely nothing to do with him.

I pretend to study my textbook, and cover my face with my hair. Look down, and he won't see me. La la la, I'm not here and there's no seat open beside me either, flyboy.

I hear his footsteps coming down my aisle, and I know I'm doomed. He flops into the chair beside me, scraping it on the floor with an obnoxious squeal. In the confined space of the two-person table, it's impossible not to smell the gum he is chewing.

Seriously? Gum is outlawed in schools everywhere. Troublemaker. I stare even harder at my textbook.

"Hey, Beautiful," he leans over and whispers into my ear, "I'm John."

Yup, definitely chewing gum.

I have no choice but to look up, and what I see both impresses and annoys me. Impresses because he is handsome beyond anything I've ever seen at this second-rate high school—well at least since Paul, my ex—and annoying because I have no time for this guy. No time at all.

I've made a pact with myself to stay single and stay sober— well, as sober as I can—for the year. I've got to get straight A's. I need that scholarship. Four years of nursing school is more than my parents can afford, even if they wanted me to be a nurse. Flyboy beside me is just bad news.

"The socially acceptable reply would be to tell me your name, now…" he whispers as I gawk at him like a slack-mouthed fish. He oozes confidence. "My name is…" he prompts.

I shake my head and glare, "Ellen. My name is Ellen." Then I turn and face the front and try to focus on Mr. Brown's incredibly boring lecture on the wonders of the sine curve.

"Nice to meet you, Ellen." His whispering breath tickles the hairs around my ear. I swear he's drenched himself in mating hormones because just about every nerve in my body is screaming to turn to him and say something alluring. Something sexy.

No! Sine curve. Cosine. Tangent. La, la, la, I'm not listening to gorgeous, bad news military brats today.

He opens up his notebook and begins to write in it. I relax, just a bit, glad that he's paying attention to the lecture and not to me. His pencil scratches on his page as Mr. Brown's chalk does so on the board. I try to follow Mr. Brown's logic, but nothing at all sinks in, and so I simply copy his squiggles into my notes, squiggle for squiggle, until John's elbow touches my chest. He slides his notebook over into my field of view.

Instead of writing notes on the class, he's drawn an incredibly accurate sketch of two people sitting in a movie theatre, eating popcorn. On the screen in front of them are written the words—"Ellen, would you do me the honour of accompanying me to the movies tonight?"

Huh? I read it again, not believing what my eyes are reading, and then turn and look at him with what I'm sure is an even more fish-like stare of disbelief. Are you serious? This guy, who I met what—five minutes ago?—is asking me on a date? He grins and nods, his eyebrows raised.

Of course, it's at this very moment that Mr. Brown chooses to ask me a question. A question which I'm sure I could have answered had I actually been listening.

"Miss McKinley. It would do you much more good to pay attention to the lecture, than to play googly-eyes with Mr. Michaels. Perhaps Mr. Michaels could answer?"

John grins at me and then turns to the board. "They are equal. The area above zero is equal to the area below it."

"Excellent." When Mr. Brown turns away John winks.

My face balloons into a red ball of embarrassed flame. I'm furious, both at him, for sitting beside me and distracting me from the lecture, and at myself, for allowing myself to be sucked in by a stupid, slimy military jerk so easily. Stupid, vile, gorgeous, conceited, rich bastard! Show-off! Asshole.

I refuse to look at him again, and spend my time mentally constructing the rudest, most derogatory insults I can. I learn absolutely nothing as the clock slowly ticks off time.

"Sorry about that," he whispers into my ear just before the bell rings. "Can I buy you a Coke to make up for it at lunch?" I stare straight ahead, ignoring him and wishing he would disappear.

CHAPTER 3
HOUSE #13

May 15, 2008

JOHN'S BOSS LOOKS AWKWARDLY INTO my eyes, pleading silently for quiet acceptance. I will my face to not betray the chaos of my mind. I want to scream. I want to scratch at this man's desperate eyes. The wind howls at the window behind me, and I want to give myself up to the howling wind. My eyes burn and my forearms cramp, but I will not betray myself. Some part of my brain records the fact that Bob is holding a small black briefcase. All of these things happen in seconds, yet it feels to me as if time has stopped.

"I need you to leave."

Shock rolls across John's Boss' face. He expected tears. He expected wailing and screaming. His arms are poised for an expected comforting hug. He cannot compute the calm, hard creature in front of him. Awkward silence contrasts with the turmoil outside the window. Bob shifts his wet toes on the Persian carpet. The chaplain holds his forced smile. Mr. Base Commander clears his throat. He is used to expected results.

"Ellen, I'm not sure that's a good idea..." John's Boss uses his 'I'm in control' voice. "We have things to discuss. There are procedures to be followed."

"Take your procedures and leave. Now."

They have taken everything from me. I will have control in my own house. I will not relinquish it.

"Ellen. We cannot leave you alone," says John's Boss.

You already have.

"Take your procedures and get...out...of...my...house." My teeth are clenched. I put up my walls, and I look him directly in the eye. It takes all that is within me not to give in to his silent command. Unconsciously I pull in my resources, which are few. Buddy sits quietly at my feet and I am thankful for his presence. This is my house. This is my fortress.

A spark of anger flickers in his eyes. He wanted to play the martyred officer. The man who helped 'the wife'. This is not going at all as he planned. Has he forgotten that I have watched it happen to others? Does he not know I have feared this moment every day for the past twenty-five years?

Idiot. He and his Base Commander have done this before. I have not. He has no idea what I feel. I will not be forced into the role of the wailing wife. Not today. Not yet.

Mr. Base Commander decides to have a kick at the can. "Mrs. Michaels", he pulls himself up as if he is sitting behind his big, expensive desk, even though he is dripping on my big, expensive carpet. "Mrs. Michaels, we have appointed Major Saunders as your Assisting Officer. His job is to represent the Armed Forces and assist you in making all of the necessary..."

"Did you not hear me?" I interrupt forcefully. It is obvious that Mr. Base Commander is not getting his way in the playground. His face flushes a deep red. I register the fact that his shirt collar is too tight. His skin bulges over the sky blue edge. His hair is light brown. I couldn't handle this if his hair was salt-and-pepper dark.

"I asked you to leave. Get out of my house. NOW." I glance at Bob and acknowledge him. This is not easy for him either, I know.

Mr. Base Commander tries to compose himself and carefully chooses his next words. "It is our responsibility to see you through the process. This must be extremely difficult for you Mrs. Mich..."

Not waiting for him to finish his little speech, I get up and walk to the closet. I grab their sopping coats and hats and throw them into their hands. Mr. Base Commander's hat falls onto the carpet before he can react to the rapidly burning fuse of a 'dependent' in front of him. Buddy sticks to my side; unsure of what is going on. Extremely difficult, my ass.

15

I walk purposefully to the door, and swing it open. The wind and rain hit my face with a vengeance, stinging and tearing at the wall I've hastily constructed. I'm not sure how much more of this I can handle—men with golden shoulders who do nothing but take. Get out now, assholes!

One of last year's oak leaves blows through the door and sticks to the tiles.

Turning my back on the black abyss outside, I take a deep breath and face the disbelieving men in my living room. Only Bob still wears his compassion. The others—even the chaplain—stare at me like I'm an errant child. Their coats are still crumpled in their arms; their faces are red and stubborn. So is mine.

"Out."

"Mrs. Michaels!"

"Out!"

"But…we need to…"

"Get the Hell out of my house NOW!" I've had enough of this game.

Their eyes, big and angry, look at me like I am a deranged lunatic. Their mental checklists are not cleared and their procedures have not been followed. The wind whips my hair into my face. Maybe I am deranged. Red anger swells beneath my ribs. Empty grief claws at my heart. Malicious forces swirl around and through me, threatening to pull me down.

Mr. Base Commander walks to his shoes. John's Boss follows him, glaring with dagger sharp eyes. Bob's wet toes stand firm on the carpet. I look up at him, searching for an ally in the madness that is my house. His face is bathed in grief. I watch, confused, as a tear slips down his left cheek. My knees feel weak and my hands start to shake. Please go. Please, I beg him silently. Bob sees my armour slipping.

He quickly wipes his face and reaches into his pocket. The tears continue to stain his cheeks. Without looking away from me, he bends over and places a piece of paper on the coffee table.

"My phone numbers are there. Call me when you are ready." He is concerned. He knows that his number is on our fridge, yet he leaves the paper anyway.

I need to be alone.

Mr. Base Commander is dressed. He brushes the wet from his coat onto my floor. He reaches out to shake my hand. I don't reciprocate.

"Mrs. Michaels, Major Saunders will take care of all of the arrangements. Whether you want it or not, the base will help you in whatever way it can. We are extremely sorry for your loss. John was a good man."

If only you knew, I think. The grief threatens to choke me. I bite the inside of my cheek to keep my face still.

Desperate to get rid of them, I give in and shake, fighting to hold on to my dignity. His hand is wet and clammy. He squeezes my fingers tightly, trying to convey his sympathies in some way I will accept. I squash the urge to snap my hand away. I bite my cheek harder as he lets go and walks out the door.

"Thank you," is all I can say.

John's Boss shakes my hand as well. "Please, let us know if you need anything at all." I look into his eyes and see that there is more than just anger there. Guilt washes over me as I realize that he is hurting too. He gently squeezes my hand and walks out the door.

I turn and see that Bob is dressed for the storm. He stands in front of me, the tears flow unchecked down his cheeks. "Ellen, I am so sorry." He sniffs and looks up at the ceiling, searching for control. "I'll come back in two hours. I'll bring Beth." Beth, his wife, is one of my friends. "If you need us before, please call." I clench my hands, fighting frantically to hold on. Bob leans over and hugs me. I stand stiff and cold in the howling wind. He pulls away and runs down the front steps into the rain. As I push the door closed, Buddy licks my hand. I look down and see that the men have left muddy footprints on the doormat. Beside the doormat, just as he left them, sit John's sandals.

John's sandals. Never to be worn again.

A tornado of wind, rain, muddy footprints, and John's sandals buckles my knees. I sink to the floor as the grief washes over me, drowning hope.

I'm not sure how long I sit on the muddy entryway floor. When the waves of grief subside enough for me to be aware of my surroundings, I feel like a void ringed with pain. My thoughts congeal behind swollen eyes. Buddy has lain down beside me, his sad eyes searching my face. The wind screams behind my head through the crack around the door. Through fog and pain, I see that John's sandals still sit beside the door.

John's sandals. Never to be worn again.

Grief hits me hard and fresh, stealing my breath.

"No!" The word ricochets through the empty hall above me.

"God... *John!*" I sob to the darkness. My limbs curl, unbidden, into the fetal position, and I lay my head down, my cheek against the muddy footprints. "John, please..." I whisper to the sandals. Aching loneliness surrounds me.

The telephone begins to ring.

Tears spill to the floor, mixing with the muck. A pebble grinds into my cheek. *Ring*, goes the phone.

Through my floor-level sideways glance, I can see the receiver on the kitchen counter. *Ring*, it taunts me. I hate the phone, hate it with every fibre of my being. A vague thought sluggishly surfaces—I was supposed to call someone...

Ring.

From the office I hear the answering machine *click.* "Hello, you've reached John and Ellen's! We can't come to the phone right now, but leave us a message and we'll think about calling you back." John's cheerful voice echoes through the house.

"John..." I whisper to the cold tiles.

"Ellen? Ellen, are you there? It's Beth." Her voice is thick. She has been crying.

Leave me alone.

"I know you want to be alone, but we can't leave you there by yourself. It's 7:15 now. We'll be there by quarter to eight. Ellen..." She takes a deep, rasping breath. "We're so sorry." My own tears run unchecked. As I stare at the receiver, it blurs and sways like the stormy night beyond the door.

Someone will be here in half an hour. I am lying on my entryway floor. John is dead.

"I can't do this." The pebble underneath my cheek scrapes my face as I speak my sorrow. Why couldn't they just leave me alone? Why can't they see I need to be here alone? Damn the world! Damn it all! Leave me alone!

Yet, like so many times before, I know what I have to do. Like it or not, I have to do it. Only now, I have to do it by myself. David, Chris, and Maria need to know. I have to tell them myself, and before Bob and Beth return.

I crawl across the floor, wiping the tears, muck, and snot from my face. I feel like a wounded animal, a wounded mother bear. I reach up and grab the receiver from the counter, swinging around to sit on the floor with my back against the cupboards. I cradle the receiver in my lap, searching for the strength to make the first call. David and Chris first. They live together and can comfort one another. How can I tell them that their father is gone? I realize that, in my haste to be alone, I didn't even ask how John died. Maybe there's been some mistake. Maybe he's not dead.

But I know the procedure—the secrecy that surrounds these things. The phone calls, the paperwork, the damned procedures that have to be followed. The dependents are always the last to know. Whatever happened, they would have held it close to their chest, like children covering up a broken vase. Like grown men hiding a monster.

If only I'd…

I need to get my babies home.

Taking a ragged breath, I clear my throat and press the quick-dial button. God help me, I think as I wipe my nose with my shirtsleeve.

Ring.

I never thought I would have to do this.

Ring.

My breath catches as someone answers the phone.

"Hello?" It's Chris.

Why do I have to do this?

"Chris? It's mom." I put my hand over the receiver and sniff wetly.

"Hey, mom. What's up?"

I ignore his question. "Chris is David there?"

"Yah, he's in his room. Do you want to talk to him?"

"Could you go get him?" I can't even think of telling him without his older brother.

"Just a sec…DAVID! MOM'S ON THE PHONE!" Twenty-two years old, and he still hasn't learned to cover the receiver. "He's coming."

"Chris, could you put me on speaker phone? I need to talk to you both." God, give me strength, 'cause I don't think I can do this.

There's a click on the other line. "Hey, mom. We're both here now. What's up?" David asks.

I take one more cautious breath and steel myself before plunging in. "Boys, there's no easy way to tell you this." Another deep breath, willing myself not to fall apart.

"Mom, what? You're scaring me." David, I think.

"Your dad has been in an accident…"

"What?" "Is he okay?" Both boys speak at once.

"No… he's not okay. He… He's not okay…" My voice breaks. "I need you to come home. I…"

"Mom, there must be some mistake… He's probably just floating in a raft somewhere…Right?"

"Chris, I'm so sorry. Please…"

David interrupts, ever the control freak. "Mom! Tell us what's going on!"

"David, you and Chris need to come home. Dad is…Your dad is dead." The words sound harsh and cold, but there is no other way. John is gone.

The receiver is silent. The tears start afresh as I picture my boys' faces. I sniff and wipe my face, already raw from tears.

Chris speaks first. "Mom, are you sure? Are you absolutely posi…" His voice breaks.

"The Base Commander was just here." I sob. "I… I kicked them out before I they got the details." *Sniff.* "Bob Saunders is coming back in about half an hour. Boys, please? I'm so… I… need you." I choke back more tears.

"We'll… be there as soon as we can," Says David. His voice sounds hollow. So far away.

"I need to call Maria now. Can you pick her up? She'll need you." Maria is taking a university degree in the same town as the boys, but she opted to live in residence for her first year. I mentally calculate how long it will take them to get home. With packing and traffic it should take them at least two hours. Two hours alone with the details.

"But." Chris sniffs. "But where?"

"Please," I beg. "Please, just come home." My nose is running into my mouth. I don't even have the energy to care.

Not surprisingly, David takes control.

"Mom. We'll be right home."

I hear an anguished sob.

"'Kay," I squeak.

"Bye, mom."

I break the connection and a dial tone drones at me. Minutes pass as I stare across the floor and cry.

What have I done?

When the phone starts to beep angrily for being off of the hook for too long I come back to reality and hang up. More raw face; more sore, snotty nose. Everything around me seems sodden, dripping. I rasp in another deep breath and hit the speed dial button for Maria.

Ring.

Ring.

Ring.

"Hello, you've reached Maria's room. I might be studying… or not! Please leave a message!"

Why is this so hard?

"Maria, Honey? It's mom. I need you to call me right away." I try, unsuccessfully to hide the pain in my voice. "Please, it's an emergency. I'm home. Call me." I look at my watch as I hit the end button. It's 7:35. Bob and Beth will be at the door in ten minutes.

I put my head on my knees and wrap my arms around my legs. Buddy's tail thumps beside me and he licks my arm because he can't reach my face. I can't do this. I can't believe that John is dead. I don't *want* to believe that John is dead. How can he be dead? I want this to be a mistake. I want to wake up. Wake up! Wake up!

I don't wake up. I'm still here on the floor. I don't want Bob to come here and tell me how he died. I don't want to think about the 'arrangements'. I don't want to think at all. My brain is heavy and thick. Thinking brings back other things. Thinking hurts.

I can't let them see me like this. That one thought holds me afloat. Strange, really. The one time that I'm expected and allowed to show my emotions, and all I want to do is hide them. So many years of putting up with whatever is thrown at me has changed my outlook. I think of my mother, and her still face, accusing and expectant all at once. I can't let them see me like this. My mother pushes me from inside. Get up, Ellen. You made your bed, now you have to sleep in it.

I somehow manage to pull myself out of the pit and stand up. Trudging like an overburdened slave, I make my way up to the bedroom, hating and grieving all the way. In the bathroom I look into the mirror and see the red blotches and swollen eyes. I reach for a face cloth and soak it with cold water. My face covered with wet cloth, I sink down onto the toilet. I cannot let them see me like this.

The soothing cool is a welcome relief, but the tears start afresh. I can feel the hot tears melting into the cloth, warming it slowly.

If only I'd told him not to go! If only I'd said something, anything!

Get a grip on yourself, Ellen!

If only I'd said...

It's 7:43. I can't let them see me like this. I will the tears to stop. I *can't* let them see me like this.

I grasp the side of the sink and haul myself up and look in the mirror again. No changes there. Eyes still red. Face still blotchy. Damn my fair skin. Another gift from my mother. I abandon the cloth for splashing water from the tap. It seems futile, but it feels calming on my skin, and my nerves. Well, John, damn you for making me go through this. I honestly don't know how I'm going to maintain my composure in front of Bob and Beth's need to comfort. The doorbell rings just as the thought flutters through my mind. Buddy barks a happy bark. He knows whoever is at the door. Why can't they just leave me alone? Why can't I wake up?

Why?

I grab a tissue and wipe my nose, then the towel to wipe the rest of my face. A terse look over my appearance and a deep breath, then I'm walking down the stairs, trying to plaster my 'everything's okay here!' face on. I'm an actor in a cruel tragedy. I'm my mother. All happy outside, all *not* happy inside.

The stairs evaporate before me and I stand looking through the front door window at Bob and Beth. I feel lost in my own home, thick and detached. Bob and Beth look like they've been crying more than me; their faces are studies in concern and comfort and grief. Buddy whines happily at the door, oblivious.

"Buddy, lie down." I pull him away from the door and make him lie on the foyer rug. He eyes me sassily but does what I say. I take one deep breath, and, indifferent face on, let them in.

Beth rushes through the door and envelopes me in a huge embrace. "Oh, Ellen, I'm so sorry!" She whispers into my hair. The detached feeling remains and I murmur something placating like "It's alright" or "I'm okay." I see Bob looking down at us with solemn, caring eyes. I quickly look away; grief threatens to erode my façade. He has changed out of his uniform since he was last here. The socks are the same, though. The toes are still wet. His coat is dripping on the tiles. I don't want to see that either, so I look out the window at the storm that blew in this morning after my now-dead husband left for work…without my blessing or my goodbye.

Beth pulls back and holds my arms, forcing my gaze to meet hers. She's searching for my pain. I try to hide it, but my eyes are burning with spent tears.

"How are you doing?" she asks.

I'm almost sweating with the effort to seem impassive. Why would she ask me how I'm doing? My husband of more than twenty-five years is dead. It could be my fault. How does she think I'm doing?

"I'm fine." And I'm not ready to talk about it, I think.

Bob reaches in now, and takes me into his arms. I feel like a puppet. Grief is radiating from him. I don't want to feel it, yet I feel him shaking through his wet coat. Bob, who knows me. Bob who knows… He sniffs absently and backs away.

"I'm sorry," he says.

I can hear quiet suffering in his voice.

"I'm sorry about earlier, too." He says quietly.

God help me, I pray silently. I can't let them see.

"Can we sit down?" Bob asks.

"Oh, yes… just hang your things up in the closet…" I walk into the kitchen.

Beth bustles in behind me. "Do you mind if I make some coffee? I think we all could use it."

It takes me a few seconds to comprehend what she's asking. "Oh. The coffee's in the fridge." She glances at my face, but quickly turns away. My unspoken grief makes her uncomfortable. My mother would make coffee. I could use something stiffer than coffee.

Bob lays his briefcase on the table and pulls out a thick binder and manila folder. Without thinking I look at what's written on the folder:

Maj. John A. Michaels. May 15, 2008.

Today's date. John's Date of Death.

CHAPTER 4
HOUSE #1

June, 1983

THE AIR IN HIS FATHER'S station wagon is sticky. I can feel my legs adhering to the vinyl seats as John drives out of the subdivision. Even the air feels liquid as it flows through the open windows. It's crazy hot for early June. My hair blows into my eyes and sticks to my neck.

John smiles wickedly as he accelerates away from my house. His hand leaves the steering wheel to turn up the radio. Then he casually places it on my bare, sweaty thigh—just below the frayed edge of my cut-offs. The flapping wind and his searching fingers make me giddy. I like it. Too much. I push his hand down toward my knee.

His chuckle is lost in the wind as he turns onto the highway, spinning the tires in the roadside dirt.

"I thought we were going to the movie!" I yell through the fresh assault of wet wind. We are driving *away* from town.

He chuckles again. I can't hear him, but his hand vibrates on my thigh.

"Baby, I've got something else in mind," he grins.

There is no question what he has in mind. No question at all. But we've discussed this before. The answer is no. I lift his hand off my thigh and place it on the seat between us.

He glances at me as a semi-truck screams past us in the opposing lane. The station wagon drifts towards the shoulder.

"John! Look out!" I yell, my heart in my throat as the wagon bumps violently on the dirt.

He casually corrects and grins, eyes toward me again. Jerk. Sexy jerk.

"Scared?" He is incorrigible.

"No," I yell. "I *like* thinking I'm going to die!"

He crawls his fingers across the vinyl and back onto my thigh, but in a somewhat less distracting spot.

"Don't worry, babe. I'm in control."

"That's what I'm worried about," I say. I reach over and gently squeeze his sweat-dampened thigh. Two can play at that game. The effect is almost instantaneous.

A bead of sweat forms on his upper lip. He groans. My pinky strokes the inseam of his shorts. Perhaps no isn't the answer.

Two minutes later he flicks his indicator and turns onto a dirt road. It's almost dark, but he drives without lights. I hold onto the door handle as we bump through the tunnel of wide-limbed oaks and maples. Their shadows stare down at us and I shiver, from excitement and a hint of fear. We're like stupid kids driving the wrong way in a horror movie.

John grins at me like he hears my thoughts.

He brakes and pulls into a clearing, stopping beside a fence. A sign on the chain link warns: *Department of National Defence. No Trespassing.* My ears are still ringing from the howl of the wind through the windows. In front of us a metal tower stands, a flashing red light strobes from its peak high above us. It looks like a radio tower or an airport beacon or something super-secret I shouldn't be looking at.

John pulls the keys from the ignition and throws them in the ashtray. Then he opens the door and hops out.

I don't move. What is he up to now? I am *not* going over, under, or through that fence. You don't trespass on military property. You don't disobey their rules. Not when they put food on your table.

The back of the station wagon opens and I hear the obvious *chuk-fizz* of a beer can. Great. Underage drinking *and* trespassing.

The wagon shifts from John's weight as he sits down in the back.

"You can sit there if you want, but the view's much better from this side," John says, and I can hear the grin in his voice. I turn to look. Deep pink sky and streetlights sparkle from behind him.

Curious, I undo my seatbelt and heave the door open.

The view from behind the car is breath-taking—but then, my breath is a little on the short side already. Runway lights line the valley below, and huge hangars look like tiny boxes on the airbase. A plane flashes and roars at it takes off away from us. On the other side of the valley a tiny copy of the tower behind us is silhouetted in the fading sunlight. The whole scene seems to shimmer in the sweltering heat.

John stands up and pulls his shirt over his head, throwing it into the back of the car.

"Shit, it's hot," he says.

He reaches into the cooler and hands me a beer, already dripping with condensation. An icy drop splashes on my leg as I sit beside him. The evening is so hot, I barely notice. He sits back down and drapes his arm around my shoulders, eyes on me, not the view. His eyes are hungry for more than just beer. I pop open my beer and take a sip, extremely self-conscious. More drops fall onto my leg. They trickle down towards my inner thigh. The feeling isn't unpleasant.

No. The answer is no. The answer is no. The answer is…

John leans over and licks the beer from my upper lip. I jerk back awkwardly, spilling beer on his chest.

I look at it in horror. I'm such a klutz! John barely flinches. Smiling impishly, he takes the beer from my hand. In one swift motion he pitches it into the grass, flips around and pushes me backward onto the floor of the wagon. I shriek. His hands pin mine above my head.

"You, young lady, are going to have to clean that up," he says, eyes flashing.

My heart is playing xylophone on the inside of my ribs.

"John…"

Things are slipping out of my control. It's dangerous, exciting, and crazy … and for once I don't care.

His lips trace my jaw. I make a last, pitiful attempt at pulling my hands from his, but he's too strong.

The answer is…

"John…" I whisper.

He switches so both of my hands are in one of his. Still I can't move—but I'm not really trying to move. Why would I move? The shadowy view of his bare chest above me, here in this crazy, beautiful place is addictive and raw and hot. His free hand slips beneath my top. My heart and my stomach melt in his heat.

"J…"

I'm silenced by his lips. And I like it. I like it a lot.

He stands up, one last time, and unzips his fly. The sound seems to echo through the car and over the hill to the town below. I know I should stop him. I know I should reach forward, push him away, brake this speeding car and pull to the shoulder. His face is a question, asking with his quirky, panting breaths.

I should shake my head; stop this before it goes too far. But my brain is foggy with need and want and longing. I don't want to be reasonable and responsible and smart. I want to be reckless. Screw the consequences.

The answer is…

I smile my silent answer and reach for him. He lifts my shirt, baring me to the sultry summer air.

His hands are on my breasts, my cheeks, my thighs…

…and suddenly I'm sweat-soaked and panting and naked beneath his nakedness. The world is spinning and he should slow down. This is crazy and reckless and I should tell him to stop! I should tell him, but his hand is there, and we are here and this is good, but no, he has to stop.

He has to…stop. He has to… Has to…

Slick and hot and full and exploding with pain and emotion and need and *oh God* and…*Oh GOD!*

Oh.

God.

Oh.

We lay naked in the darkness, the dirt from the carpeted floor stuck to our backs, the red tower light flashing on our skin, and the condom still wrapped in his shorts pocket.

CHAPTER 5

HOUSE #1

July, 1983

I'M SITTING HAND-IN-HAND WITH JOHN in the backseat of his parent's wagon. Mrs Michaels chit-chats nervously with her husband, a lit cigarette in her manicured hand, the window open just a crack beside her. My hand is sweaty in John's as I take slow, steadying breaths, concentrating on both not crying and not vomiting. The smoke is thick and sickly in the car, choking me. I reach over to the handle and turn it, opening my window as wide as I can.

Rain drips through the window and hits me on the face, but it's a comfort, not an annoyance. The coolness of it soothes my roiling stomach.

John's hand is electric with anticipation. His fingers twitch in time with the beat of the song on the radio—Michael Jackson crooning his one-gloved tune of questionable paternity. The irony is lost on John. Not that it matters—there is no question here.

I've known for exactly twenty-six hours, and still he is leaving me.

To his credit, he would have stayed. Honour has been beaten into his brain since the day he was born. A man must face his problems head-on, and a future officer must act with integrity. I told him to go because I'm not ready to share this secret yet, and the questions would be too much for both of us. My parents are going to kill me. My mother is going to have a nervous breakdown—her little future doctor is knocked up. No opportunity for a future anything now. I need time to think.

So here we sit. Me, trying not to vomit on the Michaels' shiny new upholstery, and him, looking ahead to his own future. I see Mr.

Michaels—I can't bring myself to call him Colonel—glaring at us in the rear-view mirror. His eye catches mine for a second, but he looks back to the road quickly. There's a bead of sweat on his upper lip. The gold bars on his shoulders shine brightly, even on this dark, dreary day. I take slow, steady breaths and let the rain cool my face. They will hate me when they find out, for I will be the ugly cement block that tethers their shining star. No matter that this wasn't my idea. No matter that I was the seduced, not the seducer. This will be my fault. I swallow and close my eyes as we are waved through the gates and onto the base.

The bus is there, not far past the gates, parked on a wide expanse of asphalt dotted with puddles. An ugly green school bus with simple white lettering. Small groups of parents and teens huddle around the bus, holding large black umbrellas. A mean looking man in a shiny uniform stands beside it, a clipboard in one hand. Seeing the car arrive, he snaps to attention and salutes. Mr. Michaels gives him a half-hearted wave and parks, opening the door and getting out before the engine has finished making noise.

Mrs. Michaels turns and puffs smoke into my face as she yells "Joe, dear, can you grab the umbrella? It's in the back."

I try not to gag. John squeezes my hand in support and smiles at me.

Thankfully, Mr. Michaels has already grabbed the umbrella and opens his wife's door before I barf in her face. They walk away, Mr. Michaels carrying John's duffle, and Mrs. Michaels following him like a goose afraid to get her feet wet. They shake hands with some of the other parents without looking back.

"It'll be okay," John says, all of the confidence in the world behind his eyes. "We'll figure it out."

My lip trembles, but I will myself not to cry. I need to show him that I'm strong, that this is just a hiccup in my plans for life. I don't want him to worry about me over the summer because he'll have enough to worry about. Eight weeks of guaranteed hell—meant to drain you physically, mentally, and emotionally—at basic, then four years of gruelling training at the academy to build him back up into an officer of distinction. I don't know how he can be smiling, looking forward to all of this. Will he remember me?

"I'll call the first chance I get," he says, fingers brushing my face.

"And when I get leave…I'll spend it with you. I promise. And you'll write me, and send me cookies."

"You'll look so handsome in your uniform," I say, as I fight the urge to grab his hand and hold him here with me forever. I will not cry.

"It'll be okay, babe," he says, then leans over to bring his lips against mine. A quick, firm kiss, a squeeze of my hand, a mischievous smile, and he is out the door…like he's heading to the cinema, not hell.

I open my door and climb out, but John is already beside his parents. Unsure, I close the door and stand beside the car, not wanting to interrupt their time. I think I'll get a chance to talk to him once more before he boards, but the angry man standing beside the bus starts calling names.

"Anderson, Fred!" he screams, like he's yelling across town, not twenty-five feet away. "Board now!"

Anderson, Fred, looking terrified, throws his duffle in the belly of the bus and walks up the steps.

"Allen, Robert! Board now! Boone, Patrick! Board now!" A blood vessel is sticking out on the man's temple. His face is red.

There is no more conversation. Young men with close-clipped haircuts straighten up and square their shoulders. Mothers wipe their eyes with soggy tissues. One by one, their sons grasp their duffels and walk forward.

"Michaels, John! Board now!" the man screams.

John turns to face me, a determined gleam in his eyes. "Don't wait up," he says.

I grin, half-heartedly, and finish our little saying. "Don't be late," I say. He leans forward and kisses me, then nods, turns, and walks forward, as if this were the easiest thing in the world, his legs swinging in more of a saunter than a walk. He pops his bag in the compartment and hops up the stairs. Only when he is seated by the window does he look back. He waves to his parents and then his eyes find mine.

I breathe in quickly, caught off guard by what his eyes are saying. My cheeks burn at the dangerous grin he gives me, not much different than that of five weeks ago in the flashing red glow. His gaze flicks down to the neckline of my blouse and below. It's as if he's having sex with me in his mind, as if we are alone and together, not separated by a crowd of sniffling parents and twenty-five feet of soggy paved space. I feel my body respond—my breath quickens and something flutters behind my breastbone. The rush of need shocks away my unshed tears.

I hear the sound of marching feet, slamming doors, and revving engines, but I don't look away. The corners of John's mouth twitch, and the bus moves forward. Parents wave frantically as it pulls away, calling their goodbyes and well wishes to the stench of exhaust and flying water.

I am left alone, standing in a puddle of need and lost dreams as John drives away in search of his own.

CHAPTER 6
HOUSE #13

May, 2008

PEOPLE. THERE ARE TOO MANY of them. They are everywhere. People outside wearing cameras and people inside wearing black. People with lasagne. Concerned, sincere faces and sharp, questioning faces. Some I know well, some I know vaguely, some I don't know at all. There are so many that they've stopped ringing the doorbell—they just walk in, invade my home, my personal fortress for their own comfort. Staring at me for signs of weakness. They are vultures, searching for the chink in my armour so they can push their questions, their guilt, their pain on me. It only adds to the leviathan of shame within me. Their eyes are like lead weights on my soul.

Go home. Go away. Go back to your spaces and leave me alone in mine.

After too many handshakes and too many concerned tears, I excuse myself to the solitude of my bedroom. I close the door and stare at the knob for a moment, exhausted with the effort of walking in my own home. I click the lock. A pile of unrecognizable coats towers on my bed, so I sink down and sit on the floor. The phone rings, and I jump, but not as high as I would have before. Family, friends, military officials, government big-wigs and television reporters have all called—my phone has rung off the hook since that awful night. Today I let it ring until someone else answers it. I hate the phone. I don't want to be big news and I don't want to talk to people I don't know. I want this to end.

Oh God, let this end.

After what seems like mere seconds, quiet footsteps sound on the stairs. I steel myself, knowing the knock will come. In this I am not disappointed.

"Mom?"

Maria. I need to be strong for Maria.

"Just a sec, sweetheart." Everything but the floor groans as I force myself to get up and unlock the door. Maria's tearstained face peeks through. Her innocent grief shines on her cheeks, and she is more beautiful because of it. So like John.

"Can I come in?" she asks quietly.

"Sure."

I lock the door after her and then look around. I want to sit with her, hold her, but there is nowhere to rest. The coats have covered everything. It makes me angry. I bend and grab the coats in my arms and throw them onto the floor. To hell with them.

I crawl up onto the bed and lie down, motioning for her to do the same. The scent of John catches me as I pat his pillow. I want to scream. I will never wash his pillowcase again. There's nothing left for me but a scent.

Maria's face is shredding me. What's left of my sanity threatens to evaporate, but I hold on. This is the first chance we've had to be alone in days.

Unexpectedly, I find myself as the comforter, not the comforted.

Instead of offering asinine platitudes, I simply hold her and let her cry.

⸻

I am forty-four years old. A widowed empty-nester. I abandoned my career at nineteen to follow my husband in a never-ending succession of moves. Correction: in a continuous succession of moves that brought me here, to this place that is not where I'm from—where I have no family and no roots. I've been dumped here without choice, like chattel—like a car or a bed or a carpet—as part of his DF&E—Dependents, Furniture, and Effects. In just over eleven months, I won't even have this place to call my home, and the succession of moves will cease.

"*Section II. B. In the case of the service member's demise, the surviving*

34

dependents will be allowed twelve (12) months' time to vacate the married quarters which they were allocated."

My husband gave his life to his country. And while he was giving it to them, they took mine from me.

What is left for me to live with? A meagre year's salary. Some retirement savings and mementos from all corners of the earth. An insurance policy which I will likely have to fight to receive, even though my situation is textbook easy—my husband died in uniform, while on duty, due to a tragic accident—the money that is to be mine is tied up in an endless reel of red tape.

I have no home. No future. Nothing.

Somehow I must manufacture the pieces to pick up, put them back together, and keep going.

This is not something I do well.

Maria and the boys can go back to their lives. Their friends, their lovers, their schools, and their jobs. They are young. Years of constant motion have made them resilient. And the immediacy of John's death only stalls them for a moment.

I can only crash and burn.

After the first week, the people still come, but their faces have changed. They no longer want me to ease their pain. They see their visits as obligations. They check on me because I am the poor widow down the street. I fake-smile and fake-welcome and fake life.

The house is filled with lilies. Creased and rotting white lilies on the table, in the kitchen, on the bookcases—I hate lilies. I have hated lilies since I was seven and the scent of them surrounded me at my grandfather's funeral. Lilies are death. Their stink follows me into my dreams—lilies and lies haunt me even there. I want to rid myself of both, but I have no starting point and no energy. So I ignore them and they just sit and rot.

After the second week, I have sworn off of lasagne forever. My freezer is full of it. A stack of empty, unnamed casserole dishes sits on my counter. At night I wash them by the same sink I stood by on that night, waiting for my husband to come home. I find myself searching the street for his car, listening for the slam of the door, waiting for his kiss on the back of my neck. A chance to gain back what I have lost. A chance to say goodbye. A chance to redeem myself. But all I feel is the subtle draught which this house has, lifting the hairs on the back of my neck like a ghost, while my hands are stained red in the dirty lasagne water.

One by one, the owners retrieve their dishes. I can almost hear the stories they will tell their friends and husbands.

"I went by to see Ellen today! She seemed…okay. No, the kids have gone back to the city. I know, it's so sad!"

In some corner of my mind, I know I would be doing the same thing—if the roles were reversed. I would be sipping hot coffee and speaking in a fake high-pitched voice, bringing muffins and sympathy as I walk through the door. But I am doing none of those things. I am floating alone.

Bob and his wife are my most regular visitors. There are endless reams of paper to sign. Benefits to allocate, futures to plan. Insurance companies to argue with. I hate his briefcase as much as I hate the telephone. I want to burn it, light it with gasoline and throw it out the window. I try and focus for Bob's sake, because I know he just wants to get it over with. But my mind wanders incessantly. Tonight we sit at the kitchen table, drinking hideous black coffee from the coffee shop on the base. The legalese on the paper blurs to gibberish as he reads it to me. I smile and sign. Smile and sign. Beside my hand on the dented oak is an L-shaped burn mark. Beside the pile of death certificates is a pink stain that looks suspiciously like a happy face.

This table used to be a place of joy, a place of promise and hope. Giggles and laughter echo beneath it. As Bob drones on, I see John sitting in his chair, mouth full of food and wide open in triumphant display, and I'm in a different place, a different kitchen, a different home. A high chair sits in front of me, and David is in hysterics, laughing at Daddy's silly faces. Spaghetti sauce smothers David's cheeks. Noodles stick to the tray, the seat, the floor, and David's hair. My heart is so full, sitting here watching my two favourite men laugh.

But time shifts in an instant. In this place, this place, nobody's laughing.

CHAPTER 7
HOUSE #1

August, 1983

Dear Ellen,

It's hard to believe I've been here four weeks already. It's all a bit of a blur. We get up before the sun, run until we puke, scarf down whatever crap they're serving, and try not to fall asleep standing up. They yell all day, and nothing is ever good enough for them, but I know it doesn't matter. They're just mind games.

We have to do push-ups to get our mail. The bigger the envelope or parcel, the more we have to do. Mom's boring social columns cost me 20. Ugh. Today I did 100, but it was sure worth it when I tasted those cookies. I'm glad you sent plenty, because I was suddenly everyone's best friend, and their hands were grabbing them before I even got a bite. I did have a few, though, and they were heavenly. Like a night with you.

When I do sleep, you're all I dream about. My friend Saunders says I moan your name all night long, but I think he's lying. Although he's one to talk. I know for a fact he's hot after someone named Beth.

I've thought a bit about what you said, and I'm glad you're still going to come to university here. They haven't let us leave the academy, but I know the civie university is not far away. Some of the guys from here are dating girls from there. We don't have to tell anyone yet, but when the time comes, we'll deal with it. At least you'll get a good start on your degree, and when things settle down again, we'll get you back there again. Good idea to get an apartment, instead of staying in residence.

Gotta go. I've got to get my boots ready for the morning and it's already almost midnight. I can't wait 'til I can see you again. I can't wait to touch your skin. I can't wait to…October can't come soon enough.

Don't wait up, John

"Don't be late," I whisper to the empty room.

I read the letter again and press it to my chest as I sit on my bedroom floor. I'm still wearing my Mightee-Mart uniform after a long day of standing behind a counter, being abused by stupid people about even stupider things. I couldn't care less if Coke was two cents cheaper at Jeb's Grocery. I had to leave my till twice to vomit. The smell of the hot dog machine and freezer-burned ice cream clings to the fabric of my uniform, mixed with a tinge of bile. My parents don't know yet, and I'm trying hard to keep it that way. Their anger and disappointment haunts me, before they even know.

Oh, John…why did you leave me this way? I think. Why me? I had plans! I'm lost in a whirlpool of missing John, wanting freedom, looking forward and wishing things would never change. But I know my only hope is to put one foot in front of the other and keep moving. Try not to think.

October can't come soon enough for me either.

CHAPTER 8
HOUSE #2 (APARTMENT)

October, 1983

I MEET JOHN AT A PUB downtown, where he and his friends are gathered. I push my way through the smoky air and sweaty bodies, thankful that the nausea has eased somewhat. I'm still not showing very much, and can still—barely—fit into my jeans. One of the pleasant side effects of my situation is the increased size of my breasts, and I've decided to wear something snug at the chest to showcase it. The appreciative whistles as I push through the crowd prove that it was a good choice.

I find John and his buddies at the back of the pub, and I can't help the foolish grin that spreads across my face. I am so incredibly happy to see him! He looks up and his grin echoes mine. "Ellen!" he screams as if he's just won the lottery. His buddies gawk at me, and one of them punches John in the arm. Several of them whistle—looking me over like a piece of meat—but I don't care.

John elbows his way out from behind the table and we meet in the middle, he lifts me up with a humongous bear hug and then kisses me with gusto. The kiss turns deep and passionate—and the cat-calls and wolf-whistles fly around us, almost unheard. My heart is beating so fast I feel faint. John tastes of beer and smells of clean laundry. I rub my hand over the back of his close-shaven head and the stubble tickles my fingers.

"Get a room, Michaels!" someone yells above the din.

"Hey baby, you got some of that loving for me?" says another.

John breaks off the kiss and smiles down at me like I'm a vision from heaven. He waves his middle finger vaguely behind him and then turns to face the drooling masses. "Smith, if you think I'm sharing, you got another thing coming. This beauty is mine, all mine." He hooks his arm around my waist and pulls me with him to the table, seating me on his lap. "Ellen, these sex-deprived morons are the boys. Boys, this is Ellen." He rubs the inside of my thigh with his left hand as his right sweeps the crowd. I try not to wiggle. "Smith, Mizrati, Owens, O'Neil, and Saunders." I smile at Bob, who I've heard about in John's letters.

"Hey," Bob says, smiling back.

The band starts to play, and the boys sing along with little attention to such trivialities as pitch and rhythm. John nuzzles my neck and whispers into my ear. "Let's ditch these losers and go back to your apartment."

I am so glad I convinced my parents I needed a place by myself, away from the drunken college masses.

We slide out of our seats and into the crowd to more whistles. "Where ya going, Michaels?" someone says.

"Wouldn't you like to know, Owens," John laughs and pushes me gently forward through the throng.

My apartment is three blocks from the pub, past stone houses and tall trees. The falling leaves crunch beneath our feet as we walk arm-in-arm all of the way, John telling me about the guys, his sadistic cadet leader, and how much he's missed me. I nod and smile, stupidly happy to be with him again. The past few weeks have been crazy-hard for me too, but I know things will get worse before they get better. He says nothing about the future, our future, and I don't ask.

I let us into my apartment, which is tiny but functional. It includes a kitchen, a bathroom, and a dining/living/bedroom where I eat, sleep and study. He lifts me up and carries me across the threshold like we're newlyweds, shoulders the door closed, kicks off his shoes, and lays me gently on the bed without saying a word. His eyes get that gleam in them, and his hands are unzipping my jacket.

He stops, suddenly unsure. "Is it...okay? I mean...it won't hurt him will it?"

I laugh, pleased that John's calling it a him. "No, I don't think so...I mean, I looked it up in a text book in the library, and it said it was okay."

I blush furiously, realizing that in saying this I'm admitting to thinking about this beforehand.

"And is it... okay...with you?" he asks.

I answer him without words.

Sometime later, we're spooning on my single bed in the dark. His arms are around me and his hand rests lightly on my stomach. He's asking a million questions about what I'm going through.

"So, do you feel him?" His hand brushes the small bump that's growing beneath my belly-button.

"Not yet. The books say it should be soon though. I'm going to have to go to a doctor soon."

He rubs my stomach absently, thinking his own thoughts.

There's a campus medical clinic that I know I can go to. I've walked in there and gotten pamphlets...for both pregnancy and for abortion. The clinic will help with either. I never even considered abortion, but I got the pamphlet anyway.

John shocks me from my thoughts. "We could get married," he says.

I stiffen, then turn and face him awkwardly in the small bed. "It's not against the rules? Won't you be kicked out?"

"I don't know. I guess I can ask...if we were married, then my medical would cover both of you too."

I don't know what to say. I don't want him to get kicked out of military college; the guilt would be too much.

The alarm on his watch goes off, making me jump.

"I've gotta go. There's a barrack check in forty-five minutes." He slides out of the bed and fumbles for the switch on the light beside us. "There's a dance on the campus for Halloween, and we're allowed to sign in guests. It's next weekend, and I've already put your name down... that is, if you want to come." He pulls his pants on and does up his belt, looking like something from a magazine. The small layer of fat on his middle has disappeared. His abs are washboard tight.

"Um...yah, of course." Not like I have anything else to do in my non-existent social life.

"'Kay, I'll call you this week. Don't wait up." He grins and leans over to kiss me, letting his hands say their goodbyes.

"Don't be late." I say, the blood rushing to my cheeks as his fingers slide over places only he would know. He leaves me weak and hungry.

I lie awake for hours in the wake of his departure, alone in my single bed.

The clinic workers are opinionated and pushy. Their blue polyester uniforms smell of disinfectant. There is no question at all that their preference is to end the life inside me. I let them examine me, silently submitting to their pokes, prods and comments. I feel both violated and relieved. How is that possible? Part of me was dreading this, and part of me was looking forward to it. Their cursory check leaves me feeling like an idiot, but I force them to talk intelligently to me.

I made a mistake. *We* made a mistake. But this life is as much a part of me as my eyes and my hands. I will not let some patronizing clinic worker tear it away from me.

They give me reams of information on abortion, and adoption. Then they give me a slip of paper with a date and a time for my first ultrasound. I dump the reams in the trash on the way out, and cradle the tiny white slip of paper next to my heart.

I'm dressed as a Roman goddess. Complete with gold and vine leaves, the costume fits my curves perfectly and the drape of the fabric hides the hint of roundness in my middle. The gold shines in my eyes and I swipe on another layer of mascara to accentuate the effect. I do my hair in cascading ringlets; it takes hours of standing with a curling iron, but in the end I look as sexy as I've ever looked. And, surprisingly enough, I'm feeling that way too.

John is waiting at the gate of the academy, a roguish grin on his face. I can't help but smile back. He's got a tricorn hat on, a roughed-up white shirt and his pants have the legs torn off. With the added red sash and eye patch he looks downright dangerous. Well, to me anyway.

He pays the cabbie and leads me through the tall stone buildings. They look like sentient castles, with thousands of glass eyes staring down at us as we weave between them. The air is late-October chilly, and I begin to regret my costume choice. He sees me shiver and drapes his hand over my shoulders.

"Almost there," he says, then bends down to whisper in my ear. "You look like a real goddess. Maybe we should just go back to my room."

I turn, widening my eyes in shock. Fraternization in the dorms is against the rules.

He chuckles at the look on my face. "Don't worry. We'll go to the dance…first." His breath smells faintly of beer.

The stairs into the gym are like an entrance to a palace, out of sync with the booming rock music vibrating the huge wooden doors. Two serious-looking cadets guarding the door ask John for his cadet ID. He hands it to them, and they stamp our hands with red ink before nodding us through. A man in full uniform stands just beyond them, watching the proceedings with a proprietary gaze.

John stiffens when he sees him. "Sir," he says, his head bobbing a jerky nod.

The man nods back. "Michaels," he says to John, but he is looking at me. His eyes slide down my costume, stopping at the undeniable cleavage it shows, and pointedly catching on the drape of fabric at my hips.

He knows.

"Sir, this is Ellen. Ellen, this is Lieutenant Colonel Fielding, Chief of Cadets."

I feel goose bumps rise on my arms. John shifts uncomfortably beside me. Lieutenant Colonel Fielding sticks his hand out and I hesitate—for just a second—before putting my hand in his. His fingers tighten on mine like a vise, just short of painful, for two quick shakes, and then he lets go, pulling me toward him almost imperceptibly as his fingers slide off of mine.

I stifle a gasp, and lean on John.

Lieutenant Colonel Fielding smiles like a used car salesman eyeing a great deal. "Cadet Michaels and I had a chat yesterday." His eyebrows rise imperceptibly and he glances at my stomach again.

"I'm sure we'll be speaking again," he says with dark emphasis. "Enjoy the dance."

John's hand closes on my elbow. "Yes, sir," he says smartly and propels me into the gym.

Dark heat and deafening music hit us like a wall as we walk through the door. My skin crawls as I feel John's cadet leader follow us in with his eyes. That guy gives me the creeps. John tugs at my elbow and pulls me through the gyrating vampires, brides of Frankenstein, and huge bottle-wielding babies. AC/DC screams about American thighs as we make our way to the bar. Strobe lights turn the dancers into freeze-framed photographs. John gets a beer for himself and Coke for me. The press of the bodies all around me makes me claustrophobic, and I find myself taking deep breaths of sweaty, steamy air. The icy cold can of soda feels good against my cheek.

It's too loud to talk, so John steers me over to the tables at the back of the room. An angel with far too much makeup on smiles guiltily at us, and then goes right back to trying to remove her mummy date's tonsils. I stifle a giggle at the sight of it. John takes a swig of his beer, wipes his lip with his sleeve and gestures for me to sit.

It's a bit quieter in this corner, but not much. At least it's dark and away from John's weirdo boss.

John looks at me hungrily and leans over to talk in my ear. He practically has to yell for me to hear him. "You look so amazing tonight!" he belts out as his hand slides up the bare skin of my leg beneath my thin dress. "Let's dance and then go back to the room!" His lips tickle my ear he's so close.

We each take a drink and then leave our drinks on the table, where the angel and mummy are still going at it. John winks at me as we get to the dance floor and AC/DC switches to a slow, drawling *Total Eclipse of the Heart*. He reels me in and twirls me around like Gene Kelly, and I love it. I love the feel of his hand in mine leading me around the floor, I love they way his eyes don't just look, they absorb, and I love the way I don't have to think in this moment, I just have to *be*. I am with John, and the world around us disappears in the steady beat of the drum and throaty voice singing through the speakers.

John kisses my neck as the last tones evaporate. Before the next song begins he whispers, "Let's go. Now." And I giggle and follow him, feeling sexy and strangely drunk—which is hilarious because I haven't had alcohol in months.

Lieutenant Colonel Whats-his-name has moved, which I'm grateful for as John and I half walk, half jog through the door. We sneak through the corridors and passageways to his room like bad spies. I can almost hear the background music as we round every corner. Everyone in the halls is either drunk or otherwise occupied, and with all the costumes, it's hard to tell who is a cadet and who isn't—though I suspect ninety percent of the girls are imports like me. We pretend we are invisible until he opens his unlocked door with a flourish.

His room is as institutional as it gets. Metal bedframe, single mattress with grey wool blanket and starkly white sheets, simple wooden wardrobe, a dresser and desk, white sink and industrial mirror. The only clue that a living, breathing human lives here is the solitary photo pinned to a small cork bulletin board—it's us, smiling broadly at our graduation dance. I smile at the memory.

John has on his quirky grin as he pushes the door closed, walks to the desk and turns on the small metal reading lamp. One of his hands snakes around my waist as the other flicks off the harsh overhead light.

As he leans towards me, we hear the echoes of uneven footsteps down the hall. There's a whole lot of giggling and shush-ing, and then a door slams shut. I guess John isn't the only one with an overnight guest. John chuckles wickedly and bites my neck with the tips of his teeth.

"I vant to suck your blood," he whispers menacingly as he pushes me toward the bed.

I open my eyes wide and put my hand to my forehead in mock fear. "No...! Not my blood!" I whisper. I can't stop my lips from smiling as he bites again, and I lay back in happy submission as his lips travel downward and my toga melts away.

The red numbers of John's alarm clock say it's just past two in the morning, but I still can't sleep. Perhaps it's the strange, sterile room around me; perhaps it's the occasional burst of drunken laughter beyond the door, or perhaps it's the lack of space in this tiny bed made for one. Awake, I know I should leave, but I don't. John lies on his back with his arm under my head, snoring gently. I watch in the dim light as his lip pulls in and out with each breath. I want to touch it, yet I'm reluctant to wake him from whatever dreams he is having. I'm on my side in the six inches of space his body leaves me, but I'm not uncomfortable. In fact I feel infused with happiness.

I love this boy in front of me. I've never really thought of it until now, lying here naked in his dorm room, beneath the starched sheets. It shocks me, the extent of the feeling deep in my chest. Only a few short months ago I wanted nothing to do with him, and now, without any warning, I can't imagine life without him. I love his quirky grin. I love his carefree way of dealing with life, as if nothing could hold him back. I love when he looks at me as though I am his entire world. And I love that part of him is growing inside of me.

He twitches and then rolls onto his side, facing away from me with a brief grunt. Instead of taking advantage of the extra room, I stay on my side in his shadow. His back, broad and muscled, blocks the light but makes me feel safe.

I slowly fall asleep, content in the darkness behind him.

A loud clanging outside the door shocks me from sleep.

"Up!" *Clang!* "Get up, you lazy fuckers!" *Clang!* "Out on the parade square in five minutes!" screams a furious voice as it stomps down the tiled hall. *Clang! Clang!* "In your PT gear and ready to run!"

Screaming rock music blares at full volume. Another set of footsteps runs down the hall, banging on each door as it goes. John shoots out of bed.

"Shit!" he cries, running his hand through his cropped hair. "Shit! Shit! Shit!" he says, then turns to see me lying in bed with the sheets pulled up around my neck. "Shit!"

He's pulling a t-shirt over his head, throwing obscenities out like candy. I'm frozen on the bed. There's the barest hint of sunrise beyond the ancient, paned window. The clock says 5:02 in evil red numbers. What should I do?

He rifles through a drawer and grabs underwear, gym shorts, and socks. Our costumes are strewn across the floor. My white lacy underwear hangs from the faucet of his tiny sink.

The bed dips down as he sits on the edge and begins to tie his shoes. "Just stay here," he says as he fights with the laces. "No one will know you're here, and it'll be fine." His voice is raspy from beer and lack of sleep. "When I go out, wait until we run off the parade square, and then sneak out."

He nods, as if confirming his own thought. "None of the staff will be up at this hour, and the senior cadets will either be out there yelling at us or sound asleep in their beds." He finishes his second shoe and turns to look at me, eyes nervous. John is rarely nervous, so this scares me more than the noise beyond the door.

I can hear more yelling outside of the window, and doors are slamming in the hall. Hissed curses and running footsteps follow. The music stops.

"Don't wait up," he says and hurriedly pecks my cheek. I say the rest as he grins and runs out the door.

More running steps, one last slamming door, and then the only sounds are coming from beyond the window. The hall itself is quiet. I sit there, sheets around my neck, slightly stunned. The clock reads 5:04.

I hear more shouting outside, and then as one the voices begin to sing a military chant, slowly moving away until there's no sound at all. Only then do I look around, and smile at the clothing strewn everywhere. I scoot to the edge of the bed, still wrapped in John's sheet, wiping the sleep from my eyes and yawning. My ringlets are crushed and knotted. I'm not sure how I imagined the morning would play out, but it wasn't this.

My groggy thoughts are interrupted by a slow, methodical click, barely audible at first, and then louder. *Click. Click. Click.*

I realize the sound is footsteps, and the footsteps are in the hallway. *Click. Click.*

My breath catches in my throat. I'm naked, in John's room illegally, and the footsteps are coming closer. Surely they will continue on down the hallway, and I pray they do because there is nowhere to go in this miniscule room if they don't.

Click. Click. Click.

The sound stops in front of John's door. I don't move, I don't breathe. I don't do anything but watch as the doorknob turns and the door begins to open.

It's like a bad dream, watching John's door swing out in front of me. The light from the fluorescent hall fixtures spills onto the floor with eerie slowness. Shiny black oxfords and razor-sharp creased pants step in. It's not necessary to look up, somehow I already know who is walking in John's room. The door closes with a soft thunk, and the deadbolt locks home.

I look.

The Chief of Cadets stands in front of me. I can't even remember his name, but I remember his hard face from last night. His eyes are glittering in the almost dark, surveying the room slowly. They stop on the white underwear in the sink and he chuckles.

Oh, God.

Shivers run up my spine as he turns to face me and smiles, the stiff, cold smile of a raptor going in for the kill. I frantically clutch at the thin sheet and scratchy wool blanket, tucking my feet beneath me and backing up on the bed. He closes the drab grey drapes. I look at the door—it's only a few feet away, but I'm naked, with nothing but a blanket and a sheet to cover me, and before I can act he's standing in front of me again, blocking my line of escape.

He begins to undo his belt.

"You will not make a sound," he says while dropping a small bag of white powder on John's desk. He pulls his belt out with a quiet *snap*.

I say nothing. I don't move. He sees me look at the door and frowns.

"You will remain completely still and silent unless I ask you to speak, and you will do exactly as I say, or Cadet John Michaels will find himself on his ass in jail for a disturbingly long time. Do I make myself clear?" He stares pointedly at the bag on the desk.

This hideous man can ruin John's life in an instant. I know that he holds John's future—my future—in his slimy hands. He has all of the power and I have none.

I nod.

"Smart choice," he says. He leans toward the sink and hooks the string of my underwear on his finger. "The first one you've made in a while, Ellen."

My eyes widen. He remembers my name.

He chuckles again. "Oh yes, Ellen, I remember your name. Michaels and I had a lovely chat about your…predicament…this week. A shame, really. Michaels shows such promise—too much promise to be saddled with a little teen whore and a bastard child. Perhaps I can help him with both."

Asshole. Evil, twisted asshole.

"A whore who shouldn't be in Michaels room in the first place." He twirls the underwear around on his finger and then lifts them to his nose, sniffing them like fine wine. "But we'll let that little fraternization charge slide. Besides, we all know what whores want," he says, and then he drops the underwear on the floor in front of him and threads his belt through itself, making a loop.

"Hands," he says.

I don't understand. Or maybe I don't believe that he's asking me what I think he is.

He frowns. And then he strikes out like a snake. The shock wrenches my head around. Hot, stinging pain sears through my cheek and my eye blurs. I whimper, shocked and afraid.

"Tsk, tsk," he says. "I thought we had an agreement." His voice is calm, as if we are merely having a chat about the weather, or today's stock market. "You will remain silent and *do as I say*… and I will make sure that bag does not end up in Cadet Michaels' locker during a military police inspection. Understood?"

I say nothing.

He sighs.

I begin to cry. I hate myself for showing weakness, but there are limits. This only makes him angry. He leans over and slaps me again. I flinch away, but not soon enough. The coppery taste of blood fills my mouth.

"Do…you…understand?" he asks, teeth clenched.

"Yes," I whisper.

"Good. Put out your hands."

I put them out. The sheets fall and my breasts are exposed as he loops the belt around my wrists, pulls it so tight it burns my skin, and hooks the loose end to the metal bed frame. I'm caught like a dog on a leash. He pulls the sheets off of the bed and I'm lying there, stripped of all protection. My bare skin prickles with fear and cold. I have never been so vulnerable. He undoes his fly with slow, precise movements and then rests his clenched fist on the rise in my stomach, pushing down ever so slightly. I'm terrified—for myself and the tiny life inside of me.

"Please..." I beg, realizing too late that I've broken my promise of silence.

His fist crashes into my stomach once, twice, three times, and the world crashes down around me.

On me, crashing.

In me, tearing.

Through me.

I can't breathe, and I can't move, and it hurts. It hurts down there, and he pounds, and I lie there silently praying. Praying for the world to end, and for him to stop so I can fade away to black.

Blackness.

And the blackness becomes the rising sun, and the door closes behind him leaving only pieces of what once was me.

Sometime later—hours, minutes, seconds?—I attempt to gather the pieces together. I make the bed. I dress, throwing an old sweatshirt of John's over my toga. As I close John's door, I almost run into Bob Saunders.

His eyes open in shock. Not at seeing me—at seeing what has happened to me. My lip is bleeding, my face bruised and stained with tears.

"Bob..." I whisper.

"Ellen? Are you okay? I saw the..."

I interrupt him. "You saw *nothing*."

"But I saw the Cadet..."

"You saw *nothing*!" I hiss.

Before he can question me again, I turn and flee.

I don't look back.

⊷━❦━⊶

Our baby is moving.

I haven't answered the phone for a week. The light bleeding has stopped. The tearing pain has lessened. Somehow, somewhere deep inside myself, I have found the strength to get up, wash, eat, go to class. The bruises have faded beneath the coating of makeup, and my world has turned to a horrible shade of grey—the colour of John's curtains. A non-colour. Nothingness. I am a whisper of nothingness.

People see the shadows of bruises on my cheek, but no one asks and I don't tell. I can't tell. I don't go to the clinic. I don't make any reports. I am grey.

And now, a week since that horrible night, our baby is moving. Little flutters of hope. This spark of life inside of me is my strength. I am carrying John's baby. And as scared as I am, the flutters tell me that it's okay. Inside of me grows a new life, and no vile, heartless, depraved asshole can take that away from me! Life will always find a way. This baby and I will survive.

When the phone rings tonight, I answer.

"Hello?"

"Ellen? Thank God," John says. "Where have you been? Why haven't you answered my phone calls?"

I lie.

"I've been at the library every night. Midterms." It's so good to hear his voice, but it's awkward. I pray that Bob said nothing. I pray that I am doing the right thing, talking to him now.

"Oh. I thought you were avoiding me."

"No…just really busy."

For some reason, hearing his voice is cracking the shell I've constructed around myself. I fight the tears.

"Sorry I had to leave you last week, fucking jerks calling us up on a weekend. How are you feeling? "

Bruised. Raped. Broken.

"I'm fine. I… I felt the baby move this morning."

"What?" he practically screams into the phone. "Really! That is so cool! Listen, the Cadet Chief says we can have a quiet ceremony here in the chapel, just a padre and the witnesses. I have to live here, but we'll be married and you'll be covered by my medical."

It's just days after his devil-boss raped me, and he's talking about our wedding like a business transaction with my rapist. My wedding. My rapist. The thing normal girls dream and plan for years, the day that should be filled with white, lacy dresses and virginal veils in long cathedral aisles. Not a farce sanctioned by a monster. Not a hidden comedy show where the bride wears red. Nothing about this wedding will be normal. How I long to be normal again! How I long to go back to John's room and instead of cowering on the bed, I would scream and run and never look back.

"Ellen?"

Oh, John is still on the line.

"Ellen are you there?"

"Sorry. I was just thinking. Did you say at the military college? Are you sure?" I don't want to be married anywhere near the college. I don't want to go to the college ever again.

"Yah...is there something wrong with that?"

"Um, no..." I lie.

"We won't have to pay for anything but the license if we do it here. And if we're married on a Friday evening, I can get two nights leave. Not much of a honeymoon, but I've got something planned..."

"Great. Sounds...great." And really, it does. What more could a knocked-up whore want for a wedding?

"Okay, well, do you care what the date is? When is the baby due again?"

"March. March 5th."

"Perfect. There were a few spots in February, I think. I'll ask and get back to you. Wait, are you around this weekend?"

Am I around? Jees. I have no life. Where else would I be? "Um, yah. I'm here."

"Why don't I see if I can get an overnight pass? I'll come see you."

Finally a light in an otherwise black pit. I can't help but smile. I want to reach through the receiver and kiss him. To hell with the Cadet Chief's plans for John, I need to see him. "That would be great," I say.

"I'll call you if I can. And Ellen...?"

"Yah?"

"I love you."

My heart skips a beat, and the smile on my face threatens to crack my cheeks. It's the first time he's said it. Guys never say those words before the girls...except when they're trying to get into their pants.

"I love you too, John."

"Don't wait up," he says and then clicks off, leaving me to say goodbye to the buzzing dial tone.

CHAPTER 9

HOUSE #2 (APARTMENT)

January 24, 1984

TODAY IS MY WEDDING DAY.

I am nineteen years old, roughly the size of a cow, and dressed in a white dress that would fit two people with a little alteration. My parents have driven up, and the three of us plus my younger sister, who is dressed in a gauzy mint-green dress, stand in my tiny apartment. My sister looks beautiful, and I try not to be jealous. At least my dress accentuates my cleavage, not my basketball belly.

My mom and dad's faces are a study in conflict. My mom looks like she just ate chunk of pure, unsweetened chocolate—part of her brain wants her to be happy, but the bitterness underneath has taken over. My dad is happy for me and sad for me at the same time. His face switches from emotion to emotion. I try to ignore the sad, as I know deep down in my gut that this is the right thing to do. The wiggly peanut inside me needs a real family, and I refuse to be the one to deprive him of that. It's going to be a slightly odd family, but John and I will figure things out somehow.

In honour of the occasion my father has rented a white limousine to drive us to the college chapel. He checks his watch every five seconds as it's up to him to make sure we're on time. Mom and I are crammed in my tiny bathroom, putting the final touches on my hair and pinning on my waist-length veil. Her fingers shake as she tucks a curl behind my ear with a bobby pin.

"Do you really love him?" she asks, her voice barely a whisper. "You know, sweetheart, that we would support you no matter what...whether you and John married or not..." She bites her lip, and I can see in the mirror that she's about to cry. It's a little too late for this show of solidarity, but I think she may actually mean it.

"Mom, it's okay," I say. The tears are filling up my eyes, threatening to make an appearance. Laura, my sister, peeks around the corner and snaps a picture.

I smile as she catches our reflection in the mirror and then look back at mom. "I really do love him," I say. "He's a good man. We're young, but we'll figure it out." And I'm telling her the truth.

I can't imagine a future without John anymore. We've spent every free moment together since...since last fall. He's somehow managed to get away for at least one night every weekend, except during exams. I have tried a thousand times to tell him what happened that night in his room. Tried to somehow let him know about the blood and the pain and the anger and the self-loathing...but I can't. My secret is my shame, the one thing we don't share. When we went to his Christmas Ball together, I smiled and acted as if nothing had happened. My dress hugged my belly and I purposefully made us late and then avoided the COC like the plague. I could have told John then...could have told him why my hands shook as we danced, but the words wouldn't come. I lied that it was cold and I was tired and he drove me home in his new little hatchback—courtesy of his parents.

We laughed, cried, and were amazed at little Johnny's acrobatics in my belly. We made love like the teenagers we still are, and made plans like the adults we are about to become. I have thought out every angle this crazy life of mine could take, and I've come to the conclusion that I want it all to be with John.

A tear falls down my Mom's cheek, and in an uncharacteristic display of feelings she hugs me tight, keeping her face away from the white fabric or my dress.

"It's 1:34!" Dad yells from the room beyond. "Time to go, troops!"

Mom and I giggle at Dad's attempt at a military voice. I wrap myself in the white fur stole borrowed from my grandmother, lift my floor-length dress high to avoid the messy sidewalk, and walk outside for the last time as Ellen McKinley.

The ride is silent. Dad continues to check his watch, Mom dabs her eyes with a tissue, and Laura looks out the window, lost in her own thoughts. I flip between two emotions, happiness at my upcoming wedding and the night beyond, and dread at seeing that prick of a man, Lt Col Fielding. He insisted on attending so that he could be "the first to congratulate us". Asshole. Today is my day, not his. I'll be damned if I'm going to let him ruin it. Last night, while Laura and I sat up talking about life together, I made her swear that she would interrupt the padre if she had to, push people—regardless of rank—to the side, scream, yell, whatever she had to do, to make sure that she was the one who had that honour. I'm sure she thought I was losing my marbles, but I don't care. I also warned her not to be alone with him, for any reason, and told both Mom and Dad not to trust him. It was so hard not to tell them right then. They're my parents, and even though I'm about to be a mom myself, I still haven't shaken the feeling that Mom could make it better. That Mom would fix everything if she knew the truth. But I lied to them like I lied to John—saying I'd heard some nasty rumours about the man. They believed my lies without question.

We roll through the streets of town and up the long tree-lined parkway to the college. The chapel is an ancient stone building jutting out from a larger building that houses the old gymnasium used for parties. The windows in the chapel are arched stained glass, ancient and majestic. As we pull around, snow starts to fall.

Dad gets out and walks around to help me out. I feel like I'm in a dream, and I let the feeling surround me. Softly falling snowflakes, my white dress, and this beautiful chapel have turned me into a fairy-tale princess. Even my heaving bovine bulk and an evil poisonous monster officer can't take this away from me.

I walk up the stairs behind Laura and Mom, holding tightly to Dad so I won't slip. The huge wooden door swings open, and there, at the end of a long red carpet, waits John. He is all I see. I focus on his smiling face—his handsome, kind, loving face—and refuse to look anywhere else. Nothing but John matters right now; not Laura and Bob Saunders, who walk in front of me; not the chaplain, who I know has glasses that make him look like a scared bug; not the collection of uniformed young men who we pass on our way up the aisle; not John's parents, or *anyone* else. Just John.

I know if I look only at John, the day will be perfect.

Dad lifts my veil, kisses my cheek, and places my hand in John's. John winks, and I smile back, trying to decide if it's nerves or the baby doing flip-flops in my tummy. He squeezes my hand, and I squeeze back as we turn and face the padre. I look at the Bible in the padre's hand and nowhere else. I refuse to look anywhere else. My hands shake, not because I'm nervous, but because my skin is crawling under Fielding's gaze. I take a deep breath and squeeze John's hand once more. My heart is full of love for John and my family, and I let it fill me up, leaving no place for guilt or anger or sadness. John's hand is my rock.

The padre mumbles on about dearly beloved and the sanctity of marriage, and I'm in some bizarre state of altered consciousness, like meditation, only edgier.

"And if anyone should have a reason why they may not be joined in marriage, let them speak now, or forever hold their peace."

This I hear. The silence that follows is awkward, and I hold tight to John's hand, as if I may float away if I let go. I hear the evil man to the right of the chaplain clear his throat menacingly, but I refuse to look at him. This is my day, not his.

The moment passes, we say our vows, and file to the side to sign the register and licenses. Bob Saunders signs for John, and Laura for me. We smile for pictures and file back to the front of the chapel. I glance at Mom, who is suddenly smiling like a maniac, with tears running down both cheeks. She sniffs and smiles harder. Not for the first time, I feel a twinge of regret. I've let her down in so many ways. But this is my day, and I shake it off before it digs in.

We stop before the chaplain again, and I look over to Laura. She nods. The chaplain says, "I now present to you Cadet and Mrs. John Michaels!" We turn to face the gathered cadets and family, and four things happen at once. John reaches over to pull me into a kiss, a shiny shoe moves to step around us and a mint-green heel stomps down on said shoe, while my sister screeches "Oh I'm so happy for you!" and pushes the uniformed asshole out of the way. I think I hear him groan. I want to laugh out loud at the sound. John puts his hand up toward Laura, and leans down to kiss me with all the passion of a late-night tryst, and I smile a secret, loving smile. Cat-calls fly through the air, we break, I blush, and Laura throws herself at me in a hug like only a sister can give.

"How was that?" she whispers into my ear.

"Perfect," I whisper back.

John and I practically run down the aisle and into the waiting limo, not waiting for anyone. John wanted a big reception to celebrate our wedding, the baby, and the fun life ahead of us, but for obvious reasons I insisted on a small family gathering—just our families and closest friends. Our parents agreed on a beautiful restaurant on the water that had a small side room for gatherings just like this.

When the door to the limo closes, John hits the lock button and raises the black screen between us and the driver. He leans back and surveys my dress.

"You look beautiful today, Mrs. Michaels" he says.

I blush, suddenly shy. I'm sitting in a limo with my husband.

My *husband*.

I'm *married*.

Now that I can really look at him, I see how handsome he is in his red formal uniform. His lips tilt up in devilish smile before he leans in for a kiss. His hand caresses my cheek, then traces a line downward to my mom's pearls and then to my breast, which is straining against the lacy fabric of the dress.

For the first time in months, I let myself relax, letting the tension in my shoulders flow into the vinyl seats. John's other arm is around my shoulders, and it feels so very good to just let go. I'm surrounded by a warm, rosy glow of happiness; and instead of searching for the fly in the goodness, I shut out any thought that strays toward the bad. I'm married to a wonderful young man who has a bright future ahead of him. The ceremony went off without a hitch. We're heading to a reception with only our family and friends...no one else. Everything is going to be okay. In fact, everything is going to be better than okay.

John's hand slides across my breast and onto my belly. As if in response, the baby kicks...hard. We both smile and pull away, looking down at the wondrous mountain of belly and lace.

"Well, hello there little fella!" John says as he rubs the foot beneath my skin. "It's your daddy here. I just made your momma my wife. What do you think of that?"

The baby kicks again.

We both laugh.

"He's smart. Just like his mom," John says as he turns my face toward him. "Smart and beautiful. Every guy's dream. That's what you are. And you're all mine."

I can't help but smile as he leans in and gently kisses my lips.

The reception is perfect.

Small, intimate, and happy. Just our families, Bob and his date, Barb, and Michelle. She and I have known each other forever. She tries hard to turn Bob's head away from Barb, but when it's obvious he's not interested, she goes for another guy, who is more than happy to oblige. Our childhood dreams looked nothing like my life has turned out, but she doesn't judge. Today is my day and she is happy for me.

Nothing about our marriage has been conventional, so we skip the usual speeches, instead we offer anyone that wants to speak the chance to do so, but first they have to tell the story of how they met John or me. My Dad, ever verbose, stands first. His face is dark and serious. I hold my breath, waiting to see what he has to say about John.

But he tells them how he met me.

"Ellen was born on a Friday night," he says, his frown turning to a grin. "I remember it perfectly because her mother and I were just heading out to the movies. We had paid, of course, and were just sitting down when Eleanor said "Oh!" like she'd sat on a tack. I think I almost had a heart attack right then and there. One frantic hour later, Ellen was in my arms."

He looks at me and smiles, the love on his face obvious as he raises his glass. "It was love at first sight. From that moment, I was wrapped around her tiny finger. Ellen was always one to do things her way, but yet she always seems to land on her feet, and for that, I am grateful. She is one of the two most wonderful daughters in the world. To Mrs. Ellen Michaels, may your happiness today be with you for the rest of your life." Laura grins beside me as he raises his glass. John's hand squeezes my thigh beneath the white flowing tablecloth. Everyone looks at us with smiles wide across their faces. My mom dabs at tears as she raises her glass with the other hand.

"Mrs. Michaels!" They all repeat and drink deeply. I just sit there, feeling the baby kick beneath the table, the warmth of my husband's hand on my thigh, and a full feeling of my heart expanding beneath my ribs.

How did this ungodly mess turn into such a beautiful, happy moment? I have no idea. But my cheeks hurt as I smile and smile and smile until John takes my hand and we walk side by side like grinning idiots. We fit with one another. He loves me more than I deserve, and I love him with all of my being. If we can get through this year, we can get through anything. Nothing can stop us now.

CHAPTER 10
HOUSE #13

November, 2008

GREY.

My world of blue shirts and blue skies has disintegrated to grey. Grey hair, grey clothes, grey sinks and toilets. Grey cement and walls. Grey rain.

The colour has leached out of everything and left me blind. I don't turn on the television. I don't read books. Newspapers sit in a grey pile on the kitchen counter, growing higher and higher as the weeks pass. I just stare at the grey paint all around me, unable to cry or laugh or think.

Buddy is the one spark of something in my nothingness—a small but needy presence to move the days forward. I let him into the backyard to do his business. I feed him and water him. If the sun happens to find a way out of the clouds, I manage to walk him around the block, but he doesn't pull or bark or do any of the usual Buddy things because he knows I won't fight back. I'll just concede, and he'll be free to run away, or get hit by a car, or steal some poor old lady's sandwich. His good nature prevents it, and I guess somewhere in the grey I am thankful for it.

I don't even care when a black car that looks vaguely familiar drives by me as I follow buddy down the sidewalk, or when the same black car slows in front of the house as I stare aimlessly out the kitchen window. I may know this car, but it isn't important now. My brain is too fogged to register, too numb to care.

I find myself sitting on the sofa, staring at the grey around me, lost in my head.

It has been two hundred days since John left the house and didn't come back. Two hundred days of questions—of lonely, grey guilt.

It's almost Christmas, and I have one hundred and sixty four days left to get out of this house. Merry Christmas…get out. They want to talk to me about it. *They*, ubiquitous *They*. I hate *They*. *They* took John away from me.

They, that take, take, take and never give. They.

Where will I go? I've lived on or beside twelve different bases since I left home to pursue my truncated dreams of a college education. Twelve places where I was told to go. Dictated by *They*. Of those times John and I bought twice and the rest were military housing. It was just too much effort to buy. Why put yourself through that, when you knew you were going to be packing up just as you settled in? This house is no exception. John and I were moving to the East coast this year. We had plans to live near the beach, revelling in our empty-nesthood.

Without him, where will I go? I am lost in the grey.

Buddy suddenly pricks his ears and growls as someone knocks at the door.

He barks, pulling me from my grey thoughts. I look at the kitchen, wondering who it is. I don't get up.

Knock, knock, knock.

I don't get up.

Buddy barks again, and continues barking as he jogs to the kitchen. Tick, tick, tick go his nails on the ceramic. I should cut his nails—he'll scratch the hardwood, I think.

Knock, knock.

Buddy stops barking and starts to whine happily. He knows who it is.

I don't get up.

Buddy prances in the kitchen and moves from the side to the front door.

I look up, and from where I am seated I see Bob, peering through the window panes.

"Ellen," he says, his voice muffled by the glass. "Please…let me in."

Buddy waits expectantly. His tail wags back and forth like a metronome.

I stare at Bob, seeing him but not seeing him.

"Ellen, I'm not leaving," Bob says.

Buddy turns and looks at me, his eyes confused and happy and expectant. His tail stops wagging. He waits.

"Ellen... Open the door."

Bob's breath fogs up the glass. He's wearing a knit hat. When did it get cold?

He tries the handle but it doesn't budge. Buddy walks over and puts his head on my lap, eyes big and dark and sad.

"I can't." I whisper.

"Ellen, come on. It's cold out here." Bob says.

Buddy pulls at my sleeve, like he wants to go for a walk. In the grey, I realize I haven't dressed today. Why would I dress? I'm not going anywhere.

With no thought other than to stop the incessant knocking and pleading, I get up and walk to the door, turn the deadbolt, and walk back to my cocoon of blankets. I don't even wait to look to see if Bob comes in. It's the best I can do.

Bob takes off his coat and hat and flops them over the banister. He slips his shoes off, leaving them carefully on the rug. He has a briefcase—the briefcase of doom, I think. He says nothing, just picks it up and walks in to my living room. He sits down, watching me quietly.

My eyes flit from his socks to his face. Socks...face. Socks...face. I don't want to look at the briefcase of doom. I hate that thing. Every piece of paper I've signed, initialled, read and reviewed for this whole messy business has come from that briefcase.

Bob watches me and I fiddle with the fringes of the blanket wrapped around me.

Finally, I can't stand it. "What?" I ask.

"Ellen, I'm worried about you."

Surprise, surprise, living in the land of grey is not socially acceptable. Especially for an officer's wife. Oh, wait. *Ex*-officer's wife. We're supposed to be all perky and organized with nails and clothes that match the flower arrangements on our dining room tables. Heaven forbid an officer's wife should experience an actual true, deep emotion.

I say nothing. What is there to say? Bob can worry all he wants, but it's not going to change the fact that my husband is dead and everything I've ever lived for is meaningless now.

"It's been seven months," he says, as if this should matter to me.

"Six months, and sixteen days." I say. The time matters, but what he is implying doesn't.

"Six months and sixteen days, then," he says. "John is not coming back, Ellen."

I stare at him. I'm not stupid. I know John is not coming back. I know it every second of every minute of every hour of every day. John will not come back. He is dead, dead, dead.

"Ellen you have to move on."

I squeeze the fringes in my hand until my too-long, broken, un-manicured nails dig into my palms.

"What do you want, Bob?" I finally ask.

He looks so hurt at my question, and sits there for a long time, waiting. "I want you to come back to the living. John is dead, Ellen... but you're not."

The blood rushes to my cheeks, and my eyes sting from unshed tears.

My brain screams and screams that he's not being fair, that everyone else has come and brought lasagne and told me it would get easier and patted my back. Everyone else cleaned and made coffee and left stinking lilies to die on my table. Why does he, of all people, have to be so mean?

"I don't know if I can do that," I whisper.

"You can," he says, leaving the black briefcase on the floor. "I've seen what you can do."

This...this simple statement, pulls me from the grey more than anything else could. I loosen my grasp on the blanket.

"I can't do it. I can't do it without John." The tears are so close. I don't want to cry in front of Bob.

"Bullshit!" he says forcefully. I jump.

What in the hell?

"You *can* do it. And you will do it. It sucks. It's hard. But you are one hell of a strong woman, Ellen Michaels. I *know* how strong you are."

His eyes are piercing me like arrows, and suddenly I know he's not talking about John. He's not talking about kids and postings and moves. He's talking about something I've spent my life trying to forget.

My voice cracks as I respond. "You know?"

"I know."

"But."

"Ellen, I *know*. For more than twenty five years I've *known*."

"You know?" My voice is almost inaudible.

He nods and my heart feels like it will explode through my ribs and onto the floor.

And then, instead of the tears falling from my eyes, they fall from his.

"I'm sorry," he says. I'm not sure what it is that he's sorry for. There's so much. "I...I wish..." He dashes the tears away. Add shock to the list of emotions I'm feeling anew.

"I wish I had said something—anything—then. Right then. In front of John's room."

"Bob..." I start. He can't know. No one knows. Hell, I don't even remember exactly what happened that night. I've struck it from my mind. Denial eventually leads to amnesia.

"I was late. I ducked behind a door when the COC came out of John's room. I saw him *buckling his belt*, for God's sake!" His eyes flit around the room, but they come back to me, pleading. "And then you came out, Ellen. Beaten, crying, and...and..."

"Bob, stop." The memories are coming back, and they are too much for my grey world. Vivid black and angry red.

"You were *bleeding*, Ellen! I wiped up the trail of *blood* you left! And I didn't say anything! I could have said something. I..." The tears are rolling down his face, blotching pink and streaking white. Dragging the past up in front of me after years and years of forgetting.

I can't take it! I can't! Not now, not fucking now!

"Stop!" I scream at him. "Shut up! You don't know anything!"

He doesn't know anything. He doesn't know there was more—that it didn't end there. That Fielding has haunted my every move for twenty-five years.

Buddy whines.

"I could have helped," he says as he leans forward, dropping his head in his hands. "I could have helped." His anguish is too raw for me to understand.

I'm...I don't know what I am. I'm not prepared for this. He's so destroyed over that one time, what would he do if he knew it all?

He finally sits back and meets my eyes. His are bloodshot and red, staring back at me, wanting forgiveness.

"Ellen, if you can get through that—and all the shit the military has thrown at you, yet have three beautiful children and a marriage that survived it all until now...you can get through this. No one...no one wants you to forget John. You can't. But you've got so much more living to do! You're young, and you could—"

"What?" I interrupt him. "I could what? Work at a fucking bargain mart?"

"No! Haven't you heard anything I've said over the past few months? Jesus, Ellen! John left you over half a million dollars!"

I didn't know this. My eyes widen.

"The insurance policy? Accidental death? Double the benefit? Retirement savings?"

These words I recognize...but they were just papers to sign, words to get through.

"Ellen..." his voice softens. "Ellen you can buy a house, go back to school, travel, whatever you want. Please, just come back to us. Come back to the living."

I look at the briefcase of doom, and then look at the wall. I can't think of that time, can't think of the years of denial and clothes that cover up bruises. I can't understand Bob's torment. And I certainly can't reconcile the fear and pain and guilt of that time with the fear and pain and guilt of John's loss. It's like two different Ellens in two different universes. That one moved on because there was something and someone to move on for. This one has nothing to reach toward. No one to hide behind. Only wisps of fog lay ahead of the here and now.

"Please? Ellen?"

The wall in front of me has a dark spot where Buddy has rubbed against it with muddy fur. A brown swipe on a beige background. It looks like a hand waving hello.

My head turns from the dark spot back to Bob.

"How? How can I come back?" I whisper.

He shrugs. "You have to just do it. Look all of the awfulness in the eye, and step forward anyway…Talk to me. Tell me what I don't know. Tell *someone*. And then find Ellen, and who she is."

Find Ellen.

Find Ellen.

Oh, John! Why did I let you leave that day, when I was angry and broken and lost?

And now that you're gone, how can I find who I am?

CHAPTER 11
HOUSE #4

July, 1988

Boxes, boxes everywhere and not a cup to drink with, I think as I walk through what used to look like a kitchen. I can't help but let out a long, exhausted sigh. It's so steamy-hot in here, and I could really use a glass of water. A sluggish part of my brain notes that I forgot to put the sippy cups in the 'do not pack' pile and they are now buried somewhere deep in this maze of brown cardboard. As if on cue, Christopher, now two, starts to wail at my side.

"Shit." I say, so worn out from the day of supervising packers, placating children, and cleaning cupboards that I can't even flip my mental profanity into something child-friendly. At least David, lost in his Legos in the living room, doesn't hear.

"Sit," Chris says. "Sippy?"

The hand not holding Chris goes to my forehead in frustration.

"I'm lookin' sweetie," I say, and I commence my mental search for a spare sippy as I stare aimlessly at the boxes. Each box has something written in bold, black marker. KITCHEN, POTS. KITCHEN, GLASSWARE. KITCHEN, UTENSILS. Nothing resembling KITCHEN, SIPPY CUPS.

The box beside me has 'KITCHEN, MISSELANUS' written on its side. I try very hard not to belittle the packers, but this little detail makes me laugh…with a very distinct tinge of hysteria. Missel-anus, my butt.

"Sippy, sippy, sippy" Chris repeats over and over as he whines and rubs his sweaty boogies on my shoulder.

I consider asking John if he's seen a sippy cup, but he is outside sharing a questionably legal beer with the packers. The smoke from their cigarettes drifts through the open window, making my kitchen stink. It lingers in the heavy, humid air outside. The smell dances on my frayed nerves like a spark. I'm so tired…from the day, from the week, from my life…that all I want to do is fall down and scream. Rather like my son.

"Sippy, sippy, sippeeeeeeeeeeee," Chris whines into my ear.

My mom-radar goes off and I remember seeing a cup on the van floor beneath one of the seats. It's been there for eons, probably growing a new life form, but it will do.

I push my way through the boxes to the door and yell through clenched teeth out the open window. "John, there's a sippy cup under the passenger-side chair in the van. Can you get it please?"

"Sippeeeeeeeeeeee…"

He looks up like I'm interrupting an important board meeting, not a casual beer between strangers.

"What?" John asks through Chris's whines. He has the audacity to look angry. I can see the 'how dare you disturb my social hour' roll across his face. Of all the self-centred, monumental *pricks*. He's been sitting on his ass the entire day, working on some paperwork thing or another, while I've fed, changed, cleaned, entertained, supervised and basically managed the lives of our entire family of four.

My blood pressure spikes upwards. "The van. A sippy cup in the van. Can you get it? *Now?*"

"I waaaaaaaaaaant sippeeeeeeeeeee!"

"Where?" John says, waking up to the fact that his second son is wailing at the top of his lungs into my ear.

"*In. The. Van.* Under the seat. Passenger side."

Chris's screeches have reached nuclear-meltdown pitch. John clues in to the urgency of the situation and slowly gets up to walk toward the van, murmuring something I can't hear. One of the packers chuckles. I want to kill both John and the packer with a blunt spoon. If I weren't so bone tired, and if our utensils weren't locked away for God-knows-how-long in a box marked KITCHEN, UTENSILS, they'd be dead—right now—their innards spread out under the blazing sun, waiting for the vultures to come and gorge themselves.

The packer shuts up when he sees the look on my face. In fact, all three of the large, sweaty strangers put down their empty beers and look at their watches.

I don't hear what they say, but they hop in their cube van and are backing out before John returns, blue cup dangling non-chalantly from his finger.

As expected, the sippy cup has a layer of fur on what was probably orange juice. The screaming in my ear stops like someone has thrown a switch.

"Sippy?" And then Chris is wriggling like a rabid squirrel trying to get at the disgusting, smelly cup John has handed to me. Instead of offering to help, John turns and heads back outside to clean up the beer bottles. I slam the door and half set, half drop Chris on the floor. There is no way I'm letting my child put this thing in his mouth.

"Sippeeeeee!" It starts again as he falls on his diapered backside.

"Christopher, honey, mommy has to wash it out! It's icky! Tastes bad!" I say as I fight my way to the sink. He's up again and hanging off my leg, screaming as I do so.

I am not a patient woman. I want to be, but I'm not. And the screaming dervish flailing on my leg is just about doing me in. Where in the hell is John? Why in the hell am I doing this? I can think of a million different things—useful, good-citizen things—that I'd rather be doing than sweating with a screaming snotty kid on my leg.

I glance out at the window, and a black car drives by—one that I recognize but doesn't belong to anyone our street. It goes by often, slowing as it nears our house, and today I shiver when I see it. One thing I won't miss from this place is the feeling that someone is watching me.

"Sippeeeeeeee…." Christopher screams.

The cup hisses as I open it and then fur dumps into the sink in one stinking, green blob. Yuck. Oh my God that stinks!

And then it happens with no warning at all. The donuts, the McDonalds hamburger and the French fries come flying up from my stomach and through my mouth and nose like an F-18, splattering unceremoniously in the sink beside the blob.

Oh.

The world around me sharpens down like an HB pencil as I catch my breath, thinning and compressing into this moment. Even Chris stops crying, curious as to what that noise was and why Mommy is leaning over the sink.

"Sippy, Momma?" he says.

I swallow, and wipe my mouth with the back of my hand, still staring at the bile, food, and fuzzy blob in front of me.

"Just a minute sweetie."

I rinse the cup out, pour some dish detergent in, swirl it around with my finger and dump it—knowing that there's no way I'll find a dishrag in here. The blob and half-digested food clog the sink, but I don't look at it. Even the thought makes me queasy.

When the cup is as clean as it's going to get, I fill it with cold water and squat down to Christopher's level. He reaches out and grabs it with his chubby little fist, smiling broadly with tear-stained cheeks.

"Sippy."

Overcome with a mixture of fatigue and raw emotion, I sit right there on the floor among the boxes and gather him into my arms. His body is warm and soft and the cup makes rushing, screechy noises as he pulls away at it. His other fist reaches up and grabs a lock of hair from my ponytail. In seconds his eyes are closed, and I wish like anything that I could do the same—just fall asleep and forget about moves and black cars and everything but my little blue sippy cup.

I hear the door squeak and slam shut, but thankfully Chris doesn't wake. Someone pushes through the boxes and I look up to see John, looking sheepish and carrying two cold Cokes.

"Sorry," he says.

He puts one can down, opens the other and then hands it to me, being careful not to drip condensation on our sleeping toddler. I have to shift Chris a little to take the can, but he's too far gone to notice. John picks up the other can, slides down beside me and gently brushes back Chris's hair.

"I forgot you were in here with the boys by yourself," John says quietly. "I just…offered the guys a beer, and didn't think that you might need some help."

Damn right, I think as I take a sip of Coke. It soothes my bile-raw throat. I wait for a second—to make sure it will stay down there—and then take another sip.

"I hate this part." I say. "The boxes, the mess…not knowing where anything is."

"Yeah," he says. "But you're good at it."

Incredulous, I turn to look at him.

"Good at it?" I say.

"You are! The kids have busy bags full of toys, we have a cooler full of drinks, we've got hotels booked half the way across the country, and when we get there, David's preschool will be waiting for him. I couldn't have done all that."

He's right. John couldn't organize eggs into a carton.

"I love you, you know," he says.

I nod. "I do know.'

"Good."

We sit there, Christopher sleeping, David playing with his Legos in the other room, and the light slowly dimming as the sun sinks behind the trees.

"John?"

"Yeah, Ellie?"

"I think…I think I'm pregnant."

He turns and looks at me, first in the face, then down at my stomach—which is hidden by our sleeping toddler. John smiles a big, wide-cheeked, face-splitting grin.

"Babe, that's the best news I've heard all year."

He holds up his Coke and we clink cans, and I think that today—in spite of the craziness, the heat, the disruption, and the vomit—*today* has turned out to be a pretty good day.

CHAPTER 12
HOUSE #4

December, 1988

"**Y**OU LOOK DIVINE," JOHN SAYS as he kisses the bare nape of my neck. He stops and looks into the mirror at the two of us, snuggling close. The dress makes me look fat, not pregnant, but it's the only thing I could afford. Well, the only thing on sale that I didn't feel guilty spending money on. John, on the other hand, looks dashing in his brand new suit and tie.

The invite lies in front of us, open in all it's hatefulness on my dresser. *Col and Mrs. Frank Fielding request the honour of your presence at a Christmas gathering…* blah, blah, blah. I get nervous just thinking about it, so I try not to. Why did John have to get posted here? Will I never be rid of that…that lecherous asshole?

"I look fat," I say.

"You look like Aphrodite herself," John says, "or a fairy princess just waiting to enthral me in her dancing ring." I love how his mouth quirks up on one side. His hair is cropped short to fit under his flight helmet, and it makes him look like a movie star.

His hand slides around to my stomach and rubs the bump that's forming there. "Pregnant suits you," he says. "I'll have to keep you this way."

I laugh. "Um, no…Mr. Virile. I think you'll be visiting the doctor after this one. Unless you want to quit your day job."

I'm teasing, sort of. I love our kids. Hearing them giggle downstairs with our favourite babysitter makes me smile. David is particularly enthralled with Jessica; he's told me more than once that he's going to marry her. But I'm not even twenty-five yet. When do I get to start living?

John chuckles into my ear. "I'd do anything for you."

I've managed to pull my hair up, with tendrils of softly curling hair trailing the side of my face. He nuzzles my ear, tickling me. It's sexy watching him in the mirror with his suit on, and I feel the response deep in my stomach where the baby sleeps.

"Well, let's go to this thing, so we can get back home…"

He looks into the mirror and sees my smile. The hand on my belly slides up to my breast. "And what would we do then?" he asks innocently.

"You'll just have to find out."

"Oh…well then, shall we?" He offers his arm to me and we walk down the stairs like an old-fashioned couple heading off to the theatre.

We've been here just a few months, and I've been home with the kids the whole time, so I don't recognize a soul as we walk through the doors of the Officer's Mess. John checks our coats and I stick close. I feel self-conscious in my spaghetti-strap dress with my large breasts and gently protruding belly. The hum of conversation and the big-band music in the background do nothing to soothe my nerves. I fiddle with the chain on my clutch purse as I search for someone—anyone—that I know.

As we walk through the main hall doors, we're greeted by *him*, and my blood runs cold.

"Michaels… Ellen" he says as he nods to each of us. His eyes slide down and lock on my stomach for the briefest of seconds. The resulting smile is more rapist than social. It makes my skin crawl.

"Sir," John says. He puts his hand out and Fielding shakes it. I recognize what's coming and panic, but I can't avoid it. He takes my hand and brings his to his lips. I feel the touch of his tongue, the graze of his teeth on my knuckles and my guts turn to lead. I jerk back an infinitesimal amount, and my instinct is to slap him like a stinging bug. It's all I can do to stand still and not bolt from the room at top speed.

"Oh, Ellen!" exclaims his wife with her high-pitched fake-voice, giving me the cue to snatch my hand away. Fielding holds my eyes and I glare back. I hope neither of them notices my brief look of disgust as I wipe my hand on my dress. "You look wonderful! Simply glowing," she gushes like a syrupy stream in my peripheral vision.

I finally tear my eyes away from the evil in front of me and glance at her. Is she for real? "Thank you," I manage to say, "You look lovely tonight too, Mrs. Fielding." And she does—every bit the Base Commander's wife. I'm sure her dress cost more than my dress and John's suit combined. Her hair is perfectly coiffed, her manicure impeccable. Her hand is limp in mine as we shake, ladylike and annoying.

"Pregnancy agrees with you!"

Oh my God, how does she talk like that? The energy in her voice makes me tired just listening to it. She is clueless in so many ways. How can she not know? I want to shake her, knock some sense into her. And yet another part of me pities her. To be married to such a thug—what can her life be like? Does he tie her to their bed with his belt?

The mental image makes me feel sick.

"Good to see you both," Fielding drawls, interrupting my thoughts. "Why don't you grab a drink at the bar...tell them it's on me."

"Thank you, sir," John says stiffly. Does he feel the tension shooting through me?

"Thank you," I choke out, wrapping my arm around John's elbow for support. We nod and walk away so that Fielding can greet the couple behind us. His wife gushes about the next wife's dress, our presence forgotten. Not so with Fielding. I feel his eyes on my back, like a poisonous oil-slick as we walk away. I feel faint.

"Well, that was nice of him," John says as we head to the bar. "Old Fielding's getting soft in his old age."

I don't tell him that Frank Fielding is not soft. Frank Fielding is as hard as iron.

We take our drinks—John's beer, my orange juice on the rocks—and I follow John to the gaggle of young men and women over near the tables. As we approach, I finally recognize a few of the guys, but only one of the girls—a pretty blonde with tiny everything. Jennifer, I think her name is. Beside her I see another wife staring toward the door at Fielding—her eyes wide and nervous.

"Michaels!" a beefy red-head shouts, interrupting my thoughts. John breaks away from me to shake his hand, all tough and guy like. I'm left standing just off to the side, with my back still burning and my face exposed to strangers.

"It's Ellen, isn't it?" The girl I think I know says, putting out her hand. I shake, a proper, firm handshake, and she reciprocates. I almost sigh with relief.

"And you're…Jennifer?" I ask. She nods, smiling. Beside her several other young, well-dressed ladies step forward—even the one that was staring at Fielding. I feel awkward and lumpy next to their perfect figures. More than one of them glances at my obvious bump.

"Ellen this is Anna, Jane, Donna, and Sylvia," Jennifer says. I shake hands with them all, and they smile.

"So, you've been here how long?" the girl I think is Jane asks.

"Almost five months. Just long enough to get most of the boxes put away."

"Oh, tell me about it," says a brunette—Sylvia? "We moved last year and I still have boxes. God, I hate boxes." My brain registers that she's wearing a huge diamond engagement ring. A ring that could probably feed our children for ten years. I rub my small gold band, semi-conscious of its inexpensive simplicity.

"What squadron?" she asks.

"220 Squadron." I think that's what he told me. I have so little mental energy to spend on learning John's military details. I don't even know what building he works in.

"Oh cool, same as Jennifer," says the brunette. It's like I've passed some test, they all nod and smile approvingly.

"Don't look now, but Fielding's looking this way. God he gives me the creeps," says Jane. She shudders and I whip around to face him. He's far too close to where I'm standing, and I know he's staring at me.

I wonder if any of these girls know how creepy he *really* is. I put on a mask of fake bravado and glance back to my new acquaintances, searching for anything that would suggest something more, but their faces mostly show disgust and curiosity, not terror. Except for Jane… she stares at him as though he were a viper. I turn again and watch as he greets the next couple to come through the door. His eyes suddenly look up to mine, and he smiles the same twisted smile I remember from five years ago. The nausea returns.

"Where's the washroom?" I ask, sounding apologetic. I shrug at Jane and pat my belly, "Junior is lying right on my bladder."

Now they can stop guessing if I'm pregnant or just fat. Besides, I'm not even lying. Junior and my bladder are close personal friends these days.

They titter, and Jennifer points to the door we came in. "Outside and take a left. Past the coat check and up a few stairs."

"Thanks."

Crap. I have to go by *him* to go out. And John is so busy talking with his friends that I can't get his attention to shield me.

I walk slowly, biding my time until Fielding is greeting someone and then I slip by without even acknowledging his presence. I don't care if it's rude. John's the military guy. Yes sir, no sir is his game, not mine. I walk briskly until I'm around a corner, and then practically run to the restroom, the need to pee accentuated by every bouncing step. I think I may need to vomit as well. When I get through the door, the cubicles are all empty—just one woman in front of the mirror who finishes applying her lipstick without looking my way. I slip into one of the stalls and push the lock across. Only then do I relax, slumping onto the toilet seat with my head in my hands.

Oh, God! How am I going to get through this night? I don't know anyone, John knows everyone, and *he's* here, watching me. The trapped, panicky feeling I haven't known since the Academy flutters in my chest. I knew *he* was here, I knew he was dangerous, but with the move, the boxes, the babies and everyday life, I had let the risks slip to the back of my mind. I guess I thought that if I ignored him, he'd just go away—like a virus or a bad smell. I'm nothing special, so was it that naïve to hope he would forget I existed? It's been years, now…is he always going to haunt me? Will he always be lurking at the edge of my vision, waiting…biding his time until he can strike again? I hate what he's done to me. Hate that he's turned me into a weak, snivelling fool, hiding in bathroom stalls.

I sit there, fighting with nausea and panic for a long, long time. I don't want to go by Fielding again. Maybe if I sit here all night, no one will notice. But I can't do that. Maybe I'll go out and stomp my heel deep into his foot. Maybe I'll throw my drink into his face. Maybe.

My moment is interrupted by the slam of the door and drunken giggling.

"Did you *see* her? She looks like she hasn't got a brain cell in her head," says a high-pitched voice.

Do all women talk like that? Do I talk like that when I'm drunk?

Another girl giggles. "Oh my God, he gives me the creeps!"

They can only be talking about one couple. The cubicle door beside me slams and I hear the unmistakable sounds of someone peeing. "I know! It must be a nightmare being married to that letch!" More giggles. "The boys sure are looking hot tonight!"

"Oh yeah! Oh! Did you see Michaels? God, that bod!"

Michaels? My Michaels? They're talking about John? Don't they realize I'm still in here?

Giggle, giggle, giggle…they're making me sick. My cubicle neighbour bounces out of her stall and washes her hands. I peek through the crack in the door to see if I recognize any of them, but all I see are short dresses and large hair.

"And his wife is pregnant…again! Gees, do they just bonk like rabbits all the time? They had two before he even graduated from mil-col!"

"I'd like to bonk that bod."

"Me too. We could have a threesome!"

"Sylvia said he had lunch at the diner where she works yesterday. Michaels winked at her and tipped her…really well! I think he's got the hots for her!"

My face heats and my pulse quickens. John, flirting?

I hit the flush lever. That silences them for a second, and then they burst into giggles and stagger through the door. It slams closed behind them and their giggles trail away.

I want to leave.

I've been here exactly twenty-eight minutes, my first night out with my husband in I don't know how long, and I want to leave. Right now. I'm so angry, frustrated, panicked, scared, lost, depressed…I'm so many emotions all balled up in my stomach I can barely breathe. Between Fielding's touch and those women talking about John—talking about us—I've lost my footing. There's nothing for me to stand on here. My world has turned slippery and confused.

I lean my head on the cold metal stall door, probably covered with a million germs, and take slow, deep breaths, trying to calm my heart and the headache that's creeping up over my skull.

I want to leave. I can't do this.

I open the door and look at myself in the long, wall-spanning mirror. My hair is nice, I've got a nice dress, and even though I look like a cow, I'm not hideous. What has been happening in social circles while I'm barefoot, pregnant, and possibly cowering at home to avoid Fielding?

As the emotions swirl through me, I land on one thought. John is mine. Those big-haired fakers can't have him. He's hot, all right, but he's mine. So what if both David and Chris were accidents. We had them because we were in *love*. Because John loves *me*. He's mine, mine, *mine*, and godammit! I'm not going to give him up to those giggling twits on a silver platter.

I brush back my hair and pinch my cheeks—which is not really necessary because pregnancy has put me in a permanent state of hot-flash—and as I take a last look at the mirror, the bathroom door opens quietly and Mrs. Fielding slides in. She smiles at me emptily—oblivious of who I am—and I stand there with a stupid look on my face. She slips into a stall and locks the door before I get a chance to react. And then suddenly I'm furious. My anger at the ditzy, drunk wives multiplies ten-fold, fuelled by pregnancy hormones and the fact that Fielding's wife doesn't know who the hell I am. Her husband *raped* me for God's sake! While she was lying in her expensive bed, in her expensive home, her husband was making me bleed! Stealing my chance at happiness! I want to make her feel what I felt. I want to punch her in the stomach so she can feel the pain he put me through. I wait, standing there staring at the mirror with my fists clenched and my blood pressure skyrocketing, seeing red stars and fiery flashes in the fluorescent lighting.

Ten seconds pass…twenty…a minute…and I don't know if she's hiding, realizing a viper awaits her beyond the stall or just having a little personal moment, but she doesn't come out. I hear more high-pitched voices in the hall and the anger at her slides away. I realize taking my frustrations out on this woman would do nothing. I can't help her and she can't help me. But I can help myself. I can hold tight to the things that matter—my husband, my family, my dignity.

I look in the mirror again, see my swollen, wonderful stomach, and then I stride out the door with a tenuous purpose, shoulders back and head held high. Fielding tries to catch my eye as I enter the ballroom, but I breeze by him, ignoring his pointed looks. In the dark, crowded room, I spot John's blonde head in an instant, standing with other men and their dates. I think I recognize one of the women from the washroom. I walk straight to my husband, slowly slipping my arm around him, resting my hand on the cheek of his behind.

This boy is *mine*, ladies.

He leans down and nuzzles my ear. "Hey baby," he says low enough that only I can hear. When he leans back his eyes are drinking me in, like I'm sunshine on a cloudy day.

"Hey," I say.

"How's Junior?" He asks, and unabashedly rubs my bump.

"Good. Do you want to sit down with me?"

"Always," he says. He grins that charming, lopsided smile, and the earth solidifies beneath my feet again.

He wraps his arm around my waist. As we walk toward the tables, I glance over and see the girl I'm sure is Sylvia staring at us from the bar. I give her a dazzling grin. She suddenly finds something extremely interesting about her glass.

Oh yes, he's mine, bitch. And don't you dare forget it.

We sit, we eat, and we chat with people I don't know. Jennifer sits beside me, and I quickly find I like her. She's funny and quirky, with a hint of sarcasm that makes me feel at ease, despite my pregnant state and all of the other nastiness surrounding this dinner. The other wives I'm not so sure of. Their smiles don't reach their eyes, and I don't speak their overly-enthusiastic, high-pitched language. And I can't stand the fact that some of them were talking about my husband as if he were theirs for the taking.

John is mine.

His hand rests on my thigh, grounding me as the speeches roll over me. When some poor lieutenant—Jones, I think his name is—gets up to introduce Col Fielding, I excuse myself to find the washroom again. I don't want to look at him, and I certainly don't want to hear him speak. I sit in there for at least twenty minutes, waiting for his speech to finish.

When I'm positive he can't be speaking anymore, I pat my hair, check my make-up and walk back into the hallway—straight into Fielding's grabbing hands.

"Don't make a sound, or you'll regret it," he hisses as he pulls me quickly down the hallway. At first, I'm too shocked to fight, too shocked to do anything but walk with him around a corner and through a door, into a room with a bed and a dresser and the smell of cigar smoke. He locks the door with a flick, grabbing my wrists again, and then the adrenaline kicks in. I pull and snap my arms, trying to break free.

He grips harder, his perfectly trimmed nails digging into my wrists, and I try valiantly to lodge my spiked heel into the arch of his left foot. He groans and loosens his grip—just for a second—and I slide away. But he's fast and he catches my hair, ripping out bobby pins as I strain to free myself. He yanks my head and his fist connects with my belly and then I almost black out... and I find myself face down on the bed.

"Your husband is at a precarious point in his career," he whispers into my ringing ears.

I'm going to be sick.

"Review boards next week. I think you may want to consider your actions right now." His voice is calm, but the anger underneath it is terrifying. It curls around my head like the smoke in the air, and I feel faint and I may throw up. He snaps me around so I'm facing him, arms held to my side. He bends over me, his weight pressing me down and I'm blurry-eyed and weak.

"Wouldn't it be dreadful if something popped up in his flight bag this week? Something white and illegal...There are so many things I could do to ruin your little husband..." he whispers into my ear, his hot breath smelling of whisky. I twist, but he's too heavy, too strong, and I can't breathe. Somehow he's holding both of my hands in one and his fist is pressing in on my stomach...and sliding lower.

I arc away from his hand but it's no use. I'm trapped. His breath is sickly on my neck. I know he's not making an idle threat. This monster will do it. My mind whirls, trying to find a way out, trying to justify fighting—for myself, for my unborn baby, for my family. We couldn't live without John's job. I can't work while I'm pregnant and nursing.

John needs this promotion. I need this promotion. And if John were in jail…

I am such a coward.

I stop fighting.

"Better."

And with a sick sense of déjà vu, he undoes his belt.

Ten minutes later, he watches me as I cower by the bed and pull myself together. I crawl cautiously on the floor, searching for bobby pins.

I hate this man.

I hate him, hate him, *hate* him!

"I'm going to go find your husband," he says. "And I will tell him I found you and you were ill. He will come to this room to find you, and you will go home. And if I hear one word of this anywhere…the white powder will come out…and your husband will get to know the inside of military jail. It's not nice there," he says, combing his slicked greying hair in the mirror. He reaches down to brush at his foot where I caught him with my heel. His sock is black, but his hand comes away red with blood. If I wasn't hurting everywhere I would laugh.

He looks at me with disgust, and for a moment I fear he will come at me again. But he turns and slowly, methodically rinses his hand in the sink before walking toward the door. He doesn't limp.

The door shuts firmly behind him, and I manage to make it to the small sink before supper makes its reappearance.

An eternity later, John barges through the door, and finds me sitting on the floor beside the now-perfectly made bed with the smell of vomit overpowering the smoke.

He rushes to kneel before me.

"Baby, are you okay? What happened?" His eyes are so full of love, so full of concern and there's no denying he loves me—would still love me if I told him and Fielding sent him to jail, ended his career. But I can't do that to him. I can't do that to us. I want to tell him…but I can't.

"I…I got sick." I say, and a sob escapes from my lips.

"Oh, Baby, it's okay! You'll be fine, probably just the rich food." Explaining away my horror, he pulls a napkin from his pocket and hands it to me. I wipe my eyes unceremoniously and try not to weep. I can't tell him.

I have to tell him.

"John..." I start. The words are right there, ready to explode out of my mouth like the puke in the sink, ready to erupt and wreak what havoc they may. "John, I..."

"...Let's go home," he interrupts. "It's a stupid party anyway." He draws his finger across my lips, silencing me—and squashing what courage I have.

"Can you drive?" he asks.

The pregnant lady is always the DD, even when she's just vomited.

Even after she's just been raped.

I nod and manage to stand up, blaming baby awkwardness for my difficulty as I walk with him to our car. We drive home in the winter darkness.

And I don't tell him a thing.

CHAPTER 13
HOUSE #13

December, 2008

THE KIDS HAVE COME HOME for Christmas…if you can call it home. It feels like an empty shell now, no laughter, no teasing…no John. I manage to clean up the kitchen but I leave the decorations for them. I just can't stomach it. We decide to limit ourselves to a tree and a few candles. Chris fishes the green plastic bins from the basement, and David puts together the artificial tree. No one mentions that it's usually John that puts the tree together, but we all think it. Maria finds me in the kitchen, looking out the window over the sink. A black car with tinted windows drives by, slowing but continuing down the street. My heart rate doesn't even alter, I'm so emotionally detached.

"You okay, mom?" She asks.

I'm not going to lie to her. "No." I say.

"Me neither."

We're silent, lost in our own little versions of hell.

I notice that someone has found the Christmas CDs and popped one in. Ella Fitzgerald croons softly over the boys' quiet banter.

"Mom?"

I don't want to talk right now. It hurts too much.

"What, sweetie?"

"Can we bake something?"

Oh. "Bake something?"

"Yah. I dunno, maybe some gingerbreads? What's your favourite?"

I turn away from the cold, white world outside to face her. "My favourite?"

"Yeah. When you cooked with your mom, when you were little, what did you bake?"

I'm hit with a walloping memory of standing at the table with my mom, baking little cinnamon cookies called snickerdoodles. The sight of her helping me roll the little dough-balls, the smell of the cinnamon, the sound of Christmas music in the background, it's so strong it's visceral. My mouth actually waters. I was probably six years old in that mental snapshot. So young, so innocent. So protected from the nasty, nasty world. Long before my mom started hating my choices and long before the military started making them for me. Before the military machine dumped me thousands of miles from my parents and left me a widow.

"Snickerdoodles," I say.

"Snickerdoodles? Those little cinnamony cookies Grandma makes?"

"Yep. We used to make them together. I don't have the recipe though."

"We can change that," she says, and grabs the phone.

Twenty minutes later, my daughter and I are sitting at the kitchen table making snickerdoodles, and for the first time in forever, I actually feel something. I'm hungry. Hungry for buttery, cinnamony cookies. The first pan of cookies is already baking in the oven. As we roll more of the sticky dough in our hands, Chris and David come out to see what's going on, drawn by their food radar. Both of them finger-swipe some dough at the same time. Maria hauls off and whacks David with her sticky hand.

"Hey!" He yells at her. "Get your own dough!"

Chris chuckles. "Ha-ha," he says in a sing-songy voice at David. Maria hauls off and whacks him too. Chris looks at the messy handprint on his dark shirt in mock horror. I watch, spellbound, as the boys turn to each other with evil grins. Together, almost as if they orchestrated the whole thing, the boys nod, scoop up dough, and slap it into Maria's hair, rubbing gleefully.

The look on her face is priceless. She sputters, eyes wide.

David neatly grabs a blob from the top of Maria's head and pops it in his mouth. "Yummy," he says, so Chris follows suit.

And then, the most unexpected thing of all happens.

I laugh.

I don't see it coming. It bubbles up out of my chest like a burp or a sneeze. I just can't help it. Maria has little cookie-dough horns on either side of her head, her eyes are big and half-angry, and she looks like a cookie-splatted chipmunk, like a little girl with cookie pig-tails. My stomach rocks with the unfamiliar activity, and Chris, eyeing me with the funniest look on his face, joins in. David joins in next, and then Maria, throwing her hands up in disgust, giggles too. I hold my sides and laugh from the inside out, letting the feeling wash over me, and letting the warmth and smells of the kitchen fill me up. I laugh and laugh and laugh, a rusty, forgotten sound, like an old car warming up in the dead of winter.

A little while later, we're all sitting, eating hot-out-of-the oven cookies, and not-even-a-little-bit-cooked dough, and Maria tells me about her friend's bread-baking disaster in her dorm, complete with smoke alarms and flour fights. The sun sets outside, and Maria lights candles on the table and in the living room. John's sandals still sit on the mat in the entryway. David sheepishly tells us about the girl he's been seeing, and Chris tells us about the project he's working on at his new job. I listen, but I keep thinking of John's sandals, neatly placed as they have been for months, with a light coating of dust. It's comforting knowing they are there as the kids talk, as if he's on his way home to join us. I don't participate in the conversation because my world is on pause right now, but I smile and feel the ice block in my chest warm just a little.

We move into the living room and sit by the tree when the last of the dough is cooked, and the kids finish putting the decorations on the tree. David cracks a bottle of red wine from our forgotten wine rack, and we toast silently, lost in our own thoughts. It's warm and cozy, and feels like hundreds of other nights we've spent together—laughing, teasing, and loving…only this time it's without John.

Or maybe it's not. Maybe John is still with us, smiling and feeling cozy too. In the soft candlelit night, I feel something beyond the lost, empty feeling that's haunted me for months. Like there's the tiniest light in the gloom—way, way far ahead of me—but it's there. And I think John is there, holding it up for me.

Christmas morning is a quiet affair, but we stick to our routines.

The kids get up together…well, Chris wakes the other two up and demands they come downstairs. It's sparse pickings under the tree, but I've managed to get something for each of them, and they for one another. Simple things…a locket for Maria, which opens to reveal her favourite photo—her dad hugging her on the beach when she was seven. I give David a watch, one with a special engraving on the back: *Love you always, Mom.*

Christopher was harder, but I decided to get him a satellite radio system for his car. He's always liked music.

I watch as the kids open each other's gifts, off in thoughts of other Christmases in different homes. David takes John's place and plays Santa without fanfare, handing the gifts out one by one, stretching the morning out until our second pot of coffee is brewing and there's nothing left beneath the tree.

I don't even notice the absence of a gift for me from any of the children until Maria pulls an envelope out of the branches of the tree. She looks conspiratorially at David and Chris, takes a big breath, and starts to speak.

"Mom, you were so hard to buy for this year…so we decided to get you something together. Well, Chris and David got you something, and I pitched in a little bit too. We hope…" She takes another deep breath and continues on, fighting tears. "We know that Dad…"

Chris picks up where she stops. "We know that Dad would want you to get out, do something different. So…" He nods at Maria, and she hands the envelope to me.

It's thick and decorated in hand-drawn bows and Christmas trees. I look from it to the kids. All three are holding their breath.

So I open it.

It's a ticket. An airline ticket to Venice. To *Venice.* What the hell? And underneath it is another ticket for a cruise with stops in places I've never been, never imagined ever going. I flip through the pages, knowing that it's too much. I can't accept this. I search for the price tag.

"Mom, we're not telling you how much it cost," David says, as though reading my thoughts.

I look up at them with that lost feeling floating around on the surface, threatening to pull me under again.

"But…"

"No buts. You're going. It's non-refundable."

"But…"

"Mom," Maria says, tears teetering on her lower lids, "We want you to go. It's too hard, sitting here," she gestures around the house, "with Dad all around you. David has a friend who's a travel agent in the city. There's a lady in the office who's about your age…she knew…she *thought* it would be something you'd like, and this was a deal within our budget. You've always wanted to go to Europe, always loved the beach, and this gives you both. It's just a week. Go." My lovely girl can be very persuasive.

I bow my head, overwhelmed, and fiddle with the papers. There's something else she's not telling me, but I don't have the energy to push. My hands shake.

"I don't know what to say."

"You don't need to say anything at all. And you don't have a choice because we're not giving you one," says Chris.

The date for the trip is in early May—right before I have to move. I latch onto this.

"But, the house…I have to be out of the house in May. How am I going to go on a trip then?"

"Don't you see?" asks David, eyes serious. "The ticket leaves from the city, not here. Wherever you are then, you'll be spending the night before with us. We all know the move will be hard, so this will give you something else to look forward to. And we're going to help you."

Chris reaches under the tree for another envelope. "Mom, this is a map. A map of the country. You can pick anywhere to live. Anywhere at all. And we'll help you figure it out."

They're all so earnest, so expectant, so beautiful looking back at me. My heart aches just seeing their faces. They shouldn't be looking after me, though. I should be looking after them. I need to be strong. I need to be strong. I *need* to be strong.

I can't.

My eyes burn, and the papers in my hand blur as first Maria, then Chris sit beside me on the couch. David puts his hand, strong and capable, on my knee. How did he get so grown up? When the sob escapes from my lips, they hold me locked in a family circle, absorbing my despair and making it their own.

I feel a shift, sitting here bawling like a baby with my own babies. It's a sad-happy-lost-found shift, twisting everything around. A shake-up inside and outside of me. Instead of me caring for them—for John—they are caring for me, taking John's place. They push inward with their support, squeezing without choking, and I wonder how it is—with sad, broken me as their mother—that my children grew to be so strong.

CHAPTER 14
HOUSE # 7

July, 1993

THE FIRE CRACKLES AND SENDS its sparks skyward, little offerings to the stars hanging in the canvas above us. After a long, tiring drive with cranky kids and an even crankier dog, we're exhausted, but the night is too beautiful to fall into our beds without enjoying just a part of it. Behind us the tent rustles as someone—likely Chris—twists in his sleeping bag. Their soft, steady breathing is just audible over the snap of the burning logs and the bicycle-bell chirp of crickets.

John takes a sip of his beer, and reaches for my hand. We sit this way for a few moments, just soaking in the peace. John's finger moves on mine, rubbing my knuckles, and his foot taps gently—shaking our rickety lawn chairs. He can't sit still. The stress of his job radiates from him, pushing through the soft, lake-sweet air like a heat lamp. I know that this is only the second time in his life that he's been camping—other than those times he's worn green or tan and carried a gun. The times the gun was a necessity for survival, not a pretty toy. As a pilot, those times are few and far between, but his most recent trip was an eye opener for him. Planes, people on tarmacs, and people in broken, war-torn cities get shot at. I don't know what he saw over there, but it has been with him ever since. He can't relax into the night because beyond the night are the memories.

The fire pops and he twitches, gripping my fingers tightly. I feel his urge to jump in front of me, to protect me like the fire is a threat. Spot, our black lab, sits up and watches us, his eyes glowing in the fire, then rests his head on his paws with a doggy sigh.

There's no danger here.

I have my own memories—angry and broken and painful—but I don't let them show, and he doesn't look to see them. They're a part of me, have been a part of me for almost as long as I've known John. So tonight I just rub his fingers, and close my mind to that chapter. I need to pull us both away from the pictures in our minds, whatever they are. Bring us both back to the present. The tent behind us is full of warm kid-bodies, splayed willy-nilly across the cramped space. We can't make love in that. But I have more to give him than love in the physical sense.

"Where do you think we'll be in ten years?" I ask. It's not much, but the best I've got right now. The 'Question Game' is our old standby. Something we do when the road stretches long before us or a silence needs to be filled. We ask a question and then, after we get an answer, we have to answer it ourselves. We don't play it as much lately…because there's never a silence that big.

He looks at me and smiles, probably seeing my question for what it is—a ploy to pull him from his tense thoughts.

He takes another long pull from his beer, and sets it down in the cup holder attached to his chair.

"In ten years? I don't know…I'll still be wearing a uniform, you'll be still working. David will be in college, and the other two wishing they were. In fifteen years, though, even Maria will be out of the house. I'll have twenty-five years in…maybe I could get out and work for an airline."

He's broken one of our unspoken rules, and changed the question, but I'm okay with that. At least he's talking. And it's true…we can't know where we'll be in ten years. Fifteen is better.

"In fifteen years, we'll have been married for twenty five years." I say. "I think we should buy a small house somewhere—it won't need to be as big with the kids out and on their own. Maybe a little two bedroom near the ocean. I've always liked the ocean."

He turns his face away from the fire to smile at me. The flickering light reflects off his face, warming me from the inside.

"You do." He says. It's one of things I love about our current posting: in half an hour I can be at the beach. Maybe it's because I grew up inland, maybe because I have a bit of mermaid in me, I have no idea. I just love the feel of the sand under my toes and the salt wind on my face. There's something so special about the beach.

"I would love to live by the ocean," he says softly. "It makes you happy. And when you're happy, everyone's happy."

We joke about this: when momma's happy, everybody's happy. Even little Maria jokes—as much as a four-year-old can joke with her cute little way of saying 'r's like 'w's. *Evwybody's happy.* Christopher even carefully inscribed it in this year's Mother's Day card.

John's finger rubs my knuckles and the fire crackles. He jumps, but not quite so much.

"I'd like to travel. Maybe see Europe. And I'd like to go back to school and finally get my degree." I say, surprising even myself. Until this very second, I didn't even know I wanted that, it just slipped out like a distant voice on a radio. But it's true. I want something to call my own, something other than PTA meetings and piano lessons. Something more than guilt and fear waiting by the phone for crackly calls from fun and distant places. Instead of balancing checkbooks with John's money, I'd like to feel that I'm managing *our* money. Maybe it's because I've never thought about what it would be like to be at home without kids until I was sitting here, smelling of wood smoke, anchoring John to the present with my hand.

I need something to help me be me.

"Then you should," he says.

And with those three words, John has switched the pressure from me straining to hold him with me in the here-and-now, to him pushing me into the yet-to-come. It's not an easy transition.

I don't know what to say.

"You should go back to school," he repeats.

"But we can't afford it."

"We'll find a way."

"Who will look after the kids?" The smoke is making my eyes sting and water.

"I don't know...one of the babysitters. You can do it part time. Night school maybe, or correspondence."

"John, you can't take a nursing degree by correspondence." I'm negative, only because whenever I get my hopes up about something like this, something else always happens to take it all away. Hopes, dreams, plans…they all get squished like caterpillars trying to cross a busy street when the new orders come in.

"Well, if nothing else, we can look into it. You can call, or order a course calendar. There's a university in town, isn't there?"

There is. David's swim team competes there regularly. If John were around more, he would know this. But that's an argument for another time.

"Don't sell yourself short, Ellie. You've always been smart."

Intelligence without opportunity is nothing, I think.

A log swishes as it falls over, throwing sparks into the tree-lined space above us like fireworks. John jumps but covers it up by rubbing my knuckles and sipping his beer. I stare into the flames, wondering which log will fall next. Before I can decide, John leans forward and throws another stick onto the flames, bringing what's left of our tepee down with a *fwomp*.

A loon calls from the lake—a lonely, creepy sound. Not quite sad, not quite happy. A sound that gets under your skin and fills you up with emotion.

"Maybe," I say, and close my eyes, trying to lock this hopeful, happy moment into my head before it flies away and up into the starlit sky.

All happiness comes at a price. That is what I have found, anyway. The cosmic balance is a pendulum, swinging back and forth from happiness to misery; and after three nights with my family, my husband, and the stars, I guess I'm owed some grief. Not grief specifically…I'm not sure what you'd call this emotion scrabbling in my stomach. I'm simply overwhelmed. The kids are fighting in the back yard, John is back to work—gone somewhere for three days that will turn into ten—and a mountain of dirty clothes, dirty sleeping bags, dirty dishes, and dirty dirt sits on my kitchen floor, staring me down. I'm sure if I poke too hard with my dirty finger, a rabid chipmunk, or maybe a beaver will burst out of it and attack. The heavy truth of it is that the pile will still be there tomorrow if I don't do something about it…no one else will.

They'll step around it and jump over it and decide that a little more dirt won't hurt, so they'll add a bit of crud to make it look more impressive.

Oh, God…why me?

The phone rings, interrupting my indulgent self-pity. For one brief moment I'm happy, thinking it's John and his trip is cancelled.

"Hello?" I say, breathless even though I've only taken two steps across the dirt-strewn floor. My heart beats heavily as I say it, happiness briefly turning to fear…is John okay?

"Ellen."

The touch of fear turns in an instant to dread. I glance quickly outside to check on the boys. Chris has David in a headlock. Maria is napping upstairs in her fairy dress. They're fine.

"What do you want?" I reply to the nightmare on the other end of the line.

It's *him*.

"I'm in town…and your husband is…not." He says. "I thought you might see me." His voice is like snakeskin on sandpaper. I hate this man, with every nucleus of every cell, to the very depth of my existence. He thinks I might see him.

"No." I say, before I think.

"No?" he asks, and there's a hint of surprise in the snakeskin.

"I said no." My hand trembles on the phone. Fifteen seconds of conversation and I'm falling apart. I'm a mess.

"That is a shame. I was just looking at Michaels' file. Seems he's up for his professional assessments soon. My little white bag could come out very quickly and really, his ratings aren't that great anyway."

"You wouldn't." I whisper.

"Oh, yes I would. I am a powerful man, Ellen. I would and I will. I could squash your little husband in an instant. A little forgotten bolt in an engine, a loose wheel on landing…a bag of white powder is nothing."

I don't answer. The pendulum has swung even further, and I'm about to fly off into the abyss.

No. I am in my own home. He can't hurt me here. He won't hurt John. John isn't here.

I hang up.

When the phone rings again, I pull the cord from the wall and walk away.

I sit in the middle of the pile for a long time, staring at the dangling phone cord while the kids fight like kids do outside. When I finally stand up, I walk over to the kitchen door and lock it. I call the kids in and—oh horrors!—tell them they are allowed to watch TV. I lock the patio door and close the blinds. I walk from room to room, checking that all is well, and then I attack the mountain in my kitchen with a vengeance. It's not a mountain I can climb, so I fight to bring it down to my level—laundry, dishes, dirt. I beat them into submission like he would do to me. I'm terrified of what I've done, what he could do. We can manage without John's promotion, but I know he won't stop there. He is pure evil. He would take food from the mouths of my children. He would take my husband from me. I know he would.

When Maria toddles down with her hair mussed and her sparkly dress twisted around, I lift her up and kiss her. When the kids are fed, bathed, and tucked into bed, I pour myself a tall glass of red wine and plug the phone back into the wall.

It doesn't ring.

I finish my wine and wait, building my liquid strength. If he calls again, I have no idea what I'll do, but I can't keep the phone unplugged forever. What if John calls?

At 9:40 pm, I decide no one is going to call. I put my wine glass on the counter, double check all of the doors, and turn out all of the lights—well all of the lights except the one over the stove. That one I leave on. It's my John-is-away ritual. As I flick the switch on, a black sedan drives by and slows down. My heart goes into overdrive, thudding almost painfully against my sternum, and I slip into the shadows as I watch it almost stop in front of our house. I glance from my hiding spot at the lock on the door—it's bolted tight. Spot sits up and looks at me, curious, then whumps his head back down on the floor. I see a shadow of a face in the driver's seat, and even though I can't see who it is, I know. It's a shadow that haunts my nightmares. But the car drives on and I breathe out shakily.

He can't hurt me. I am in my own house. The doors are locked.

I'm heading up the stairs to bed when the phone rings. My heart nearly flies out of my chest.

Ring, ring, ring... it goes, taunting me. I creep back down the stairs, with no intention of answering. I let the answering machine pick it up. It might be John. It might be *him*. I can't answer until I know.

"Hi! This is the Michaels family', says Chris. The little red light flashes ominously.

"Leave a message after the..." says David.

"...Beep!" says Maria.

I wait.

"Hey babe, it's me! Are you there?"

It's John. Thank God. It's John. Just John.

I rush to the phone and pick up the receiver "John?" I say quickly, before he hangs up.

"Hey gorgeous," he says. "What's up?"

"Oh, sorry! I was in the bathroom upstairs." I lie. We only have one phone on each floor, so it happens frequently.

"I figured. How are the kids?"

"They're good. All asleep, though..." He's probably forgotten the time difference. He always does when he flies west.

"Oh, well you'll have to tell them I called."

"Of course. How was your flight?"

"Not bad actually. Weirdest thing, though. When we landed on the base, the military police were waiting with dogs. I guess they'd had an anonymous call that there were drugs on board or something."

The breath catches in my throat.

"Anyway, they searched but found nothing. We all had to do drug tests too. I haven't had to pee in a bottle like that since pilot training..."

It's *Him*. He did this as a warning to me. His voice echoes in my head—"I am a powerful man..."

Shit.

"But you're okay?" I ask, trying to keep the panic at bay.

"Yeah, like I said, it was just an anonymous call. The MP's searched, but they found nothing. Just a precaution."

It's like a flashing red light in front of me. A warning call from *Him*. John is oblivious to the danger he was in, that I am in, that we're *all* in.

His life, the lives of his crew…would Fielding stoop that low? Would he murder his own men, just to punish me for locking my doors?

He would.

"John…" My voice cracks. I wish I could tell him. But how can you tell the man you love that he may lose everything because of you? That your secret has grown so big, so ugly that even he is in danger? Especially a man who is just barely holding himself together right now? How could I explain that this started before we were even married, and I haven't got the guts to finish it?

"Ellen? You okay?"

"Yeah," I squeak, swallowing the sob bubbling up from below.

"You sure?"

"I just miss you, that's all…and…I worry," I lie.

"I miss you too." We're both silent, lost in our separate thoughts, islands on opposing sides of the continent.

I try to rein in my emotions, taking slow, even breaths as John tells me about his trip—the turbulence over the prairies, the flight over the Rockies, the obnoxious jokes bantered around in the cockpit. I make the required noises, the "Uh-hums," the "Yeahs," and the "Ohs" that he wants to hear. The normalness of the conversation is soothing. He goes places, I listen to his stories, and live my life through his excitement. He longs for time with the kids, sitting at home, and I long for the excitement of new places and unknown skies.

"I gotta go," he says after a few minutes more. "Meeting the crew for a debrief at seven."

"Okay," I say, and the panic starts to rise again.

"I'll call you tomorrow if I get a chance, 'kay?"

"Okay."

"Don't wait up," he says.

"Don't be late…" I reply, and then he hangs up.

I put the phone on the cradle slowly, the familiar emptiness expanding within me. I'm a thousand miles away with him in his hotel room, and I'm right here on this slowly disappearing mound of laundry. I shouldn't really miss him yet, he's only been gone a day, but I miss what he is to me. He's safety and warmth, and someone to talk to. He's a raft in a windswept sea of insanity. He's normal and happy and calm and silly and all of the things that make life bearable. I miss that.

I'm still staring at the phone when it rings again.

I know I have to answer it. I see no other choice. John's drug test...

I pick the receiver up, and drag it to my head. "Hello," I whisper.

"You'll meet me now, won't you Ellen?" he says.

And I say yes.

Lies.

I tell lies to the children. Lies to the babysitter. Lies to John.

I drive to the park he has suggested. I lie to myself that it will be okay.

It's dark, and the parking lot is empty. The moon is in that in-between place, not quite full, and its light is dimmed by the evening haze. I get out, but don't lock the car. What's the sense? What's the worst that can happen? I'm stupidly walking into the shadowed woods to meet with a rapist. My rapist. I can't stop shaking and I can't stop walking. Stupid. Stupid! *Stupid!*

My footsteps mingle with the noise of the crickets and the frogs as I walk down the path to the gazebo. I know where it is, I've been there a million times before with the kids. It's a little hidden spot in the trees where the kids play house and I read my book. In the daytime it's innocent and magical. Tonight it's evil. I know without a doubt that I will never bring the children here again.

He's not here. I step up onto the platform and sit on the bench inside, heart pounding so loudly that I don't think I could hear him if he came thundering through the bushes on a motorbike. My heartbeat swallows even the screeching mating calls of the frogs. I suck air in and push air out, but it does nothing to dispel my fear of what I know is to come.

"Wise choice," he says behind me and I jump. He steps out of the shadows into the pale moonlight. He's dressed in black, his face shadowed by a black hood. In any other situation, he would look ridiculous. But here in the dark, with no one else near, his face is not funny at all.

I'm too panicked to do anything but nod. My legs are too weak to rise from the bench. He steps onto the gazebo and stands in front of me. The buckle of his belt glints in the moonlight—hard and ominous.

He sees my recognition of the belt, and fingers the clasp. "I thought you would see reason with my little drug search. Drug tests are so easy to manipulate. It would be such a shame if Michaels' test came back positive. Nice touch, don't you think?"

I say nothing. Why am I here? How can I get out of this mess?

"Ah, yes. You remember how I dislike unnecessary noise."

I don't correct him, but I don't speak either.

"So you will make no sound—unless I ask you to. You will walk with me and you will do as I say. If I am…displeased…your loving husband will be found guilty of so many charges that he will never fly again. Or perhaps his plane will malfunction… Do you understand?"

I stare at him, tall, strong and evil, still searching for an out, a way to run, but there is none. I'm weak and pathetic. Blind, deaf, mute. I see no other option but to do as he says…and I'm terrified.

He walks to my side, unclasps his belt, and slides it free, the tip snapping like thunder in the night. The frogs go silent. "I said, do you understand?"

Oh why, why, why is this happening?

I hear the belt whistle over my pounding heart, and then the pain crashes across my back. I fall to the floor of the gazebo and land—hard—on my knees, gasping. Again the belt whistles, and again the sharp, cutting burn crosses my back.

He reaches down and grabs my jaw, wrenching my neck to face him. My eyes water and my heart flails under my ribs.

His teeth are clenched and I'm positive I am looking at the devil.

"I said, do…you…understand?" With each word he squeezes my bones in his hand. I flinch back, my instinct to run warring with my resolve to see this through, but he only squeezes tighter. The belt whistles and the pain stabs down again, and I slump and gasp, and the world goes even darker.

"I'm waiting, Ellen," he says. "Do you understand?"

"Yes," I whisper.

I understand perfectly.

I do what he says.

He leaves me in the woods, naked and cold, and I let him. He's ordered me to stay here and stay silent until he's gone…and that's what I do. I don't scream, don't cry, don't do anything. I'm numb from pain and anger and despair and self-loathing. I lay there, the rocks and crawling ants beneath me, and wait for his footsteps to disappear. My back stings. The crickets chirp, the frogs call, and I wait.

When I'm sure he's gone, I get up, get dressed, brush myself off and go home.

What else can I do?

The bruises are there, inside and out, but in his sick, demented, vicious way, not a single bruise shows past the edge of my jeans or the collar of my shirt. It's all hidden, just below the surface. I put on a brave face, pay the babysitter, who is too tired to notice anything out of the ordinary, and crawl upstairs to shower. I *have* to shower. I have to get every last ounce of me clean from that beast.

While the water heats, I glance at myself in the mirror. I look normal. My wrists a bit red, and my lips a bit swollen, bruises here or there that can be explained by general clumsiness, but mostly I look fine. The only thing out of place are the two wide welts on my back, one of them just barely open and bleeding in the small of my back, the other just a dark red line.

The welts will be gone before John gets home.

The scalding water stings on my back, washing away the dribble of blood, and my eyes water but I don't cry. I lean against the wall and refuse to give in. Somehow the shame and anger mingle and harden into resolve. I don't care what happens to John. I *don't* care. If I ever see Fielding again, I won't be weak. I'll fight. I'll run. I'll scream.

I can never, ever do that again.

This.

Has.

To.

Stop

CHAPTER 15
HOUSE #13

January, 2009

THE MAP IS ENDLESS. A wide, wide expanse of roads and streets and green and blue. Terrifying, yet familiar.

When the kids left last week, Christmas packed away and the new year ahead of them, I promised I'd look. Promised I'd think. But I'm stumped. How do you pick somewhere to spend the rest of your life? How do people do that? We've moved so many times I've almost lost count...Twelve? Thirteen?... But not once have I had even an iota of say in where we go. *They* said go here and we went there, end of story. So much easier that way, not having to think. We may have hated where we were going, but there was always the promise of another place after that...and really, you can live anywhere for a couple of years. No one has ever asked my opinion before. Now I'm ashamed of my inability to process the map in front of me and spit out a destination, a destination based solely on my own desires.

The obvious choice would be closer to the kids. A city only two hours from here, a quick move by military standards. For some reason that doesn't sit right with me. They've got their own lives. They're doing so well without me, and I'd just be a chain around their neck, a burden. I want them to be free and independent. They can't do that with their mom living just down the street.

I could do the easy thing and just pin the map to the wall and shoot darts at it. Leave my fate to fate and just go somewhere, anywhere. But the permanence of this move won't let me do that. I have to decide.

So I make a list.

What do I like? Oceans. Beaches. Lakes…water in general. A view, but not enough view to swallow me up.

What do I like to do? Nothing lately. I'm functioning on broken cylinders. I can barely focus on any task for long. I like to escape. I'd like to escape this choice.

Who do I want to be near? The kids. My mom. It's been so long since I've lived close to my mom. It would be so nice to just drive over and say hi, not spend all of my savings on airline ticket every time I want to see her.

Who do I want to avoid? *Him.*

I don't know where he is now, but he's likely on a base somewhere. So all military bases are out. That's a good idea anyway…the farther away I can get from this…life—for lack of a better term—the better. But it's hard to imagine any other life than the one I've always lived.

I sold my soul to the military when I married John, and now it doesn't want me anymore.

My head falls onto the map, and I wait for the ever-present tears to drown me, but they don't. I feel…empty: empty of tears, empty of sorrow, empty of empty. A vacuum.

A dependent with nothing to depend on but myself.

Finally, after hours of staring and hair pulling and coffee drinking, I pick a place near the ocean, four hours northeast of where the kids live, and five hours south of where my mom lives. I don't know what it is that attracts me, but it looks nice on the computer. Perhaps it's the name, Sophia Beach. It sounds exotic and sweet, and Sophia reminds me of Maria. The pictures on the Internet show a quiet town, long stretches of lonely beaches, and tall pine trees. I pick a real estate agent from a list of about five. I take a deep breath and call him. I can do this. I can.

"Trent Wallace speaking." He sounds young, perky, and ready to run a marathon. I'm exhausted just from those three words.

"Hi, I was um…wondering if I could come and look at a few houses…in the next few weeks. Sort of a house-hunting trip."

Trent Wallace is ready to help. "Sure can, ma'am. What sort of price range are you looking at?"

I tell him.

"How many bedrooms?"

"Um…two? Maybe three?"

"Waterfront, waterview, or doesn't matter?"

Wow. So many questions. It's 69 degrees in the house, but I break out in a sweat.

"Um…" We've bought and sold so many times…but John always did this part while I watched kids and cleaned up puke. "Water-view?" I finally spit out. Somewhere I can see the beach, but not be afraid of it washing me away.

"Excellent. I can go through the listings and pick out a few things. Can I email you…?" He waits for my name.

"Ellen. Ellen Michaels."

"Can I email you Ms. Michaels?"

"Okay,"

I give him my email address, and he double-checks it.

"And when would you like to come for your showings, Ms. Michaels?"

"Next week?" I ask, because I hadn't thought that far in advance.

"Will there be a Mr. Michaels with you?"

And with that one question, he's hit the nail on the head. There will be no Mr. Michaels with me. I'm on my own.

"No," is all I say.

He doesn't miss a beat. "All right then, I'll send you the listings, and we can go from there. Did you see anything online that you'd like to look at?"

"No."

What little bravado I had is gone. I'll be going on my own.

I can't do this.

"Okay then, I'll send you the listings tonight. Thank you, Ms. Michaels. Good bye," he says, and we hang up.

I sit there for a long time, looking at the little blip on the map between the blue ocean and the green shore. What if I don't like it there? What if I don't know anyone? What if there's nothing for me? What if I can't get a job? What if? What if? What if?

Moving from military town to military town guarantees you at least one kindred spirit—like Jennifer, like Barb—someone who understands what you're going through because they were in the same situation themselves not long ago. Maybe not a best friend, but a friend you can meet for coffee when you are lonely. This time there's no guarantee. Do I want to chance that, as lost as I am now and without John to support me from behind?

Every time we've moved John has done so much. Well, he's done the military paperwork and bought the packers beer—which is fine by me, because I don't want anything to do with unknown beefy men. How am I going to do it this time? And how do I buy a house, a three hundred thousand dollar purchase, without him to haggle the price and check the walls for cracks? How?

I guess I'm going to find out. This dependent only has three more months to vacate the premises.

CHAPTER 16

HOUSE #7

August, 1993

JOHN HAS BEEN GONE FOR eight days. As much as I would like to cower, hide, and wallow in self-pity, there is no time for my pain. Today has not been an exception to the drudgery of life. Wash, clean, play nurse, work, moderate sibling rivalry, repeat. I now sit on the sofa, some soft piano music in the background, and stare at the wall. I'm drained.

The phone rings.

Why didn't I unplug it? Stupid, stupid, stupid. I hate the phone, hate it with a passion but I can't let it ring, or it will wake up the kids. I stand there, heart racing, staring at it across the room.

Ring. Ring.

Please, please, *please* let it be John. I jump for the phone before it can ring again. "Hello...?" I say, trying to keep that tinge of fear from my voice.

"Ellen? Is everything okay?" It's Jennifer, my friend. Relief rushes through me. Just Jennifer.

"Jennifer! So good to hear from you," I say, my held breath rushing outwards as I speak.

"Sam told me that John's been gone on a training flight for a few weeks. He said there was some trouble at the beginning, and they've been re-tasked en route. So I thought I'd call and see how you're doing... Are you sure you're okay?"

"Yeah, I'm fine—I just had to run to get the phone. I was in the bathroom," I lie.

She giggles, an honest, sweet sound. "Oops, sorry about that."

"No problem! I was just washing my hands anyway."

"Oh. Well I was wondering if you'd like to come over for coffee tomorrow. You could bring the kids if you want, it won't be anything fancy. Just you and me."

It's like a lifeline to a drowning woman on her last gulp of air.

"Sure! You don't know how much I'd love that. I'll try to get a sitter if I can." I need to get away from the chaos of my house. I love the kids dearly—really I do—but I *so* need a break.

"Around two tomorrow afternoon? Sam is home, and he's planning to take Josie for a walk to the park after her nap."

Josie is Sam and Jennifer's two year old. Oh how I miss the napping days!

"Two sounds perfect."

"Okay, well just come, you hear? Don't bring anything but yourself and your kids if they're coming."

"Yes, Ma'am," I joke.

"Good…" she pauses for a minute. "Are you sure you're okay, Ellen?"

"I'm surviving, Jennifer. The best I can be after more than a week on my own." I fail miserably at keeping the despair from my voice. I hope she doesn't hear it.

"Chin up, girl," she says. "He'll be home before you know it."

"I hope so."

We say our goodbyes, and I go back to staring at the wall, not bothering to hide the tears on my face.

No one will see them anyway.

I manage to secure our babysitter for the afternoon, and decide to walk rather than drive over to Jennifer's. It's a sunny, hot summer day, and the birds are singing as I walk down the crumbling sidewalk toward her street. The military powers that be (or rather were) lacked imagination when setting up the quarters here. John and I live on Tenth, and Jennifer and Sam live on Eighth; no flowery street names, just the bare essentials. Weeds grow between the cracks in the sidewalk, but in spite of its neglected look, life blooms everywhere in our little corner of the world. Kids bike, dogs bark, and birds sing. I meet Sam on the street with Josie in the stroller. He smiles kindly and Josie mouths her sippy cup.

"Go on in, Jennifer's waiting," he says but doesn't stop.

I knock, and Jennifer opens the door mid swing as I go to knock again.

"Ellen," she says, without a trace of high-pitched fakery, "I'm so glad you could come." She looks nice, but not perfect. Her nails aren't done, her hair is pulled back in a common-sense ponytail, and her clothes, though brand-name, are loose and comfortable. It's such a soothing relief from so many posing, magazine-model, rank-conscious wives I know.

"I've got coffee on, and I managed to whip something up really quick for a treat." She points at the counter where sits a very obviously store bought coffee cake.

I laugh, "You shouldn't have!"

"I know, I slaved all day." She wipes her brow in exaggerated exhaustion. "Those little walnuts are a bugger to dig out of their shells. And I nearly burnt the caramel sauce! Coffee?"

"Please."

We take our coffee and cake out to the back patio, which consists of a few patio stones thrown half-heartedly over grass. Laundry blows from her line, a few scrabbly flowers poke from the tired dirt, and a baby pool lies within arms reach of the table. An asphalt walking path separates the back of her yard from the one across from it. It's all so…normal. Relaxing. Like I walked into my own back yard. I want to hug her.

We sit down on the simple patio chairs in the shade of the house. It's really hot back here, so hot that I slip my long-sleeved over-shirt off and hang it from the chair, enjoying the breeze on my limited bare skin. Jennifer has brought out a pitcher of ice water. I relax into the chair, and close my eyes.

"So, Ellen… how *are* you?" she asks.

"I'm fine," I say, opening my eyes again and trying to look like someone who hasn't been raped in the past week.

She frowns. I've been doing this routine for what, ten years? And a friend who's spent barely twenty-four hours with me in total can see through my façade. Not good.

"Really? 'I'm fine' is something someone says when they don't want to talk about something."

Maybe I don't, I think. What I say is: "Really, everything's as good as it can be with John away and three wonderful but emotionally-draining children to look after." There. That sounds realistic.

I sip my coffee slowly and try for a smile.

"Yes, that would do it for most people," she says, and I hope I've fooled her.

"How about you? How are things with Josie? Sam must be busy at work, with a whole crew gone for almost a month."

"Yeah, this is the first weekend this summer he's had off. And he's still carrying the pager. We were hoping to go camping or something with Josie, but no luck. She's pretty good, but she still gets up during the night. It's exhausting."

I've sidetracked her for the time being. Like every mom with kids at home, she loves to talk about her children. And like every military wife, she likes to compare spousal horror stories. We don't try to outdo each other, we share to let the others know they aren't alone. The true, realness of the moment relaxes me more than anything else could. I'm myself, just for a moment, coffee and ice water and conversation acting as medicine for a tired, broken soul.

After two cups of coffee, my bladder is so full, I feel like I'm going to burst. I excuse myself and head to the washroom. As I stand up, the breeze catches my tank top, flapping it against my back. I must wince as I move toward the door.

"Ellen?" Jennifer says, stopping me before I get there.

I turn to see what's up.

"Ellen, what happened to your shoulder?"

My heart rate explodes. Surely there's nothing on my shoulder. Surely.

I turn to look, but of course I can't see my own back.

"My shoulder?" I ask.

"Yeah, there's a huge black bruise."

I twist again, pretending to look for what she's talking about. I feel sick. There can't be a bruise. Why in the hell did I take off my shirt?

She walks toward me, and touches me gently on my shoulder blade, just where it peeks out from my tank. I can't help but wince. It hurts.

Damn.

The look on her face terrifies me.

"I...I must have hit it on the doorframe," I say, trying to cover up the fear that is ballooning under my diaphragm. No one can know!

But to my never-ending relief, she buys it. Or at least, I think she does. She looks at me funny, but says nothing else.

"Oh, I do that all the time," she says, God bless her. "And the kitchen counter. I *always* have a bruise right here from whacking that." She points to the bone on the front of her hip. Some nursing student part of me mentally spews out the name—anterior superior iliac spine.

"Oh, me too," I say.

The shock of Jennifer's comments coming on the heels of my over-full bladder is not a good combination. I really have to go, and I say so. I hope she takes the desperation in my voice as bladder tension, not cover-up.

"Oh, yeah," she says with a half-hearted tone, but she's still looking at the bruise. "You know where the bathroom is." Our houses are mirror images of each other. Every house in this block of quarters has the same basic layout.

I laugh, a strangled, fake sort of laugh, and nod. "Be right back," I say, and escape to the safety of her house.

I practically run to the bathroom, and when I've done what I needed to, I twist myself around so I can just see my back in the mirror. Sure enough, a brilliantly coloured bruise peeks from beneath my flimsy tank top and stretches diagonally upward to the corner of my shoulder blade. The edges of the bruise are bright red and scabbed, where the force of his belt dug into my skin. With even more horror, I also see marks I hadn't even known were there. On the backs of both of my arms are four small, oval bruises.

Fingerprints. Very obvious fingerprints. *His* fingerprints. On my skin.

Oh God. And Jennifer has seen them.

What must she be thinking? Does she think that John put those marks on me? She must, because how could she know about *him*?

It's cool in the bathroom, but I am covered in sweat, standing here gawking at my own arms like they belong an alien.

"Ellen?" Jennifer says from the kitchen, and I jump. "Would you like some fresh coffee?" she asks, her voice sounding just the slightest bit forced.

Coffee. She's asking me about coffee, not rape. There's no way she could know.

"Oh, sure!" I say. "I'll be right out!"

She can't know. She *can't.*

I flush the toilet and wash my hands, splashing some water on my face as well. I'll just act normally, and she won't ask anything. I'll put my shirt back over my tank. I'll smile and chat and go home.

I nod at my own instructions and open the door.

When I get to the patio, I put on the famous military-happy-happy smile and act as if the world is a lovely place. Jennifer doesn't even look at me, she's watching the kids on the other side of the path. They are blowing bubbles with dish soap, running and catching them. Their younger sister is slathering suds on her bare belly.

"The coffee will just be a minute." She says without looking. We sit there and quietly watch the neighbour's kids. A normal day in a normal backyard. I quietly slip my arms into my shirt, even thought the temperature has gone up about five degrees already.

When the kids run around the corner of their house, Jennifer turns to me, her face serious. The noise of the children fades away. Even the crickets are silent.

"It wasn't John, was it?" she says. It's more of a statement than a question.

I try to look like I don't know what she's talking about.

"The marks. On your back and arms. They aren't from the door frame, Ellen."

Tears burn my eyes, and I will them not to fall. Her gaze is strong, but kind, it's killing me, digging into that deep part of my being that I've been fighting so hard to hide. The part that knows I should have fought back. The part that knows I'm a coward.

"Jennifer, please…" I whisper.

She doesn't look away, doesn't give up.

"There's more aren't there? More marks? More bruises?"

I say nothing. I don't nod. If I acknowledge the pain is real, it will hurt even worse.

"Whoever did that to you should be stopped. *Was* it John?"

No, not John. Kind, loving John. I shake my head quickly. Several tears fall from my eyelids and slide down my face.

"I didn't think so."

I sniff. I want to leave, escape. It hurts too much to even think about how those marks got there. I can never tell anyone. I need to go.

"I have to go," I say quickly. I stand up and look toward the door.

She reaches out and grabs my hand. "Ellen, no. Don't go. Please...I want to help."

I pull my hand away. "You can't help. No one can help. I have to go."

"But..."she reaches out again, but I've moved out of her reach.

I think, just for a moment, about how good it would be to tell someone, to get this hideous, awful secret off of my chest. But even telling someone wouldn't free me of the guilt, the self-disgust, and the pent-up emotion seething deep in my bones. If I tell her, she'll look at me with pity—pity I don't want; pity I don't deserve.

"Jennifer, you can't tell anyone," I whisper, looking frantically around for eavesdroppers. "If you're my friend at all, you'll keep this quiet. Not even Sam can know!" I hiss.

"But, Ellen!"

"Not. Even. Sam."

She nods. "I won't tell Sam, I promise. Just tell me what I can do. Are you in danger? Is...is he here, on base?" She automatically assumes that it's a guy that has done this to me, that no woman would be so cruel.

I shake my head. "No," I say, "he's gone. Not here." I sniff again, and wipe away the tears on my cheeks.

This satisfies her for a moment and I take another step backward. "Look," I say, "he's not here, and...I don't..."

I want to tell her. I want to open my heart and let it all out. Get this awful, hideous, debilitating secret off my chest. Maybe if I told her I could catch him. She could help me. I could make him hurt like he hurt me. We could stop him—make him pay.

"Ellen you can tell me anything," she says. "Stay. I'll listen." She reaches out and grabs my hand again before I can go any further. I let her.

"It wasn't John. John would never…It wasn't…" I look around us. There are open windows everywhere, listening ears and people that could hear.

"Come into the house," she says, sensing my discomfort. "You can tell me there. No one will hear. I promise."

What if Sam comes back?

No, this is a burden I must deal with on my own.

I shake my head. "No, Jenn. I have to go."

She smiles then, a sad, still smile that barely reaches her eyes.

"It's okay, Ellen," she says. "I'm here, though. If he comes back…let me know okay?"

She means it, I can tell. And I know right now that if he did come back, I would tell her…and she would listen.

"I will," I say, but I turn away from the first lifeline I've seen in ten years.

CHAPTER 16
HOUSE #13

January, 2009

A s a personal treat for the big and scary step I've taken—planning a house-hunting trip to a completely unknown destination—I decide to take a day and head into the city to go shopping for myself. Yup, *myself!* The last time I walked into a women's swimsuit section was just after Maria was born. If I'm going to go on a cruise, I need a bathing suit that actually *fits*. It's a concept so foreign to me—shopping for myself, and only myself—that I feel like an errant child as I manoeuvre through cars on the highway, listening to a CD John bought years ago.

I'm stressed about the traffic, but even more stressed about trying on a bathing suit. This body has not seen the light of day in years. I don't even know what size I am any more. I'm sure there will be a pushy-yet-obsequious salesperson ready to help me with that.

The mall I'm heading for is just outside the city where the kids live, and I consider calling them to justify the trip. Driving several hours just for a bathing suit seems sillier and sillier as the miles flash by. But I don't. They have their lives. I won't intrude on them.

I find the exit, turn into the mall parking lot, and drive around to the back. Without even thinking, I pull into a space right by the sports store, where John always parked at this particular mall. I stare at the sign, its big red letters glaring down at me, daring me to come through its doors and re-live the hours spent watching John try on runners and ice skates and flick hockey sticks.

I put the car in reverse and drive to another spot.

Walking into the mall is no better. I've only ever come here with

John or the kids, never alone. Why would I drive all the way here when I could buy groceries, underwear, paperbacks, or most other things at the commissary or the local mini-mall? John's favourite fast-food joint, the place where John bought his suit last year for the Christmas party, the little pub where we'd go so John could have a beer after shopping…all the memories I'd locked away, only to have them come smashing back into my mind like a sledgehammer.

The wide walls seem to close in on me, squishing and grabbing, and I walk quickly to the map in the middle of an intersection, searching for the right store—physically running my finger down the list until I find it. Anything to not think about John. Anything to avoid the stream of memories. I find the appropriate store on the map and practically run to that section of the mall, hardly focusing. People pass by me like ghosts until I am there and in the shop, realizing I don't want to shop for bathing suits any more.

"Can I help you, Ma'am?"

Instead of old and professional, the salesclerk is about Maria's age, wearing fluorescent pink lipstick and very obviously bleached hair.

"Uh…" My brain is lost somewhere between John and get-there-and-get-it-done.

"Are you looking for something specific?"

"Uh…" I say again, and then I manage to grasp a thought. "A bathing suit. I need a bathing suit. For a cruise."

"Oh! Right back here," she says, and then walks back toward the back of the store, not waiting for me to follow. I do follow her, and she jabbers away about colours and styles and then turns and blatantly looks me over.

"Your shape…hmmm…would look best in something like this…" She grabs a suit and hands it to me, and I just nod. "You're a 6 right?" She asks.

"Um…" I have no idea what size I am. She looks young and ditzy, but she obviously knows *way* more about swimsuits and body shapes than I do. She must think I'm some sort of mental case. Who am I kidding? I *am* some sort of mental case.

I grab what she hands me, head to the fitting room, and try on the black one. I hardly look at it. It fits…I think. I want to ask John what he thinks, but he's not here.

"Are you okay in there?" bounces the dyed blonde.

"Fine!" I yell the socially acceptable answer before she barges in to check. I am not okay. How could I be okay?

I somehow get through the fitting process, buy two suits—trying not to gag at the price on the receipt—and then escape Blondie as fast as I can. What a disaster I am.

I'm standing out in the corridor, holding my bag like it contains plague rats, when I see it—the travel agency the cruise tickets are from. The sign is a stylized bird; I would know it anywhere. I walk over and peek through the window, wondering if there's a pamphlet or something I could pick up, something to help me plan ahead for seven days on a cruise ship, when the agent stands up and sees me there.

Oh *shit*. Shitshitshitshitshit!

Mrs. Frank Fielding is the travel agent.

She waves at me, and I freeze.

"Mrs. Michaels?" she says, all high-pitched and fake-voiced, and I want to kill her. I want to rip out her little fake-voiced throat. I want to tear out every one of her perfectly manicured nails and dump acid all over her perfectly tailored suit. Me, standing here in my ten-year-old bargain-rack jeans and my ponytail.

Oh, God help me, I want to kill the woman for her ignorance.

"Ellen? I'm so glad to see you!" she squeaks. "Wasn't it the sweetest thing your kids did for you? You have such a wonderful family."

Had a wonderful family. *Had*. Your dick-head of a husband tore my family apart, and you don't even have the slightest, do you?

"Yes," I say from some silent, well-behaved part of my head. "Yes, I do."

"Well, I was so pleased I almost told Frank!" She covers her mouth and gives me a fake look of shock. "I didn't, of course—client confidentiality and all—but I sure wanted to!"

A cold chill runs down my spine. She wanted to *tell* that *monster*. She *almost* told him.

Oh. Sweet Mary, Mother of God!

What if she's lying? What if she really did tell him?

"Well," I say, clutching my bag so tight my fingers hurt. Goose bumps stand out on my arms and a cold sweat trickles behind my ears.

Sweet Mother.

"He's probably too busy to care about my vacation anyway," I say. Probably too busy raping people.

"Yes, he is that," she grins.

The bag jerks, and I come *this close* to bludgeoning her to death with my swimsuits.

"I have to go, now," I say through clenched teeth. "I have an appointment."

"Well, If I don't see you, have a fun trip!" she says.

"Thank you," I say and turn away from Mrs. Smiley-Happy-Rapist's-Wife.

I'm always fleeing my insanity, running away from the crazy that is my life. I can't get out of there fast enough. I burst through the door, jog to the car and unlock it with shaking fingers.

Frank Fielding's wife booked my escape with my children.

Holy crap.

I don't know if I should laugh or scream, really. If she didn't tell Fielding, how will he ever know? But I want to call my kids and ask them if they are okay, call Maria and tell her to stay away from the Fieldings because they are bad, bad news. I want to rip up my tickets and fake pneumonia, because I don't want to go on that trip at all now.

I shake my head. I'm being silly. He doesn't know. He *doesn't* know. He *does not* know.

But as I throw the bag into the back seat and start the engine, I know my luck is never that good.

Somehow this fact will come back to haunt me.

Life always does.

CHAPTER 17

HOUSE #7

August, 1993

THE DAMNED PHONE IS RINGING again.

John is due home today, and I'm relatively sure it's him, so I answer.

"Hello?"

Such a loaded word, hello. All of my hopes and fears flow through the receiver with that single word.

"Hey gorgeous, it's me."

Thank God.

"Hello, handsome." I say. "Are you home?"

"Well, not yet…but I will be in about half an hour. Just gotta finish the paperwork, and I'll be home."

I'm happy and terrified at the same time. The bruises are still visible, eleven days after my nightmarish walk in the park.

"I was just heading up to bed," I say.

"Music to my tired and lonely ears," John replies. "I'll meet you there." I can hear the implication in his tone.

I say goodbye and trudge upstairs. John will want to make love. He always wants to make love after long trips. And I usually feel the same way. Except for today. Today I want nothing to do with that part of my body. I'm still bruised and torn and *violated* there. I want to forget that part of my body ever existed.

I wash, brush my teeth, and crawl into bed as quickly as I can, leaving his bedside light on, but turning mine off. I'm not tired at all;

in fact my veins are pumped with adrenaline. I'm terrified that my own husband will want to have sex with me.

I stare at the ceiling, waiting for the familiar sounds of the door unlocking, the clink of the keys in the dish, the clunk of his suitcase on the kitchen floor, the thud of John's flight boots on the boot rack. They all come, faster than I had imagined—faster than I'm ready for.

The light switch clicks and I hear his footsteps on the stairs.

What in the hell is wrong with me? He's my husband, for God's sake. I *love* him. I'm happy to see him. I *want* to be near him. So why am I hiding under our covers, trying not to hyperventilate?

I can hear his quiet, sock-muffled footsteps as he peeks into the kids' rooms, pauses in each doorway to blow them a kiss. They're dead to the world, of course. They don't even know he is there, but he does it anyway. Such a good dad.

The bathroom door closes as he brushes his teeth, and then he's walking toward my—our—room.

"Ellie?" he whispers, "you up?"

For a second I almost don't answer. I don't want to be awake. I want to just sleep and avoid talking to him.

"Hey," I say.

The bed dips as he sits on it, and I peer up at him from beneath the covers.

"Hey gorgeous," he says. "I'm home."

I smile at him, because he's too sweet not to smile at. He smells of sweat and wool and jet fuel. I love that smell. It's a smell of going places, being somewhere other than my bizarre, multi-faceted, soul-sucking life.

"I'm glad you're home," I say.

He slips off his flight suit and lets it fall in a crumpled pile on the floor. His undershirt and long johns are out of place on this warm evening, but familiar to me—safe. He rubs his hair back, and what there is of it goes everywhere in little blonde spikes.

"How was your trip?" I ask.

"Long…" He bends down to take off his socks. "Crazy…" He shoots them into the laundry basket. "Odd." He pulls his army green t-shirt off and tosses it after the socks like a basketball. Then he looks at me, and the corners of his lips quirk up. "But I'm home now. It's good to be home."

He leans over and kisses me—a chaste, night-time kiss, not a let's-have-sex kiss. I almost sigh with relief.

"You must be tired," I say.

"Yeah. Nine hours in the seat today. It was choppy too. Storms over the prairies."

He rolls down his long johns, and stands naked in the dim light. His six-pack has softened over the years, but he's still beautiful. A small spark lights up somewhere in my middle, but I don't listen to it. I don't follow through because I don't want that kind of love right now. Safe and quiet is what I need.

John turns off the light and rolls the bed sheets down. He flops onto the mattress like a man ready for a good night's sleep. Somewhere outside the window a neighbour's dog barks.

"How were things here?" John asks.

Violent. Scary. Awful.

"They were okay," I say.

"Okay?"

Busy. Insane. Painful.

"Hey," I say. "Did you know that your old Chief of Cadets was in town?"

Oh my God. I did not just say that! I cannot believe I just said that.

"No," John says sleepily. "That man is an asshole." He yawns a big, jaw-cracking yawn and absently reaches over to grab my hand. His fingers knead my knuckles.

"Yeah," I whisper.

I stare at the dark ceiling and *will* him to make the connection. Will him to see the bruises and sense my pain and finally figure it out.

"Yeah, he really is." I say, louder this time. "I think he could be dangerous."

I hold my breath and wait for him to ask why. Why is he dangerous? Why do you think that?

But his fingers start twitching with the quick movements of someone falling asleep. His breathing slows and a soft snore slips from his lips. He didn't hear me. Or if he did, he was too tired to care.

I lay there in the dark, slowly letting the night take me, holding my husband's hand on our bed and hating myself. What have I become? I have become a puppet, a marionette that dances only when someone else plays my strings. Friends, my husband, the kids, the military, *Him...* They all twitch my strings and I move. Go here, do that...without a thought for myself anymore.

I don't remember how to think.

A tear trickles from the corner of my eye and sinks into my pillow. I let it go, let it do what it must. I'm not even in control of my own tears.

I want to make love to my husband. That's what I want. I want him to make love to me. I want him to hold him me and want me and take away all of this awful, scary hideousness that has become my life. I want him to possess me, and make me his, erasing away all traces of that monster and reminding me of how I got to this place.

This is what I want.

"John?" I whisper as I squeeze his hand gently. "Are you still awake?"

"Hmm?" he's not awake, but he answers.

I squeeze his hand again, and sit up on my elbow, looking at him in the light filtering through the window.

The movement rouses him even more.

"What's up, gorgeous?" he asks, all sleep and slur.

"John, will you...will you make love to me?"

I'm suddenly shy. I shouldn't have asked. I should have just let him sleep. Sleep was safe.

I feel, more than see, him smile.

"Beautiful, you don't have to ask me twice."

And when he holds me, gentle and sleepy-soft, for the briefest of moments, I remember why I wanted this life. Why I never questioned my belief that this was my path.

He gives of himself freely, loves me delicately and his half...makes me whole.

He sleeps in the next morning.

I get up and he barely even moves. His blonde hair spikes on the pillow, his hands curled around the comforter. I know he is tired, and I imagine there's some jet lag there too. He deserves some rest.

I feel better somehow, even though I ache in places I probably shouldn't. I make coffee and dole out cereal and juice to kids. They giggle and laugh and ask if they can watch television. I nod, my mouth full of fresh coffee.

When they're gone from the kitchen, I sit down at our little table, admiring the sun as it shines through our tiny kitchen windows. I feel more peaceful than I have in weeks—years, maybe. In one night, John has almost fixed what was broken. Or maybe I've fixed what was broken in me.

A timid knock at the door makes me jump. My coffee slops over my fingers and onto the table.

Who could be here this early on a summer morning? It can't be more than eight o'clock…and I'm still in my flimsy nightgown and ratty housecoat. I'm not dressed for social calls.

I peek timidly around the corner, trying to see but not be seen.

It's Jennifer. The cozy feeling evaporates, and my flimsy nightgown is all of the sudden too tight. I don't want to see Jennifer. But she sees me and knows I am in here. I can't ignore her…she's the only friend I have.

I walk forward and open the door, enough to say hi, but not enough to let her in.

"Hi," I say.

"Hi," she replies.

We stand in awkward silence.

"Did John get home?" she asks.

"Yeah, last night. He's still sleeping."

"Oh."

More silence. Somewhere on the other side of the street a baby is crying. She looks toward it and then looks back.

"Ellen, I…I just wanted to tell you that I won't talk about it if you don't want me to." Her eyes are big and shining with tears. I want to look away, but I don't. "I just don't want to lose your friendship over that." One of the tears slips down her cheek.

I step outside the door and close it quietly. I don't want John or the kids to hear her. I don't want to hear her myself.

We sit down on the crumbling cement step. I flick a little flake of it off into the sad, wilted garden. The baby stops crying. A jogger runs by on the sidewalk. Jennifer brushes the tear away, but says nothing. The morning has that peaceful, not-quite-awake feel to it, externally anyway. Internally I'm anything but peaceful—my mind is whirring and spinning like a propeller.

"Jenn, I…I'm fine, okay?" I finally say to break the awkward silence, although I know I'm not fine. I'm a mess. Officer's wives are not allowed to be a mess.

She turns and I feel her eyes searching, weighing my words.

"Are you sure?" she says.

No, I'm not sure. I'm a wreck. "Yeah. I'm sure," I say.

I can see, quite clearly, that she isn't convinced.

"Ellen, if you need to talk—about anything—I'm always here to listen," she says. "Anything. The price of milk, the wart on your toe… the bruise on your shoulder…" She's trying to lighten the situation, but it's not working. Her tight smile shows that she knows it.

I wait, because I have no answer to that.

"There are people other than me you could talk to—counsellors, social workers—I could help…"

There is no fucking way I am going to talk to a complete stranger about this! The military *owns* this town. I am a little wife of a little pee-on officer with no power whatsoever, and I'm pretty damned sure that they would slam the door in my face if I accused one of their chosen few of rape. Not only in my face, but in my children's faces. And then the rumour mill would take care of any shred of dignity I have left after being raped by said chosen one.

The military community does not take to tattle-tales. Tattle-tales find themselves ex-communicated, stepped-on, abandoned, and left to die in everything but the literal sense. And in my case…well, even I don't know what Fielding is capable of. Left to die in the literal sense is a very real possibility.

"Jennifer, I am not going to talk to anyone about anything," I say. She's trying to help, I know she is, but this is not something that can be helped. "I'm going to drink my coffee, get up, go on with my life… nothing you can offer to me will make me change my story. My shoulder hit a wall, okay?"

I've given her a little in that statement. The veiled acknowledgement floats in the air between us. I wait until she's looking into my eyes before I continue.

"Other than John, you are my best friend. Hell, you're my *only* friend. And if I could tell anyone about things going on my life, it would be you. But. I. Hit. A. Wall. It happens. Bruises heal and then… and then in a few weeks there will be nothing to see. Nothing to help. *Nothing.*"

She stares at me silently as the dogs bark, my heart beats and the television blares in the house behind me. Her eyes give in, slowly, and she nods.

"You're my best friend too," she says. "Is there any of that coffee left?"

And in those few words, she has mended the rift between us. She has accepted my lies; accepted me in all my broken, simple, nobody-ness; accepted me, as I am, warts and all.

I smile. "I always have coffee for you."

And when I get up, it's as if another weight has lifted from my bruised and battered shoulders. One thing the military can never take away from me is a good friend .

CHAPTER 18
HOUSE #13 (CRUISE)

Early May, 2009

I'VE NEVER FLOWN ACROSS THE ocean. The space beneath me is so... *big*. And then there are just waves and waves, so small that they look like tiny wrinkles on a giants face. I should be sleeping like the strange couple beside me, snoring softly over the hiss of the over-processed air, but I can't settle. Instead I press my face to the window and search for boats in the early morning light. I'm like a kid. I want to comment on everything, but John's not here to talk to. It's just me and a couple of heavy-breathing, sleep-masked strangers crammed in with several hundred other strangers. That, combined with the fact that I had to go to the bathroom an hour ago but haven't gone because I don't want to disturb the sleepers, makes me one wiggly woman.

I still can't believe that the kids have done this for me. Well, I can, because I'm here, but I can't believe that they would take the initiative and make it happen. It's likely that at least half the money came from my own bank account—John's bank account—but I don't care. I'm here, going there, and that's what counts. I just wish John were here to share it with me.

There was a moment, as I was passing through security earlier today, that I thought I saw someone—someone who looked like *him*. He was far off in the distance, and when I looked again the man was gone. My brain does stuff like that when things are going well, just to remind me of my secrets—a little background nudge to stay on my guard. I can't let myself enjoy something this frivolous, something solely for me. Mrs. Fielding at the travel agency did nothing to help my paranoia. And I'm sure Fielding is behind the wheel of the black car that haunts my street, wherever I live. But crossing the Atlantic to stalk *me*, a forty-something widow, is a step that even hell-born Frank Fielding is unlikely to take. I haven't actually interacted with the thug in years.

Other than that one time...

No. I don't want to think about Fielding today. Fielding is in the past—in another time and place. I look out the window and wait for the land to appear out of the waves.

As we land in Venice, the lagoon and the island stretch to the left of the plane, looking solid and surreal. I gather my one suitcase, and follow the rest of the sheep through customs. There is a shuttle waiting to take me to the ship. I walk up to the short, fifty-something Italian fellow, and he takes my bag and gestures for me to hop on. It's very hot, very noisy, and the air smells of exhaust. I can't see the lagoon from my seat until we pull up to the port.

I follow, follow, follow, surrender my passport to the cruise check-in people, follow again along a gangway, and suddenly, I'm in my room. It's beautiful, all bright purples and reds and dark furniture. The sun shines brightly in from the balcony. A nice young man from the Philippines introduces himself as Joselito, my room attendant. He shows me the coffee maker, points out the lifejackets, explains the seating arrangements in the main dining hall, and asks me if I need anything. I say no, thank you, and he smiles.

"The ship will be departing in two hours, ma'am. The buffet is open, and there's music on the pool deck if you'd care to join. Your bag should be delivered by the time we sail." He points to the phone. "If you need assistance, just dial 3 and I'll answer. Enjoy your trip, Mrs. Michaels," he says, and then closes the door, leaving me in the hushed silence of my stateroom.

I stand in the middle of the room, shell-shocked.

I am in Venice. On a cruise ship. Alone.

I am going to see the Greek Islands.

John is not here.

I am alone.

I drop my purse on the floor and stand and stand and stand, until exhaustion takes over and tells me I need to sit. Then I grab the bottle of water from the counter and step over the small lip onto the balcony. I collapse on the deck chair, sipping water as my thoughts whirl and Venice watches me through the glass railing.

I am in Venice. John is not here. I am alone.

And it's okay.

Venice is everything the tour guides said it would be, although I know I have yet to see its heart. It's hot, smelly, damp and beautiful. Ornate stone buildings rise over the ugly, flat buildings of the port. People, boats, and seagulls flow around and over. A dull roar of sounds, most of which I suspect comes from this boat, assaults my ears, but it's okay. In fact it's more than okay. It's good. The sights, the sounds, even the light is different. New.

I don't know a single soul on this ship. I don't know anything about this place. I'm anonymous and alone. But in this crazy, different place, I can escape my past. Here on the Mediterranean, I can almost feel safe.

I doze, sitting there on my warm balcony, too tired to move to my bed, and too comfortable to care.

I awake to the ding-dong of the intercom. "Good afternoon, Ladies and Gentlemen, and welcome to Athenian Cruiseline's *Seastar*," says a deep voice with a slight accent. "This is your captain, Gregorio Vallante, speaking. We'll be departing shortly for an evening at sea, and I'd like to now invite you to head to your stations for our mandatory life-boat drill. After that, you're welcome to dine in any of our fine dining establishments, join us for our opening night show in the *Seastar*'s own Diamond theatre, or just relax in your room and enjoy the view. I'd like to thank you for choosing Athenian Cruiseline, and wish you a pleasant trip."

I sigh, the warmth and the smells of the city holding me to my chair. I could stay here for the whole trip. No uncomfortable social situations, no too-energetic people pushing activities. But if this drill is mandatory, I should be a sheep and go. I drag my jet-lagged self back over the threshold and grab my ugly, orange life vest as the announcement drones in several vaguely recognizable languages, and then the alarm tone goes off, calling me to my life raft station—as if the ship alone could save me.

The ballroom is full of happy, loud strangers. I sign in at my station—6B—and have a seat beside a couple that personifies the Texan tourist to a 'T'. A tall, beefy, loud man with red cheeks, and an overly made-up, fake blond with too-tight jeans and too-high heels. They are louder than loud and are completely confused about how to do up the buckles of their life jackets. The poor twenty-something Croatian girl helping them, Vanna by her nametag, looks like she's about to explode.

I look around and consider moving, but the place is so packed there's nowhere to go. A sea of unknown faces and orange vests boils and changes in front of me. I'm positive they are all couples, and I am the lone single—the lone widow in the group. I haven't been single since the eighties, before John. I'm too young to be a widow. How many women are widowed at forty-five? Most of the be-jacketed minions in the room are in their sixties or older, and I sincerely doubt that any of them are widowed. A few families, a few honeymooners, maybe a few couples my age, a group of forty-something men wearing business suits by the windows, and other than that, all oldies. I can't wait to escape back to the comfort of my room because I just don't fit here.

I sit, and realize that I'm being strangled by a life jacket that my husband didn't have. A life jacket could have saved him, and maybe we'd be sitting here together, complaining about the heat like the Texans beside me. Why did we never travel together? And more importantly, where was his life jacket when he needed it? Where? Under his bloody seat, that's where. I've seen the picture in my mind a thousand times. John, fighting to get out of his seatbelt. John, fighting to free himself. John, taking his last breath, alone...

When the 'all clear' finally comes, I push past all the obnoxious tourists and little old ladies and flee to my room.

What were the children thinking? What was *I* thinking? I'm on a boat! A fucking boat! I tear the life jacket off and slam it on the floor in disgust. It seems harmless enough lying on the colourful floor, all orange and blocky and uncomfortable, but that piece of orange might have saved my husband from death and me from this choking uncertainty. The excitement of newness has vanished. I don't want to be here, surrounded by reminders of him. I don't want to see the water, the love in the eyes of the elderly couples, the beauty of the ship. Even the overwhelming urge to joke at the expense of the florid Texan...all of these things bring memories of John to the surface of an already perilous façade.

This is crazy. A boat. Me. Not John.

I need to run. I need to get off. My suitcases are sitting in the room, beside the bed, and I stare at them and the sprawled life vest and I know I could just grab them and go before the boat leaves.

But that would be giving up.

I don't give up. I've shovelled vomit at 2 a.m. in a power outage. I've moved across the country while pregnant and lugging two kids.

I can't give up.

I just got here. And if my kids had the gumption to buy these tickets, I should at least have the intestinal fortitude to see this through.

I give the life jacket a kick, just to show it I'm in control, and then step out on to the balcony. I see that I've been fighting with myself over nothing, because we're already on our way. The soft rusts and pinks of Venice are already sliding by; somehow we've left the dock without even a whisper. It's beautiful out there, the architecture, the milling tourists, the black habits of the nuns. Like a fairy tale of history in sunlit miniature.

And then, once more, it hits me hard.

I wish John were here.

I wish John were here.

I. Wish. John. Were. Here.

CHAPTER 19
HOUSE #1 (BEFORE JOHN)

September, 1980

THE BATTERIES ARE ALMOST DEAD, but the radio still spits out a quiet, careful rendition of AC/DC's song. AC/DC is neither quiet, nor careful and I would rather to listen to someone else, but Michelle loves this band. She's such a rebel. She takes a drag on her cigarette, and I stare at her in awe.

"You're sure you don't want to?" she asks, flicking her ashes out the small window of the tree-house. They fall down silently through the night and she grins. "Chicken," she says after a moment's silence.

"Of pulling that crap into my virgin lungs?" I ask. The word virgin has been used at least four hundred times in the last hour. We've discussed every girl in all of our classes—who is a virgin, who isn't, and who wishes they weren't. Virgin. Virgin. Virgin.

That's what I am.

She shrugs. "Your choice."

I'm glad she leaves it there. My parents both smoked at one point in their lives, but they quit together when mom's asthma got too bad. I think they were very brave.

"I think it will be Paul Donovan," she says, looking cool and introspective as the tip of her cigarette glows, then dims. "I think it will be Paul…behind the school dumpster."

I throw my pillow at her and she just barely lifts the cigarette in time. "Shut. Up!" I say, the words like a joke. But I don't mean it. Paul is tall and hot. And he's the captain of the hockey team.

"Seriously, he wouldn't look at me if someone had his head in a vice." I lean back against the uneven wooden boards and smile. Maybe Paul would look at me. But all he'd see is the book in front of me, and then he'd look away, seeing beautiful, bold Michelle beside me with open arms. "Besides, I think he likes *you*."

This makes her blush, I'm sure of it, but it's too dark to see her cheeks.

"I wonder what it feels like," she says. She is so much braver than me.

"Sex?" I ask.

"Yes, stupid. S. E. X. Making love... L'amour." She grabs my pillow and jambs it over her body, rubbing up and down. Beside me the radio screams silently "aaaaaall niiiiiiight loooooooooooong! Yeah, you...".

My face is hot, and I think of what it would be like to have a boy, any boy, laying naked on top of me. A tiny part of my body would like that, but a much bigger part of my body wants nothing to do with it. The thought of anyone putting anything that close to my private parts makes me nervous. I've never even kissed a boy. Unless you count Joe in first grade when I was six, and that was on a dare.

I say the first thing that comes to mind. "Sweaty." Trust me to go all scientific.

Michelle laughs, a giggly, snorty laugh, and throws the pillow back at me. It lands on top of my knees and I pull it up to hug it. A soft, snuggle kind of hug, not a lewd, sexy kind.

"You're a prude, Ellie," she says and then sits up puckering her lips. "Let's just say Paul comes your way at the dance next week. Asks you to dance... pulls you in tight..."

"Michelle..."

"No, really! What are you going to do if he tries to kiss you?"

"Firstly, he's *not* going to ask me to dance. And second of all, he's *not* going to try to kiss me." Now it's my face that's blushing.

She throws the cigarette out the open space called a window that's letting in the bugs and the starlight. Her face is beaming.

"You like him."

"No. I don't"

"You do! I can see it in your eyes!"

"Michelle, it's pitch black in here. You *cannot* see it in my eyes."

She slides across the small space where our sleeping bags are and gets as close as she can to my face. I know she can't see anything. I know it. I squirm under her gaze.

"You like him! You want him!"

"Michelle. I do not like him. He's seventeen. He drives a motorbike. And his dad's military."

"So?"

"So I'll never, ever, *ever* end up with someone like that. He'll join up and be some annoying pilot boy that's always flying away and leaving. You know me…I'm all about stable."

Michelle laughs. "Ellie, you're whacked."

"What?"

"You're crazy! It's just a dance. You're *almost fifteen* for God's sake. No one's asking you to marry him. Just a little lip dancing. You know… *fun*?"

That's the problem—I don't know fun. I know studying. I know my family and looking after my little sister. When I'm feeling particularly crazy, I bake cookies. I know doing what's right. And I'm pretty sure if Paul tried to kiss me, I'd freeze up and he'd laugh his head off at my juvenile spazziness. I want nothing to do with those fly-boy wannabe's anyway. They're just pale comparisons of the real thing. In four years I'll be off on my own at university, studying to be a doctor or a nurse and far, far away from anything that wears a blue uniform. In four years, the military won't own the street I live on or the school I go to.

Or the boys I kiss.

Friday evening comes, and Michelle and I walk to the school from her parents' house. I swear she's got ten pounds of hairspray in her hair, and enough makeup for both of us. She looks great. I, on the other hand, look like the brainy kid on a television sitcom: button-up shirt; jeans; straight, simple hair. Michelle leans over and undoes my top button.

"Honestly, Ellie, it's just a dance."

I nod. She hands me her lip gloss. Root beer flavored.

I'm not good at these things. Really, I'm not. I can't understand why I go. Michelle shines, and I wilt while the AC/DC crashes in the background. On one side of the gym, the boys stand with their hands in their pockets, saying nothing and looking uncomfortable. On the other side, the girls stand close together and cup their hands to each other's ears, whispering secrets. The teachers and parent supervisors look bored. I'm sure I saw Mr. Maynard beside the school smoking a joint with Shawna—a girl in eleventh grade—as we came in. More loud, screamy music. Some of the girls rush the dance floor and dance together. The guys stand and watch.

I feel Michelle tap on my shoulder and her hand beside my ear.

"Paul is looking this way," she half whispers, half yells over the music. I want to be somewhere else. She winks at him and he looks away. I wonder who it was he was looking at. Was it me? Was it Michelle? My cheeks feel hot.

"I have to go to the bathroom," I say.

"Wait!" Michelle grabs my arm. "It's going to be a slow song next. He's going to ask you!"

Michelle is right on both counts. The screaming stops and a slow, steady beat kicks in. Michelle whispers something else in my ear but I don't hear because a guy almost three years older than me is walking toward us, and he's definitely looking at me. I think I'm going to puke.

"Hey," he says to me. Just me.

I smile and brush at my polyester shirt. "Hey."

Michelle giggles.

"Do you want to dance?"

I don't, but I do, but I don't, but I do.

"Okay," I say.

I can't even hear the music anymore, but I know it's there. I smile at Michelle, she winks back, and then I follow Paul out onto the dance floor, weaving between the couples until we're surrounded by slowly swaying teenagers and I can't see Michelle anymore. He turns and puts his hands on my waist, catching my eyes with his as he does so. I awkwardly reach up and put my hands on his shoulders. His hair is shorter than most, and his teeth, when he smiles, are just a little bit crooked. He must be six feet tall, because my measly five-foot-two frame barely reaches his chest. He's wearing a t-shirt with the arms rolled up...and his biceps actually fill it out.

He leans down to whisper in my ear.

"You look nice tonight," he says. I wonder if someone put him up to this. I wonder if he's just trying to get some fresh meat.

I turn my head to the side so I can speak into his ear. His short hair tickles my lips when I reach too far. He smells of sweat and deodorant. It's not unpleasant.

"Thanks," I say, "so do you." I'm not lying, or saying it because it's the correct reply to his musing. It's the truth. I'm trying my darndest not to get all starry-eyed, dancing with the captain of the high school hockey team.

We go round and round in circles, and as the music peaks his hand slides up my back. I feel light and flittery, but it's nice. Round and round and round. His left arm slides down again, and his hand rests on the waistband of my jeans. I like it there.

All of a sudden I realize the music has ended. We separate quickly and look at our feet.

"Well, thanks," he says.

"You too." I say. *You too*? What the heck is that supposed to mean?

"Maybe...we could...dance again?" He says, but I barely hear the last bit. The bangy loud music starts up again, making it impossible to talk.

"Okay!" I yell, and escape back to Michelle before I say something else I shouldn't.

Michelle and I spend the rest of the dance with our loose group of girlfriends, trying to ignore the boys with out actually ignoring them. I see Paul looking my way several times, but he never comes over. He dances with a big-haired junior a couple of slow dances, and I think maybe I was just imagining his interest.

Jerk.

At our school they always play two slow dances at the end of the night. It's like a signal for the horny, drunk teenagers to take their groping elsewhere. The unattached girls stand in one corner, chatting and searching for someone, anyone, to break away from the jumble of testosterone on the other side of the room and pull them onto the dance floor. I generally don't bother looking, but tonight I do. And, to my utmost disbelief, Paul detaches himself from his shoulder-punching buddies and saunters across the gym toward me.

He must see the shocked look on my face, because his lips quirk up in an incredibly cool half-smile.

"Hey," he says over the music.

Michelle is out on the floor with some other hockey player, so I have no backup. "Hi again," I say.

He flicks his head back toward the gropers in the centre of the floor. "Do you wanna dance?"

"Sure," I say. It's steamy in the gym, and I'm sure my sweat glands kick into overdrive. I thank God and all of the Saints that I put deodorant on tonight.

He reaches out and grabs my hopefully-not-too-slimy hand, and pulls me on to the floor, as close to the middle of the crowd as we can get. I awkwardly lift my arms up and over his neck and his hands are back on my waist. I let my head rest on his chest, and the smell of sweaty male and aftershave hits me hard as he kneads my back with his fingers. Oh. My. God. I am dancing with the captain of the hockey team. Me! I think I've entered another dimension, because why the hell would he bother to even look at me, let alone single me out for one of the last two dances?

His left hand traces slow circles on my back and I can feel his chest vibrate as he sings to the music. He has a surprisingly good voice. Well…what I can hear of it. We sway our tiny circles in the crush of teen bodies, and I'm happy but confused at the same time. I'm pretty sure cute, popular Paul is only interested in getting into someone's pants, like ninety-nine percent of all teenage boys, so why does this feel so good?

The song ends, and when it does I let go and turn to leave, expecting him to go find the junior he was dancing with earlier. She, I'm convinced, will put out for him.

But he grabs my hand, anchoring me in place. "Hey," he says in the brief silence between songs, "don't you want to dance again?"

"Oh," I say stupidly. "Okay…"

As the couples around us reorganize, some with new partners, most with the same ones, he wraps his arms around me again, and I try to squash the confusion in my head. It's just a dance. Don't over-analyze. Live for the moment!

The song continues and I let his hand travel up my side, brushing my breast and tilting my chin back to look at his face. He's hot, in both the literal and figurative way, and I feel my pulse thrumming in my throat. I lick my lips, tasting root beer from Michelle's lip gloss. He smiles, oozing sexiness, and as Bonnie Rait croons out the lyrics of her song, he leans down and kisses me.

Just like that. My first real kiss.

More of a brush of his lips than anything, but my heart and body say it's a real kiss. He leans back and grins, without letting me go. I feel like one of those girls in the movies that stands there, spellbound, while angels sing around her. The over-bright gym lights flick on and the kids file off the dance floor, more than one of the junior and senior girls staring daggers at me. Who the hell am I to be kissing Paul Donovan? But he doesn't see them. He smiles and says, "The boys are going over to the bridge, wanna come with me?"

He just kissed me, and now he's asking me—*me*—to the bridge— A.K.A. the get drunk and make-out spot? Alarm bells go off everywhere in my head. But my body is screaming *YES!*

Before I can answer, Michelle comes barrelling over, grinning like a Cheshire cat.

"Hey, Ellie! *Hi,* Paul. Hate to interrupt." She winks at me, and my face flares beet red. She is *loving* that she's interrupting. Paul drops his hands, but slowly, like he wants to keep holding on to me. Michelle's eyes follow his hands, and she grins even wider.

I want to sink into the floor.

"Ellie, the girls are all going over to Sheryl's. Ready to go?"

"Um…" I say, torn completely between options. Go with the girls, and have a fun, but relatively safe, time with them, or go with Paul, and likely repeat the kiss that just turned my insides to jelly…and maybe more?

I'm all about safe.

I shrug my shoulders, and turn to Paul, my side still tingling where his hand was. "Maybe next time?" I ask. I'm such a dried-up prude. Like there will be a next time. You don't get a second chance with guys like him.

He nods, as if it's no skin off of his back. "Deal," he says, jams his hands in his pockets and walks away.

He's barely across the gym before Michelle detonates. "Did he ask you to go with him? And you said *no*?"

I nod.

"*What?* Are you *insane*? That was Paul Donovan. Paul. Donovan. Go!" She pushes me toward the door. "Go with him before it's too late!"

I shake my head. "They're going to the bridge," I say, as if this should be enough explanation for my cop out. But I'm talking to Michelle, queen of the dare.

"He invited you to the bridge?" She slaps her forehead with her palm. "You must be insane. *Serious* make-out possibilities, Ellen. Why are you still here?"

I watch as Paul and the boys jostle out the gym doors, so I don't miss Paul's quick glance back. He tilts his head and waves toward the door—*Do you want to come?*

I frown and shake my head. He shrugs and follows his friends.

"Ellen, you are one crazy chick," Michelle says beside me. "One crazy chick."

And I can't help but agree with her. Sometimes safe and crazy are the same thing.

CHAPTER 20
HOUSE #13 (CRUISE)

Early May, 2009

WHEN THE GREEN ISLANDS AND villas have slid by, and there's nothing to watch but the waves and the setting sun, my stomach growls unceremoniously and I realize I haven't eaten since the plane. That's at least twelve hours. I could hide away, here in my beautiful room with the quiet-ish balcony. I could order room service and sit on my bed and feel sorry for myself and talk to John in my head. It would be easy to do, because I know it's what I've done for almost a year. But I can't.

I can't sit here with just myself. I'll only think of John. John, John, John. He swirls in my head like the wind on my balcony.

There must be some place I can go where I can eat without interacting. Not the main dining room. The buffet? It's sure to be packed, but I can grab something and escape to a quiet corner on the deck.

I pass Joselito in the hallway, and he nods politely.

"Everything to your liking Mrs. Michaels?"

"Yes, Joselito. Just fine." I say, forcing a smile.

"Are you heading out to eat?"

"Yes."

He somehow sees my need for simplicity.

"Might I suggest the Culture Café on Deck 3, Ma'am? Usually it's not that busy on the first night. The view is beautiful and the food is excellent. "

"Thank you, Joselito. Sounds perfect."

He nods, and points down the hallway. "Take the elevator to Deck

3, and turn left. It's on the port side almost all the way to the front of the ship." He nods and smiles again.

"Thanks."

Not having a better idea, I take his advice and head to the café on the third deck. As I emerge from the elevator, I can hear the loud party music on the deck, and the booming voice of a twenty-something trying to convince the old fogies to get up and dance. I cringe and veer away toward the front of the ship, and see the open door of Joselito's café. He's right, it looks like an oasis. Plants, sunlight, secluded tables, and a order-at-the-bar style menu. I walk up, order a pasta dish and a glass of wine. I take the number that goes with my order. A small table beside the window is empty, so I sit.

There's not much to see from my perch, except the waves and a few straggling boats. I'm so high up the boats look small and unreal, like a television image. As I sip my wine, a gentle old French melody rolls from a speaker somewhere, masking the crazy strains of party music. Below me is the walking path on Deck 4 that travels the entire perimeter of the ship. A few of the suits from the life-vest drills walk by, deep in conversation. One of them looks vaguely familiar, probably was on the same flight or something. It's not bad, here.

I watch the waves and the people, and just let the peace of the moment take me. The server comes with my pasta, tells me to let the bar-staff know if I need anything else. I order a second glass of wine, and then she leaves me with my thoughts, which are many and confused.

I'm stuck now. I guess I was stuck when I stepped on that plane, but now there's nowhere to go but my room on this floating resort. Little flutters of panic roll around in my stomach with forkfuls of pasta and sips of wine. I'm here, on a couple's trip without the second half of a couple. I don't know how to act. Really, other than Paul all those years ago, the only person I ever dated was John. John was my first…the first and only except for *him,* and even I know that doesn't count. I knew John's rhythms and he knew mine. Our life was simple. I loved John, he loved me, and there was no question of who we would spend the rest of our days with. There were no games.

Do people come on these trips to hook up? Crap, what if someone tries to hit on me? I doubt it would happen; I'm old, for God's sake!

Forty-five is dangerously close to fifty. I have wrinkles on my wrinkles, and my bikini body bit the bullet when I was pregnant with number two. How could someone find me attractive enough to make a move? I probably look like death on stilts. And if someone did find me attractive enough to talk with me, what should I do? I haven't dated since high school. I pat my hair, pinch my cheeks and then glance around the room to see if there are scary, single-looking men glaring at me. There aren't, just a few couples, chatting quietly and sipping their drinks. I'm safe for now, because the thought of talking to another man without John nearby is terrifying. The kids *couldn't* have thought about this when they signed me up.

I take another furtive glance around, order a third glass of wine, and turn myself to the window, secluding myself in my own little space. They can't talk to me if I don't look at them.

The pasta is good. Really good. In fact it's excellent. And the wine isn't bad either, but I've never been one for wine. I always feel guilty drinking it, and it makes me feel drowsy. Who'd look after the kids if I got drunk? Of course, now the kids get drunk themselves, without me. With that thought I suck back a few more gulps and try to look mature and confident.

When my fourth wine glass and dessert plate are empty and I'm more relaxed, I embrace my liquid courage and explore the ship. It's huge and opulent and filled with things that remind me of John. Not in a bad way, not in a way that makes me sad, but in a way that makes me want to talk to him. Opulent is more his thing than mine—all of those hotels and airports and fancy ceremonies are par for the course in his world. Or were.

I walk along the same path I noticed from my perch in the restaurant, looking out as the last glimpse of land slips away on the horizon. The deck lurches a bit, but I put it off to my lack of sea legs. It's really windy and my hair blows all around my face and into my eyes. It's nice though—the warm buzz in my stomach, the full feeling there too, and the fresh ocean air. I lean over the railing and look down at the rushing waves, the deep blue darkness.

It's mesmerizing…the wind, the waves, the darkness. When I finally lean back and move away, I feel dizzy. Really dizzy. I stumble away from the railing, watching my feet to make sure I don't fall, but that only makes it worse. Maybe that extra glass of wine was a bad idea. Maybe I shouldn't have gulped it back so quickly. When a pair of men's loafers blocks my way, I look up and the world tilts.

The owner of the loafers reaches out to steady me. His hand is firm, but not intimidating, and I close my eyes tightly and then open them as I look up from the deck. The hand drops as I try to focus, which is a good thing because pulling away from Loafer Man would result in my face meeting the floor very quickly.

"Ellen?"

Whoa. He knows my name. His face slowly defogs as my eyes fight to focus.

"You know my name," I say.

"Ellen McKinley?"

"How do you know my name?"

His face looks familiar, vaguely, but I can't place it. I'm on a boat in the Mediterranean. I shouldn't know anyone here. No one should know me.

"I'd recognize you anywhere. You haven't changed a bit," he says.

His voice is familiar too.

He chuckles, and it's a nice sound, not menacing or scary. "You really don't know me, do you?" The smile that lights up his face is handsome and assured. He's tall, dark-haired, muscular...who is this guy?

I study his face—well, as much as I can study his face with the world doing circles around me—and a vague hint floats just under the surface of my thoughts. My maiden name. He knew me before John...

"Paul?"

His smile widens, showing just slightly crooked teeth. "In the flesh!" He glances behind me, and then around the deck. "Your husband in your suite?"

My stomach falls to my toes, and I must visibly sway because he reaches out again to grab my arms with both hands. He looks around, locates a bench, and walks me to it while I try very, very hard not to burst into tears.

I slump down into the chair and hide my face in my hands. The wind blows, the waves crash beneath us, and Paul sits there silently, waiting for me to get my emotions—and my equilibrium—back under control.

It could be minutes or hours before I finally sit up. I've lost all concept of time in my inebriated, sea-shifting state, but he sits there without moving, without touching and without saying a word. John's death and my mourning were plastered all over national television and in the national newspapers. I can't believe he hasn't heard. How could he not have heard? When I look at him, his face is curious, but compassionate.

And holy cow! Have the years been good to him, or what?

"John is dead." I say, failing miserably at keeping the tears from flowing. God, I'm a wreck. They leak, unceremoniously, down my face and drip into my lap. It's been almost a year, for crap's sake. How can he not know? When I last saw Paul, he was cute but a lot less muscular, and heading off to army military college. John's death cannot have gone unnoticed in any military circle.

"Oh," he says because, really, there's nothing else to say.

"I should go." I say as I stand up, brushing at my legs and trying to hide my intoxication. I fail at this too, and Paul's hands catch me once again.

"Damn!" I growl at myself.

"Here," he says as he stands up too, his hands not leaving my arms. "Let me at least help you back to your suite."

I recognize the practicality of his offer. God knows what will happen if I try to make it back to my room in this state. The fourth glass of wine on a jet-lagged and over-tired stomach was a really, *really* bad idea.

"Okay," I say.

His left arm wraps around me, and his hand holds my waist, guiding me gently down the deck and through the doors to the elevator lobby. I lean on him, not by choice but by necessity. I can't help but notice the feel of his chest against my shoulder—the pressure of his fingertips on my waist.

"What floor?" he asks.

"Shouldn't you get back to your wife?" I ask. There's no way a guy like Paul would be on a ship like this without some eye candy to keep him company. I feel his laugh more than hear it.

"No wife," he says. "We divorced about six years ago."

"Oh," I say as the elevator dings and opens up. We walk in and I tell him the floor number. He presses the button, but his other arm stays firmly around my waist. Some part of my pickled brain registers the familiarity of his touch (we *did* almost have sex a gazillion years ago) and the fact that I'm taking a single, buff, handsome man to my room. Or rather *he's* taking me to my room. I can barely stand up. This is not good.

Where is John when I need him?

Dead. That's where.

I try to peel his fingers from my side, and he takes the hint and lets go. Of course, that's the moment when the elevator decides to stop with what's probably a slow deceleration, but which feels like a train crash. I wobble ungracefully and almost fall over. Paul once again grabs me before I face plant. My cheeks burn with embarrassment. I'm such a stupid, pathetic cheap drunk.

"I think I better help you walk," he says.

"The wine was stronger than I thought."

"Mmm-hmm." He's smiling, but not with condescension. I have to admit, I must look hilarious, falling all over the place.

We walk out of the elevator—or should I say, he walks, I stumble—and then he stops, fingers pressing firmly so that I don't fall.

"What room number?" he asks.

Holy freaking shit, I don't remember my room number. What in the *hell* is my room number?

"Um…" I say, and pull my purse around, shuffling to find the key-card. Please, God, let me find *something* with the room number on it. I pull out the card, and hand it to him, but of course it's useless.

Just my name. Ellen Michaels. Nothing else.

"Um…" I say again as I dig further into my purse. Thank the good Lord above! I find the little folder that held the key. On it is my room number, 8225.

"It's 8225!" I say, sounding all proud of myself and looking ridiculous.

He grins, and as we head down the corridor, I say "I didn't intend to get this drunk." For some reason I want him to know I'm not a lush. I've never been a drinker. Surely he must remember that.

"It's okay. Did you just fly in this morning?"

I nod, and then stop because my head feels like a heavy bowling ball that might just fall off.

"Jet-lag can do it to you. And the wine is different here..." he says. His arm guides me to a stop, and he deftly swipes the key card and opens the door without letting go. Just at that moment Joselito walks by. Nodding discretely at us both.

"Ms. Michaels," he says as he squeezes by in the narrow hall.

My cheeks flame up with embarrassment again. What Joselito must think! Here I am, drunk at my door, with a single and very handsome man. But the hall sways again and Paul leads me in before my brain has time to really process it. The door clicks closed.

I am such an idiot.

The life vest is still where I kicked it, twisted up against the wall, and my suitcase still sits against the bed. Paul surveys the room for a minute as it spins around and around in some sort of cosmic roller coaster in front of my eyes. Ugh, ugh, ugh.

"Some fresh air would help," he says, more to himself than to me, and then I let him walk me through the room and out onto the balcony, where he deposits me in the very chair I sat in this afternoon. It's full dark out, and the waves are black beyond, but they're adding to the distortion in my head, so I just close my eyes and listen to the rush of the wind. He must go inside and make coffee or order room service, because soon he's in front of me with a steaming cup of salvation under my nose.

"I thought you'd like some coffee."

I grunt, take it, and swig some back. Oh how attractive that must be. Somehow I manage to take two sips without splashing it all over myself, and he takes the cup and places it on the small table before sitting down himself. I still don't dare look out beyond the balcony, so I look at the floor.

"Well, this is embarrassing," I say, to break the silence. He watches me but says nothing, so I hide my embarrassment in a sip of my coffee.

"I had four glasses of wine with dinner. That's all." I say, as though he's accusing me of being a drunkard. He's not, but I say it anyway. He just sits there, thinking who knows what, while I squirm under my skin. Maybe I'm justifying my actions to myself.

We sit there for a few more minutes in silence, and the world seems less topsy-turvy as the caffeine and fresh air clean out the cobwebs. I look at him again, and he's still watching me, coffee cup held in his hand. Rather than look away, I watch him back. He has *definitely* aged well. There are a few greys in his hair, but it's still dark, almost black, and short but not military short. His face has lost that teenaged look; now it's more chiselled, with a faint hint of scruff. He's wearing fashionable cotton pants, and a button-down shirt that looks expensive. Even his shoes look like something from a GQ magazine.

"Paul, are you still in the army?" I finally ask. When I last saw him, I was in eleventh grade and he was off to be all that he could be.

He swallows his coffee and sets the mug down on the table.

"I never finished mil-col," he says. "Hated it. It made no sense. So I released, transferred to a civie university, and graduated with a Bachelor of Business Admin."

"Oh." I say. This night is just full of surprises. I had pegged him as a future army-army-army guy.

I'm still drunk enough to be bold, so I keep going. "Your dad must have hated that."

"Yeah. But I worked two jobs to pay my own tuition. It was worth it."

"Oh," I say again.

We sit there a few more minutes saying nothing. I can't stand the awkwardness. "So what brings you on this cruise?" I ask.

He looks out over the balcony. Another cruise ship is sailing off in the distance, brightly lit in the dark night.

"I'm working out of the London office of a world-wide engineering firm, and this is a business trip. We've got a few meetings scheduled each day we're at sea, and our Italian group is meeting in Venice after the cruise."

Wow. Must be a pretty huge company if they can afford to spend the cash on a business trip like that. It also explains the fancy clothes. My musings are interrupted by his question.

"And what about you?"

What about me? He sees my dazed look and clarifies his question.

"What brings you on this cruise?"

Well there's a good question.

"Christmas present from my kids." Ugh. Makes me sound like a stupid, frumpy, diaper-changing moron.

Ugh.

"Your kids?" he asks.

"My three kids…" and because of the way his eyes raise, I feel the need to clarify to this fancy, metropolitan man that I spent more than one steamy evening with in a 1970-something Chevelle.

"Chris, David, and Maria. Maria's the youngest—nineteen, and David, the oldest, is twenty-five. I…uh…had them pretty young."

I can almost feel him doing the math. I need to take the conversation away from myself.

"Do you have any? Kids, that is?"

He nods. "Two girls. Jenna is twelve, Jordan is nine. They mostly live with their mother and visit over the summer and holidays. I'm okay with it. My work is pretty hectic. Takes me all over the place, and my ex doesn't approve. She hates travelling—part of why we split up, I guess."

"John used to travel a lot too," I say, and then I wish I hadn't. I don't want to talk about John. "I would have loved to have gone with him."

Did I just say that? Now I sound like I'm trying to win Paul's favour or something.

Note to self: Never. Drink. Again.

I hide my face in my coffee cup.

"Have you ever been to Greece?" He asks.

I shake my head. The wine must be wearing off because I only have to close my eyes for a second to regain my equilibrium, and I manage to set the coffee down without any major catastrophes.

"Tomorrow we'll be in Corfu. I'd be happy to show you around, if you'd like."

No pressure, no forced lies behind this statement. And it is, actually, a statement. He'd be happy to show me around. For the barest of seconds I think I should ask John before I comment, and then I recognize the futility of the thought. John isn't here to care.

So, in a rare moment of Ellen recklessness, I answer. "Yes, I would like that."

Why not?

CHAPTER 21
HOUSE #13 (CRUISE)

Early May, 2009

I LIE IN BED, EYES FOCUSED on the fire-proof ceiling above me, while the wine and caffeine war with one another in my bloodstream. Paul is off to his suite, somewhere on the expensive floor, and I'm attempting to deal with the guilt I feel from saying yes to his offer. I left the sliding glass door to the balcony open, and the white noise washes over me as I sink deeper and deeper into my incredibly comfortable—and incredibly empty—bed.

How can I go with Paul tomorrow? What if he gets the wrong idea? Do I *want* him to get the wrong idea? I am *so* not prepared for this. When I married John, I married him forever. All other interested parties need not apply. And now, somewhere on this ship, in his opulent, first-class suite, an extremely well-preserved ghost from my past is sleeping, ready to get up and escort me around a Mediterranean island for the day. It's a bizarre twist of karmic fate that we're on the same ship, at the same time, and then I practically fall on him in my drunken stupor tonight. How can he *not* get the wrong idea?

Somewhere after the second trip to the bathroom, I finally fall asleep, no closer to the answers than I was before.

The bright, clear sunlight streams through my balcony door as I pace nervously, waiting for Paul to arrive. My embarrassment at my intoxicated idiocy last night almost overtakes my nerves at going out with a relatively strange man. The good thing about being a cheap drunk is that the day has dawned relatively hangover-free. I'm still tired, but a shower, juice, and two cups of coffee have taken the edge off.

I'm primping in the bathroom mirror when the knock on the door comes. I jump, dropping the brush on the floor. Gees, Ellen! He's just taking you for a tour. It's not like he's going to jump you. I squash down all of the unpleasant memories that thought brings to the surface.

I answer the door, face bright red.

"Hi." I say, letting him in.

He's dressed more casually today, in shorts and sandals. "Hi," he replies. "How are you feeling?"

"Oh, God, Paul! I'm so sorry for last night. I can't believe how quickly that wine went to my head. You must think I'm such a lush."

"Not at all. I'm just glad you're okay." His eyes *look* sincere. My blush lightens a tiny bit.

"Are you ready to go?" he asks.

"Just got to grab my bag." I grab my small daypack, throw a bottle of water in it from the bar fridge, and smile at him. I'm wearing a flowery skirt, comfortable sandals, and a fitted tank top—probably the most figure-flattering top I own—but I still feel old and flabby next to him as I walk out the door. He's wearing a spicy cologne that reminds me of John.

The concierge at the disembarkation door recognizes Paul and ushers us to the front of the line. He offers us more bottled water and to help find a taxi, but Paul refuses both, saying the day is too nice for cars. We hop on a shuttle that will take us to a drop-off point in the city. It's a fast, narrow road, and my stomach complains a bit, so I'm happy to walk after that.

"We're heading to the Agios Spyridon," he says as we squeeze in between pushy tourists and wizened old Greek men. "See that spire over there? The one with the red dome on the top?"

I nod, glad to at least have a destination. It doesn't take long to reach it, as the roads are narrow and packed closely together.

We enter from the front, and find a seat in the silent pews. To the front of us, lit by sunlight streaming though small windows, is a silver casket.

"The remains of Spyridon himself are in that casket," Paul whispers to me. "seventeen hundred years old."

All I see is a casket.

A casket.

In a church.

It takes mere seconds for the tears to well up again, and I'm rushing out the door, pushing past nuns, Japanese tourists, and who knows who else, trying to get away, trying to breathe, trying to escape the feeling that the world is closing down on my chest like a giant, unfeeling clamp.

I run down the street, past crowds and shops and jewellery racks, wiping tears and barely seeing where I'm going.

"Ellen!" I can hear Paul behind me, but I push on, push forward.

"Ellen, wait!"

He's faster than me, of course. I'm out of shape and he's trim and toned and probably runs marathons every Tuesday.

"Ellen, stop…Please," he says. He touches my shoulder, and I stop right there in the middle of the crowded street. I turn around, my chest heaving and my arms hanging at my sides like a lost marionette. His face is a study of concern.

"I didn't think, Ellen. Jesus, I feel like such an ass! I was just thinking about the story, and the architecture, I didn't even think about what it might mean…"

He runs his hands through his hair, in a surprisingly John-like gesture, and I start up afresh. Will I ever be able to remember John without dissolving into a blubbering, snotty mess?

"I just…I…" I sniff wetly, rubbing my eyes with damp fingers. "I…"

He pulls me in and holds me in his arms like I belong there. But I'm not ready for that. I push away—grasping my elbows and shutting him out.

"Sorry. Shit." He says, and grabs his hair in his fingers. "Okay, um… would you like to go for coffee?"

I can't speak, so I just nod.

We walk further down the street, away from the church and toward a green space that looks like a sports field. We sit, he buys strong coffee and baklava, and we watch as men in white pants gather on the field.

"How long ago did he die?" he finally asks. I don't think I've ever seen such compassion on a man's face. Ever.

"Almost a year," I say, my insides numbed by the strong coffee and sweet pastry.

"You really miss him."

I nod and rub my eyes with my napkin.

"That's hard. How many years were you together?"

"Twenty-five. It would have been twenty-six in January." I wait as he adds up the years in his head. He knows how old I am.

"But that would mean…"

"I was just nineteen when we got married. The year I started university. I was pregnant. He was in Military College." The tears keep coming, but I wipe them away and keep talking. It's good to talk to someone who doesn't know, who doesn't have all of the military baggage holding his opinions in place, someone that knew me as Ellen the motivated, not Ellen the used-up and discarded, Ellen the dependent.

"We were young and stupid, but I loved him. Three kids, twelve moves, and a lifetime later, he went out on a training mission and never came back." I watch as the men on the field form up three sticks in a row like a child's building set. My voice is surprisingly steady and I feel lighter, less weighed-down, just by telling him those words. He listens, quietly and without judgement, but I don't even care what he thinks about it. It just is. I can't take the past back, and I can't make everything better.

"The kids bought me this trip because, without John, I had nothing to anchor me." I look at his face. He owes me nothing, almost thirty years after we dated. "No career, no kids at home, no John to help me cope. They thought it would help, I guess. Get me away from the world that is…was…Ellen Michaels."

He nods, an I-understand-but-I-don't kind of nod. I wonder, briefly, if the kids had something to do with Paul being on the ship, but they can't have. They wouldn't know about Paul. I don't even think John knew about Paul.

I take a deep breath and continue my story.

"I've never, not once, travelled without John, and when I saw that casket, it brought it all back. The funeral, the flowers, all of it. Only John's casket was empty." I watch a scraggly cat walk up to the café beside us. A Greek man in an apron bends over and picks it up, like it's the most exotic cat in the world, like it's beautiful.

"I'm sorry," I say, and turn to Paul. "You must think I'm crazy."

He shrugs. "Your story is no worse than mine," he says.

"Not possible," I say. He has no idea of the skeletons in my closet.

He smiles a rueful smile. "I can tell you, if you'd like."

I take a sip from my water bottle. "Sure."

He leans back in his chair and crosses his legs like a storyteller about to spin a yarn. "Francesca and I met in university. She and I dated, on and off, but nothing serious. Well, not for me, anyway. I was still reeling from being dumped in the last month of high school…"

Oops. I don't miss the look he gives me. Somehow I think he's not joking.

"…and I wasn't looking for serious. I got a job at the company I'm with now, right after graduation and moved to New York City right away—and she didn't come with me. I should have known that it was doomed from there. We kept running into each other, and after a year of being in Dallas together, I proposed. We got married, had kids, and then my job moved and she didn't. The commuting thing worked okay for a couple of years. Like I said, she hated travelling, even to fun places. And I thought she was being selfish. We fought a lot. She didn't work, was caught up in the socialite scene, and lived to get our daughters on the top cheerleading squad. I *hate* cheerleading." His jaw clenches and unclenches. I suspect there's more to that story. "Jordan loved it, but my oldest—she's an intellectual…"

The crack of a ball on a bat echoes across the open area we're seated in. The game has started. Three tables over from us, the loud Texan couple from the ship are harassing the waiter. An island this big, and they have to be right beside us.

"Anyway, things got nasty, we both said stuff we shouldn't have. I left, and that was that. Maybe I should have fought for it, fought for the girls, but it seemed like it would just make it harder for them. And I didn't love her anymore. I'm not sure I ever loved her."

I watch his face as he remembers, dark brown eyes scrunched up in the sunlight, dark brown hair glinting. I don't want to think of him as anything but an acquaintance, but he really *has* aged well.

Stop! How can I be thinking about this? This is crazy. My husband is dead. My husband is dead. My *husband*, the man I loved with all of my heart, is dead and I'm sitting here in Greece, looking at a guy that

I dated in high school. The huge hole in my heart, still raw enough to explode at the sight of a centuries-old casket, can never, ever be filled with someone else. It's wrong that I'm looking at Paul that way. Wrong that I find him attractive. Wrong that I want to touch his biceps and feel his arms around me. Wrong that I want to slap his ex-wife for leaving him, when I did the same thing years ago.

Wrong, wrong, *wrong*!

Paul turns, and his lips quirk up in a bare, sad smile. "Maybe I was an ass. I took the job in London, I let her take me for all she could, and now the girls come and visit me a couple of times a year." He shrugs.

"There's nothing wrong with that," I say. "Life is too short to be with someone you don't love."

The words are out before I can take them back. Crap.

"I thought I loved you in high school," he says. I cringe inwardly.

Double crap.

What can I say to that? I hide my face in my hands, wishing that, just for once, my life could be easy. He's baring his soul to me, and I'm just as heartless as I was back then.

"I was stupid in high school," I finally say through my fingers. "Stupid with how I treated you, stupid with John, stupid to get pregnant...stupid."

I hear him shift, and feel his hand touch my shoulder, gently—tentatively like he's afraid I'll break. He might be right.

When I look up from my hands, he's right there, perched on his seat like he would pick me up and hold me. If only I deserved that kind of compassion.

He tilts his head to one side. "What happened back then made us who we are now. I have no idea who I would have been if I hadn't dated you, hadn't married Francesca. And your time with John formed you into who you are now. We can't go back, Ell. There's nothing to do but move forward, and see where life takes us...one day at a time."

He's right. I can't go back. John is dead, and I wouldn't give away my time with him, or the kids, for anything. I have many regrets, but my time with John is not one of them.

Paul looks at his expensive watch, stands up and puts his hand out to me. "And today, you're on Corfu...and I just happen to be here too.

Call it coincidence, call it whatever you'd like. Would you like me to show you around…around places that don't have caskets?" he grins.

I look at his hand and feel the guilt; like I'd be betraying John and all of the time we had together by taking it. But I squash that feeling down. This trip isn't about feeling guilt or mourning the dead. This trip is about being alive. And my heart, however damaged, is still beating in my chest.

"I'd like that," I say. And then I take a deep breath, I reach up and I take Paul's hand.

CHAPTER 22
HOUSE #1 (BEFORE JOHN)

November, 1980

TWO WEEKS AFTER THE DANCE, Paul asks me out to the movies with him. Well, sort of. He asks Michelle if we are going, and when she says yes he then turns to me, his hands buried deep in his pockets, and then asks me if I'm coming too. My heart jumps into my throat and I feel both light as air and like I'm going to barf.

"Sure, I'd love to come." I say before I can think about it.

"Awesome. Do you need a ride?" he asks, looking up from the very interesting patch of dirt by his feet. But he's asking me, not Michelle.

"Oh, um…yeah, probably."

I don't look at Michelle, but I can *feel* the silly grin on her face. She's been bugging me to talk to him since the dance, and here he is, asking me to a movie. My cheeks blaze.

"What's your number?" I know he means my phone number, because in this little town everyone knows where everyone else lives. I'm surprised he doesn't already know my phone number.

I tell him the last four digits. The others aren't needed here, as there's only one exchange. He pulls a pen out and writes it on his hand and then closes it tight as if it might slip off and float away.

"Okay, I'll call you after school."

He smiles at me, and I feel my cheeks burn even more red.

"See you tonight," he says, before readjusting his backpack on his broad shoulders.

When he leaves, Michelle explodes.

"Holy shit, Ellen! Paul just asked you out! You dropped him like a hot potato after the dance, and he still asked you out! Holy shit! It'll be your first real date!" She's jumping up and down, and I'm feeling dazed, shocked, and still a bit sick. I need something to lean against, but there are no trees here in the dusty schoolyard.

He calls at 4:52, just before my mom puts supper on the table. She answers, and glares at me as she hands it over.

"It's for you. And it's a guy."

I'm sure he hears. Thanks, Mom.

I take the phone and wrap the cord around the corner into the entryway, they can still hear me in the kitchen, but it's a bit more private.

"Hello?" I say.

"Ellen?" asks a deep male voice.

"Paul?"

"Yeah, it's me."

"Oh."

"You still on for tonight?"

"Just a sec," I say and then cover the receiver before yelling around the corner. "Mom, I'm going to the movies with Michelle and some friends tonight. Is that okay?"

Of course she doesn't leave it there. "What friends?"

I name off everyone I think is going, including Paul.

"You're all going together? Not alone with the boy on the phone."

"Mo-om," I sigh, rolling my eyes.

"What movie?"

I tell her, and she humphs before saying yes.

On a crazy whim, I keep going, blocking the receiver with a firm hand. "I'll be staying over at Michelle's after, 'kay?"

She glances at me, and I can see the suspicion in her eyes. "Michelle's parents know about this?"

"Of course they know about it."

"And this has nothing to do with the boy that is on the phone?"

"Just that he's going to drive us. *Mom*, we're all going as a group, and then he'll drop us off at Michelle's later."

She thinks for a minute before speaking.

"Fine. Just the movies, and then to Michelle's house."

"Yes…Just the movies and then Michelle's"

Her eyes narrow, but she nods. I'm boring and truthful and I've never had a boyfriend, unlike my younger sister who has already had three, so she doesn't doubt my story. In fact, the huge lie I've just told shocks me. I didn't even know I was capable of lying like that. It comes so easily that it almost scares me.

I turn back around the corner, and lift up the phone. "Yeah, I can go." I say.

"Awesome. Pick you up at six?"

Holy crap. That's barely an hour from now.

"Okay," I say.

"See you then," he says and hangs up.

I stand there, leaning against the wall, cradling the phone, and wondering what the hell I'm getting myself into. He's dreamy, no doubt about that, but do I want to go to a movie with him? Do I want to see it through to what comes next?

I think I do.

I don't see much of the movie. There's a lot of shooting and car chases, but with Paul's arm around me and his fingers touching places where I've never, *ever* been touched, I'm not really interested in the plot. Michelle is making out full-force with her date-of-choice beside me, and the sexual tension in the air is almost palpable. I swing back and forth between embarrassment that someone might see where Paul's hands are, disgust at where Michelle's date's hands are, and a new and alien feeling of need. At one point Paul kisses me, and I forget all about the embarrassment and disgust.

When the movie ends, Michelle detangles herself from her date and suggests we go to the bridge, eyes locked on her date. Paul is still holding my hand, and my resolve is fading.

"Wanna?" he asks.

I can't find an excuse, and I've sealed my fate by lying to my mom about where I'm supposed to be tonight. The safe option would be to just suggest another place to go, the pizza joint, or the coffee shop, but his hand in mine is not safe, and Michelle is *not* going home right now. No question as to what she has on her mind. The drooling red-headed guy she's with is *toast*.

"Okay," I say.

He grins.

"See ya there, children!" Michelle says, and heads out the door, dragging Red-head without looking back.

We hop in Paul's dad's Chevelle, and stop to get milkshakes at the Dairy Barn on our way. He gets vanilla and I get strawberry. The shakes are so sweet and thick that the straws collapse as we pull at them, and the sides of our cheeks pull in like fish-faces. When we get to the bridge, Michelle and her date are parked in the shadows over by the trees. The windows are already steamed, with fingerprints trailing downward. Paul pulls his car closer to the river, and turns the key so that the radio keeps playing. We sit there in awkward silence, and it comes to me that I'm sitting in a car, in a very obvious indication that I want to do more than just sit, with someone I've never had a real conversation with. Not good. I search for something to fill the dead air.

"So are you going to college next year?" I blurt out. That's a safe topic.

"Yeah, mil-col. My dad's choice, not mine."

"Oh?" He doesn't want to go military? Didn't see that coming. I thought he was all *Hooah* and *gung-ho*.

"He wants me to be a general, I swear. Taking arts-history." He brushes his left hand through his hair as if he could wipe away his dad's wishes by doing so.

Another curve ball. "History?"

"Well, they don't care what you take if you're going to go army. I suppose I could take engineering, but it seems like a lot of work."

"What's your dad think about the army part?" I'm pretty sure his dad is a pilot.

"He's okay with it. Well, maybe a little pissed, but he'll live. He's just glad he doesn't have to pay my tuition."

"Oh."

We lapse into awkward silence. My conversation-starting skills have completely abandoned me.

He reaches down, and pulls the lever to shift the bench seat back away from the dash. We both lurch as it lets go, and I giggle. He shrugs and then leans toward me. I brace myself for the inevitable move, suddenly terrified of what's next.

He turns to me, his face lit by the gentle glow of the dashboard lighting, and I try to slow my breathing down.

"Ellen, we don't have to do anything, if you don't want to," he says, sensing my distress. He reaches toward my face and cups the line of my jaw with his hand. His fingers are surprisingly soft.

Oh, I want to, yes I do. I want to very badly. I also want to jump out of the car and run away very, very fast.

I reach up and take his hand before the run-away part of me takes over. Leaning in toward his lips and stamping down the voice of reason in my head, I kiss him. This kiss isn't like the one on the dance floor. It's full and needy; hot and bold, not quiet and secret. I don't understand the feelings in my chest, but they feel good. Really good. He pushes me back against the seat and his hand moves from my head, to my shoulders...to my breasts.

I feel a moment's pang of alarm, and Paul pulls back to look at me, questioning but not moving his hand away.

"Ellen, we don't have to... Just tell me when to stop and I will."

I nod, not trusting my voice, trying to calculate in my head just how far I'm willing to let this go.

He leans in again, and I let him search for my limits while finding them myself.

Oddly enough, it's me that breaks the relationship off. After six months of cold rides on motorbikes and Paul following me around like a hungry puppy, I don't want to see him any more. Every moment that I'm not studying and he's not playing hockey, we've spent in some state of undress, and I've been so close, so many times, to saying yes that it scares me. Michelle thinks I'm insane. I really want to be with him, I do. He's gorgeous and smart, and his body is to die for! He can do things to me that I never thought were possible. But I keep thinking... what's going to happen when he leaves? I don't want to be left. I don't want him to take that last bit of innocence from me and then leave me. Years of being a civie kid in a military town have made me cautious with my heart, and I know that the temptations of his college life will be too much for a long-distance relationship. I already get jealous when he comes out of class with some senior skank chatting him up, eyes all glittery and hair spray-painted in place. What's it going to be like at a college party, with temptation inundating him at every turn?

I need to protect myself. I need to get away.

We're sitting on a brick half-wall by the school, two weeks before exams, when I finally get the guts to do it.

"Movie tonight?" he asks.

A movie? Tonight? With exams two weeks away?

"Paul…I have to study."

"So?"

"So? So some of us actually have to *work* to do well in school."

"And?"

He reaches over to grab my hand and I pull away.

"And making-out with you at a movie is not conducive to a good history mark. Paul, you know it's important to me to do well."

"Yeah," he says, but then he leans in and tries to kiss my cheek.

I turn my cheek away and jump up.

"Paul, I can't do this anymore."

He looks confused, his dark eyes even darker.

"Can't do what, anymore?"

"This. Us."

The hurt on his face almost undoes me. I feel the tears behind my eyes, but I can't cry—not now when I'm the one doing the leaving.

"You're…you're breaking up with me?"

He says it like he's never even considered the possibility, like we were a done deal, forever. My eyes burn, and my heart stings like I'm cutting myself, not him.

"Paul, you're going to leave and go away to school, and I just can't do it."

"But…" he reaches out and tries to grab my hand, his fingers closing on my forearm.

"I have to go." I say, and then—coward that I am—I pull my arm free and run, leaving him there with big eyes and nothing to hold on to.

CHAPTER 23
HOUSE #13 (CRUISE)

Early May, 2009

Paul and I walk to the old ruins, shop for a few souvenirs for our kids, and make our way back to the ship, talking and enjoying each other's company. It's surprisingly easy to be with him. Maybe it's the fact that we spent several pseudo-intimate months together as teens, maybe it's our own histories, maybe it's just that we're two broken people who want honesty and friendship. I still see John everywhere: in the plane taking off over the city, in the uniformed guard at the museum, even in the way Paul brushes his hair out of his eyes. But I don't let it get painful.

When we reach the elevators on the ship, he presses the button for my floor, and walks me to my door, but doesn't ask to come in.

Instead he asks me to dinner.

"Do you like steak?" he asks.

I nod.

"Would you care to join me at Jeremiah's tonight?"

"Jeremiah's?"

"It's the steak restaurant on deck four. Quiet and classy. I think you'd like it."

"Oh. Um…" I search for an excuse to stay in, but after our day together he knows I have none. "Sure."

"Meet me outside the restaurant at about seven?"

I nod again.

"See you then." He smiles and turns away.

I walk through my door, shocked at my own behaviour. I just said yes to what can only be construed as a date—with an ex-boyfriend.

John, will you ever forgive me?

Not surprisingly, John doesn't answer.

I'm on my own.

I scrounge through my still-packed suitcase for the little black dress Maria insisted I pack. It may be ten years old, but it's a classic design. The fabric is light and clingy in all of the right places, smoothing over the bits that need smoothing over and snugging in on my undergarment-assisted curves. I curl my hair—something I haven't done in years with my natural waves—and brush on what little makeup I own. I pass over the perfume John bought me, because I just can't match that scent with the situation.

The heels are uncomfortable, but nice, and when I look at myself in the mirror, I don't appear hideous. I actually look...nice. One thing my mother gave me was good genetics, and I'm ever so thankful that my metabolism has kept me somewhat slim. At least what fat I have can be hidden by the right choice in apparel.

With a final brush of lipstick, I head out the door before I can lose my nerve and cancel.

Paul is standing with his back to me, looking out the floor-to-ceiling windows when I walk up. He's wearing a tailored suit, the pants just skimming his own curves, and the jacket showing off his muscular shoulders. I shouldn't look at him that way, but it's hard not to with him standing there, deep in thought. When he turns, I swear it's like something out of a movie. He smiles at me, like I'm the light he's been waiting for.

"You look lovely this evening," he says.

I can't help but smile.

"Shall we?" He points toward the restaurant door, and the hostess shows us to the table.

"The wine list, Mr. Donovan?" The hostess hands him the list.

"Please."

He orders us some red wine, tossing me a grin when the hostess asks if we'd like a bottle or glass.

"I think the bottle, please." His eyebrows arch conspiratorially and I blush.

The hostess nods and leaves us alone, promising to send the waiter to our table with the menus.

"I'll have a *small* glass," I say, face still flaming.

"After all of these years, you still look beautiful when you blush," he says, and I blush even more.

We order steaks and appetizers, and he tells me about his girls, pulling out their pictures. One has dark hair, the other golden. "Jordan looks like her mom, Jenna looks like me."

I fumble in my purse for a picture of the kids but all I have is our family pictures. The most recent with John and I front and centre, the kids at our side. The other is older and of the five of us, standing outside our quarters with snow banks taller than Maria. I debate showing them to Paul, but he reaches out to take them before I can decide.

"So this is John," he says.

I nod, biting my lower lip so as not to cry. Paul would never have met him—John came to our school after Paul left for the Army academy, not the Air Force one. And Paul would have been at civie university before John graduated from high school with me.

"He's a good looking man."

I nod again.

"And good looking kids. I still can't believe you have children this old. You're so young! I wasn't kidding yesterday when I said you haven't changed a bit."

I must look shocked because he keeps going.

"No, really! Your eyes, your skin..." He reaches out to gently touch my hair. "Your hair... Don't sell yourself short, Ellen."

Before I can respond, our appetizer comes.

After the meal, we walk out onto the deck and to the back of the ship. It's windy but warm. We talk some more about the places we've lived, the things we've done, the fun times we had in high school. It's so easy to talk to him, so calming and...normal. He teases me about my wine tolerance—I had just one glass tonight and sipped it slowly—and I tease him about his dislike of seafood—something I discovered over dinner.

And then he walks me to my room.

It's awkward standing by my door, but once again he doesn't ask to come in.

"Tomorrow I have meetings all day," he says.

I feel like he's taken the wind from my sails. We must be at sea tomorrow. I'm shocked to discover how disappointed I am, though I'm not sure if it's because we'll be at sea or because Paul will be busy. Apart from my meltdown, Corfu was paradise, and I can't deny that Paul was the one who made it that way.

His fingers lift up and touch the frown line that's formed on my forehead. I don't lean away. "Would you care to join me for dinner again?" he asks quietly as his hand trails across my cheek and rests under my chin.

"Yes," I whisper, as all of the air in the hall seems to have disappeared.

The pressure of his fingers increases ever so slightly and then he drops his hand, leaving the line of my jaw tingling. "Meet me by the pool at six? Casual at the pasta place?"

"Sure," I say.

He brushes his finger one last time on my cheek and walks away.

I wanted him to kiss me.

That realization cracks me on the head as I walk into my room and straight out onto the balcony. The wind is cooler now and goes right through my dress, but I'm so warm that I stick my head out over the railing and let it blow through my hair. I've fallen from hell into some sort of widow's twilight zone. I shake my head in hopes that the ocean breeze will blow away this craziness—untangle the emotions rolling around in my brain. I'm angry with John for leaving me alone, I'm sad and lonely and guilty and happy and shocked at the errant thread of desire running through my veins. I *really* wanted Paul to kiss me.

I've had sex with exactly two men—my dead husband and a sadistic rapist. The only other man I ever even remotely considered it with is somehow on this ship a million miles away from my home—and is not only single, but also handsome, kind, and possibly rich.

And courting me. Me!

What the hell?

The sea air does nothing to dispel the heat in my veins. Maybe I'm having a hot flash. I remember my mother talking about her mid-life hot flashes. Menopause should be hitting me sometime soon. But then why do I want to walk right back out my door, find Paul, and ask him to finish what he started? Holy crow, I've not even been on this ship for 48 hours and I'm ready to throw myself at someone whom I haven't seen in almost thirty years, just because he touched my cheek?

I'm losing it completely.

Or maybe I'm just finding what I'd lost.

CHAPTER 24
HOUSE #8

February, 1995

I T IS SO COLD OUTSIDE that the entire car protests as I put it in park, even after the fifteen-minute drive home from work. The squeaking, crunching sound it makes reminds me of a huge and crabby rat. I find it ironic that the heat decides to kick in just as I turn the engine off. The clock on the dash reads 2:48 just before it blinks out.

I sigh a deep, body-shaking sigh, and steel myself for the frigid air before opening the door, grabbing the two bags of groceries in the passenger seat. The stinging wind tries to claw my cheeks off as I rush from our tiny hatchback to the back of our quarters, where at least I'm out of the wind. My fingers fumble with the keys and I unlock the door, trying not to breathe. The cold air hurts my lungs.

The clock on the microwave says I have exactly fourteen minutes until the kids hop off of the bus and destroy what peace exists in our house. Cereal bowls still sit on the table in our tiny kitchen. Blotches of dried milk have glued cereal O's to the placemats. Half-empty orange juice glasses are scattered on the counter. Beside them sits our cat, Humphrey, looking devious as he licks his paws.

"Hi, Humph," I say, and he hops down to come and rub against my leg. Fourteen minutes is just enough to make a cup of coffee and read a few pages from my book. After my day at work, I crave a few minutes of me-time. With my work, kids activities and John's crazy schedule, me-time is becoming a thing of the past. Even fourteen minutes is a treat.

I drop the groceries on the floor and shrug off my coat, immediately wondering at the coolness of the air inside the house. It's almost as cold in here as it is out.

"Crap." I say, throwing my coat on a chair and checking the thermostat. 62 degrees. "Crap!" I flick the dial all the way up to 90. Nothing happens. "Shit!" I yell, as crap doesn't quite seem to fit in this situation.

Without even pulling off my boots, I run down the stairs to look at our prehistoric furnace. Other than my strangled breathing and Humphrey's questioning purr, the room is silent. I whack it for good measure, but nothing happens.

"Fuckity-fuck fuck!" Every explicative in the book comes out of my mouth. Humphrey scampers back upstairs, eager to get away from my now vile temper. I flick the reset button, just in case. Nada.

Our oil tank is full; I know this because the oil man was here yesterday, just as the kids left for school, getting in our way. We changed the filters last month. The exhaust is cleared of snow. John is nothing but thorough when it comes to home maintenance. He keeps the house in tip-top shape for me, just in case he is deployed without notice. It's one of the few things he can do to help me stay sane.

The furnace is dead, no question.

I trot back upstairs, grab the phone and rifle through the pile of papers beside it for the Defence Housing's pamphlet. Drawings, school notices, birthday cards, and old bills fly through the air. One of them settles on the spilled milk.

I find the pamphlet, and frantically search for the help number. I dial it, the receiver stuck between my shoulder and my ear as I dump old orange juice into the sink.

"DHO," a male voice says into my ear.

"Hello, this is Ellen Michaels at 28 Green Crescent."

"Just a second, Ma'am, I'm going to put you on hold." He doesn't wait for my reply, and the elevator music starts up. Eight minutes until the bus stops. I silently count to ten three times to calm myself.

The line clicks and the elevator music stops. "What can I do for you, Ma'am?" the voice says, somehow managing to sound bored, self-important, and over-worked all at the same time. The quarters are allotted to members according to rank, so he knows exactly what rank my husband is—somewhere between pee-on and know-it-all.

I cringe, readying myself for battle. "Our furnace stopped working while I was out this afternoon, and the temperature in the house is already down to 60. Can you please send someone over right away?"

"Well Ma'am, our technician is on a call right now, and he's got two other calls today and one tomorrow, so the earliest we can get to you is tomorrow afternoon."

"By tomorrow afternoon, the pipes will be frozen, so you might as well send a plumber too," I say, barely controlling my voice. I'm furious. If I could jump through the phone and strangle this turd, I would.

"I'm sorry Ma'am, that's the best we can do. Did you hit the red reset button on the side?" Now he sounds like he's talking to a three year old.

I take a deep breath. "Yes, I hit the pretty red button on the side. Nothing happened."

He still hasn't caught on to my tone. "And is it possible you forgot to get the oil tank filled?"

"No, the tank is full, the exhaust is clear…and the filter is clean," I say before he can belittle my intelligence any more. "The temperature has fallen ten degrees already. You need to send someone over now, not tomorrow." My teeth are clenched. I grab the coffee pot and fill it with water. I need caffeine.

"Well, Ma'am, I'll see what I can do, but it looks like it will have to wait. I'll take down your phone number in case anything changes."

I am too mad to even argue.

"Fine," I say. I give him our number. "I'll look forward to hearing from you." *And I'll look forward to punching you in the face!* I think as I hang up, not waiting for his response. Idiot. Twit.

I have five minutes now, and the coffee is slowly dripping into the pot. I slam the phone down on its receiver and start to undo my boots. Wet footprints are scattered over the floor. Great, another mess I have to clean up. At least I made this one myself.

I trudge up the stairs to find a sweater and a second pair of socks, wondering if this day can get any worse.

As it turns out, it can. The kids come in with loud voices just as I do up the last button of the warmest sweater I own.

"Mom?" Chris shouts from the bottom of the stairs. "We're home!"

"Hi sweetheart!" I call down, trying to control the resentment in my voice. My fourteen minutes of peace has been snatched from me like a dangled carrot.

"Why is it so cold?" David's voice is slightly quieter than his brother's.

"The furnace is broken! Grab a sweater!" I answer.

"Can I have some chips?" Chris again.

The yelling is getting to me, so instead of answering I walk down the stairs to face them, trying to hold in the resentment that bubbles up in times like these. The resentment that John, the man I love, is off doing something exciting, while I drudge around a freezing-cold house. I dole out quick hugs, before speaking in a forced, but calm, voice.

"So the furnace is broken, and they say they can't fix it until tomorrow. At least we still have power," I say. "And no, you can't have chips."

"Awww...Why can't they fix it until tomorrow?" asks Chris.

"You got me. The dispatcher said they were too busy."

"Oh," says Chris.

Maria is sitting in the living room. I can see her from where I stand at the bottom of the stairs. She's fiddling with the tie on her sweater, not looking up.

"Hi sweetheart," I say as I walk in and sit on the arm of the chair.

"Hey," she says. Something isn't right—Maria is usually louder than both boys put together.

"What's the matter?"

"I don't feel good."

"Oh?" I reach over and feel her forehead. Sure enough, she's hot. *Crap.* "Did you eat your lunch?"

"Not all of it."

"Hmmm. Why don't you go get into your comfy pj's and I'll grab a thermometer."

"Okay," she says and then trudges up the stairs.

"Mom?" David says, "Don't we have a little heater thingy downstairs?"

I'd completely forgotten! "Yes, we do! Can you go find it?" Maybe not all is lost.

Just as I finish that thought, I hear Maria gag, and then the unmistakeable sound of spraying vomit hitting something other than the toilet echoes from above.

Sweet Mother of God, give me strength!

I turn and run up the stairs, just as round two hits the toilet. The stench of puke hits me like a punch in the face. Maria is leaning over the toilet, crying.

"It's okay, sweetie, it's just the flu," I say, though a torrent of swear words is rolling through my head. *Crapfuckshitdamnittycrap.* I grab a facecloth from the closet, wet it, and help her wipe her face. "It's not your fault. Rinse out your mouth and go lie down while I clean this up." I dump the garbage can on a puke-free spot on the floor and hand it to her. "If you feel sick again, use this."

She whimpers an affirmative and heads in to her room.

Chunks of undigested pasta, tomato sauce, and carrot sticks litter the hardwood floor and one of the basic beige walls. Ick. Pasta. Why is it always pasta? I grab some cleanser from under the sink and a roll of paper towels, wiping down the worst of it while I try not to breathe. The donut I grabbed before I left the mall threatens more than once to make a reappearance. Body fluids seem to be my lot in life.

"Mom! I found it!" yells David.

Oh, the heater. I'd forgotten.

"Great! Can you plug it in? In the living room?" I say, trying not to inhale through my nose.

"Yeah!"

Maria groans from her room, and heaves into the garbage can. I wipe up the last of the barf with a cleanser-soaked paper towel, and then head to the washroom to clean off my hands. I flick on the fan although I know it won't help.

The phone rings.

"Mom! The phone's ringing!" one of the boys says.

"I'll get it up here," I say through clenched teeth.

I jog into the master bedroom and pick up the phone, hoping it's DHO calling to come fix the furnace, not…someone else.

"Hello," I say in my business voice.

"Hey, Ellie, it's me."

Not DHO. John. This means one of two things: A) the plane is broken and he won't be flying tonight, or B) he's leaving—soon—for more than just tonight. I hope it's A, because I'm rapidly reaching my stress limit.

"Hi…" I say cautiously as I sit down on the bed.

"Is everything okay?"

I curb the urge to laugh like a madwoman. Is everything okay? Is everything okay? Of course everything is not okay! We've no heat, it's minus a million degrees outside, puke-fest 1995 is just getting underway in Maria's bedroom, and I haven't had any coffee!

"Sort of," I say.

"Oh, well…I just wanted to let you know that our crew has been tasked." He stops, leaving out the nasty details like where and how long. This isn't good.

I'm a sucker for punishment, so I ask. "Tasked?"

"Well, there's been a ceasefire called in Serajevo. The UN needs us to airlift humanitarian aid to the people there."

My brain hears 'ceasefire' but not much else. Ceasefire means war. War means people being killed. Shot at.

"So our crew isn't doing a trainer tonight, we're leaving for Bosnia."

"Oh."

John is pumped. I can hear the excitement in his voice. This is something big, something different than the endless practice trainers. The first excitement he's had since his last big trip, the one that left him edgy and jumping at shadows for three years.

"We're leaving in a little over an hour to go pick up the UN stuff—we've got to get out before the storm hits," he says. Storm? I didn't know there was a storm coming. "All of my UN kit is here in my locker. It should be a couple of days. I've got an overnight kit with me, so I should be fine. "

"Oh." I try to sound cheery, like this hasn't just deflated what little bit of wind was left in my sails, but I fail miserably. I can picture his animated face, his excited grin, and if I wasn't exhausted before this trip of his even started, I'd be grinning right along with him. It's one of the many things I love about him: his enthusiasm for life. But he is so caught up in his world-changing moment that he doesn't even notice my worry, and my lack of world-changing anything. He's moving ahead, and I'm stuck here in the snow.

"Gotta go. Give the kids a hug for me, and tell them I love them. I'll see you in a few days, 'kay?"

"Okay. Be safe," I squeak as my legs give out from underneath me, and I sit like a dead weight on the side of the bed. I breathe through my nose, trying not to cry. Humphrey, intuitive as ever, hops up and rubs against my side. He's not allowed on the bed, but I scratch behind his ears anyway. He purrs as if life is perfect, not going to hell.

"I will. Don't wait up," John says, his voice sincere. Those three words mean more than what they say. Don't wait up has come to mean goodbye, good luck, I love you... please wait up for me because I'll be hoping you did.

"Don't be late," says a voice that I'm not sure is mine. A quiet, forgotten, desperate voice that sounds strong but isn't. He hangs up before that voice says anything more. I stare out the window cradling the receiver in my hand like a baby, like it's my lifeline to sanity. I keep waiting to feel the strength that military spouses are supposed to have, but I'm not a solid, hardworking, dependable spouse. I'm angry and jealous and spiteful. I want to call the base and tell them that my husband can't go—that I need him here more than they need him there. Screw their stupid rules and laws and discipline! But I don't. Is that strength or cowardice?

It's almost dark outside, and delicate white snowflakes have begun to fall. If my life wasn't such a disaster right now, it would be almost pretty.

"Mom?"

I jump, the voice at the door startling me. I turn to see David standing at the door. His eyebrows are crunched together. David has always been a worrier.

"Is everything okay?" he asks, unknowingly echoing his father. I can feel him watching me, assessing my features for signs of distress. He's such a smart kid. I school my face into a smile, but decide to tell him the truth.

"Come here, sweetie," I say, patting the bed beside me. He walks around the bed and sits cautiously beside me. I put my arm around him.

Eleven years old, and his shoulder is level with mine as we sit side-by-side in our inner turmoil and stare out the window at the thickening snowfall.

"Dad is going on a mission tonight. He's flying overseas with some UN aid," I say. "It would just be easier if he came home tonight, that's all."

"He's going to Bosnia, isn't he?"

David watches the news. He knows—more than any of us—what's going on in the world. "Yes," I say. No use hiding it. I glance at him, watching how he takes this news.

His face crinkles a bit more, but he says nothing.

"He'll just be gone a couple of days," I say, turning back to the window. How do you tell your eleven-year old that his father is flying a giant metal bull's-eye into a war zone? There's no way to sugar coat it, but I try anyway. "He'll be okay."

The wind has started to pick up, and the snow is swirling around the icicles on the eaves of the house. A piece of siding rattles as the wind shakes it. The streetlight in the park behind us flickers on as the night settles in with the snow. We sit there staring out as he processes this. Not for the first time in my life, I wish John had a normal, 9-to-5 job. I wish he worked in an office somewhere, that he left his job at five o'clock and came home to ask me about my day, that the military wasn't such a damned greedy employer that devoured everything our family had to give.

I glance down at David and squeeze his shoulder again, but say nothing, because there's really nothing else to say. His hands are clenched into fists, but he leans into me. I know he is fighting tears.

Somewhere behind me Maria heaves into the trashcan again. I close my eyes and pray once more for strength.

By 10:00 pm, the storm is raging with unbridled fury beyond our walls. Within the house, all three children are sleeping with buckets beside their beds. Christopher managed to spray his meat and potatoes all over his sheets just before he climbed into them. David appears okay so far, but I know from experience that it's only a matter of time.

I'm standing in our dark dungeon of a basement, unhooking the dryer hose from the wall so that it will pour its leftover heat into the house, not out of it—I trick I learned from my frugal mother. Needless to say, the furnace repairman did not show up. Our house is hovering around 56 degrees, even with the heater going in the living room. I've filled the bathtub with steaming hot water, hoping it will help. The power is still on, but with the wind howling the way it is outside, it can't last. I've got one load of laundry thumping away in the washer and another in the dryer, with Chris's sheets rolled up in a reeking pile, waiting to go in. Humphrey sits on a shelf behind me, watching. The entire house smells of moist puke.

The dryer hose pops off suddenly, flying out of my hand and hitting me in the face.

"Shit!" I scream at it. Humphrey hisses.

Well, that was stupid. I should have turned the f'ing thing off first. I brush my hand across my cheek, and it comes away with a streak of blood. A not-so distant memory of blood on my face resurfaces, but I don't have time to feel sorry for myself. I squash that memory down because the cold air from the now bare vent-hole is rushing in fast. The past is not important right now. I cram an old towel in the vent as hard as I can and secure it with criss-crossed duct tape for good measure. It holds. God, I love duct tape! I pop an old nylon stocking over the hose to catch the lint. A piece of slimy red pasta flies into the nylon as I secure it with more duct tape.

When I've done all I can do with the laundry, I trudge up the stairs and start working on the dishes. I'm so tired from six hours of nasty people buying clothes that don't fit and four hours of cleaning up puke and washing floors. I want to dissolve onto my bed like half-set Jello, but the dishes won't clean themselves any more than the laundry will. The view from the kitchen window, which faces the street in this house, shows me three inches of snow blanketing the road. I haven't heard anything from John, so he must have gotten away okay…good for him, not good for me. I really do hope he stays safe, but I'm irrationally jealous of the adventurous life he lives, so separate from ours. What he does makes a difference. He hops in planes and takes food to where people need it. Takes soldiers to where they can fight for freedom. Takes himself to amazing places that thrive with colour and excitement. What do I do? I clean up vomit.

It's not that I want to hold him back from his worldly existence. I love that he does what he does. It's just...just that I feel trapped here. I feel closed in by the snow and the puke and the needs of others. Just once I'd like to walk out that door and get away from it all, live a different life than this one. A life where I'm making my own plans, not reacting to the plans of others.

The clock on the stove says 11:34. If you turn 11:34 over, it reads 'hell'. Funny fact, that. I can't remember when I noticed, but ever since I've hated that time. It's surprising how many times in a week I look at the clock at exactly 11:34. I put the first dish in the water, staring the clock and waiting absently for it to turn from hell to sell.

Before it does, the lights go out, and I'm left with wet hands, tired eyes, and a bright red phantom image of upside down hell in the cold, pitch-black kitchen .

I wake to the smell of vomit and the too-white brightness that can only be the aftermath of a blizzard. The outside world is smothered in snow, and the reflections of blue sky and cold yellow sun burst through our windows as if trying to prove their dominance over the storm. The three kids and I are snuggled on the pull-out couch, in front of our solitary heat-source—which, thankfully, is blowing heat full tilt into the living room. I am so glad I convinced John to buy the thing, because we would be frozen solid right now, along with every pipe in our house. It has been forty-two hours since Puke-fest '95 began, and somehow we've weathered it—no pun intended. The power outage only lasted until the next morning but the furnace is still broken. My dryer vent switcharoo, the full bathtub of hot water and our tiny heater have kept the house in the high fifties or low sixties.

Outside the snow is still falling gently, but the wind has died down and it's almost pretty. I thank God for my strong, flu-less constitution, because I don't have time to be sick right now.

Maria's arm is draped over me, and she's kicking out heat to rival the electric heater, but it's not a fever, just warm kid. I extract myself from her arm and go to find the phone, hopeful that there will be at least someone on the other side of my trouble call today. Unlikely, but still, I'm hopeful.

Before I call, I open the oven and turn it on, set the coffee machine to burble out the only thing I have to look forward to and peek out the window. Everything is white. The plough has been through, leaving banks almost six feet tall, and much to my surprise…our driveway has been shovelled.

Wow! Our driveway has been shovelled! When did that happen? Don't remember any sounds outside, but then again, the washer, dryer, and heater have been going full tilt since our power came back on, not to mention constant moaning and retching. I'm so glad that's over with.

Just as the coffee finishes dripping, and I pour myself a cup, the phone rings. I say a little prayer that it's the furnace repairman.

"Hello?" I say.

"Ellen?"

"John!" He hardly ever calls because he's so busy on these things. "Where are you?"

"We're in Lyneham…in England. Crew rest for 24 hours and then we're heading back in."

"Oh!" I sit down at the table with my coffee, grinning. "It's so good to hear from you."

There's a slight delay on the line, like a waiting period in the middle of the conversation. A poorly placed punctuation mark. "Same here. I got an outside line from the base, so it's free. How are things?"

"Um…they're okay." I can't tell him we've been sick, snowed in and without power and heat since he left. He'd worry, and the last thing I need is to feel guilty for making him worry while he's over there being shot at. "Everything's good. How about you?"

Another delay. "It's good, and a bit crazy. Can't really tell you about it on the phone, but it's nuts flying in there."

"I bet." I pause a second, and when I start to speak again he speaks at the same time. "We miss you…" I say.

"…How was the storm?" he asks. This delay is really annoying.

Both of us pause, waiting for the other to speak…and then we both speak at the same time. "We got twenty-four inches of snow," I say, just as he says "I miss you too."

He keeps speaking, powering through the pause like he powers through life. "It's really nice here, cold but there's no snow. The boys and I took a drive out to this castle place not to far away. Just a huge, round mound on top of a hill now, but you can see for miles. We're going to Bath for supper, one of the RAF guys is a relative of Terry's, and he's going to take us."

I sit there, drinking in his voice as he talks. He's so happy to be flying, and travelling, and it's like my own brand of drug. I suck it in and can't get enough. I have no life, but he lives enough for the both of us. His life is addictive—the excitement, the unknown. Mine is all puke and power outages and grade-school homework. He is in England, for God's sake! When will I ever get to cross the ocean? My pre-John self would be appalled, but this is what I've become: a whiny, stay-at-home, bon-bon-eating wife. Without him I'm lost, floating without an anchor.

"…you sure you're okay?" He finally asks.

"We're fine. Someone even came and shovelled out our driveway for us."

"Oh, must have been the squadron," he says after the pause.

I say nothing, because suddenly everything that has happened over the past few days is right in front of me, staring me down. Instead of pushing back my despair, speaking to John has brought it to the surface. Like a jug full of air forced below the water, it flies upwards with a vengeance, defying gravity and everything else to break free. I'm fighting tears and I can't start, because if I do, I'll never get stopped again. I'll explode. It's too much.

"Well, I should go. Give the kids a kiss for me, okay? Don't wait up," John says. He quietly fills the long empty space between us.

No! You can't go! I can't do this without you here!

"Sure, I will. Don't be late…Love you," I say.

"Love you too, Ellen. I'll be home before you know it."

And then the line clicks, and he's gone; and even though I wanted him to call, wanted to hear his voice…I wish he hadn't.

CHAPTER 25
HOUSE #13 (CRUISE)

Early May, 2009

THE NEXT MORNING I WAKE up with the sun. It's another gorgeous day—does it ever rain in the Mediterranean? The itinerary newsletter slipped under my door says it will be hot and sunny at least until tomorrow. I slide on one of my two bathing suits and my cover up, then I make my way up to the buffet, dodge the tacky Texan tourist couple who seem to haunt my every move, and take my fruit, pastries and coffee out onto the pool deck. The sun is hot, the coffee is good, and it's too early for the heavy partiers to be hanging around the pool, so I pull off the cover up and let the sun touch my skin.

I can't remember the last time I sat, in public, with my skin bared just to soak up the sun. I fight the little voice that says I'm too flabby to be hanging out on the deck in nothing but a bathing suit. Looking around I see a whole lot worse.

Without realizing it, I start searching for Paul, looking up every time a dark haired man walks by. I tell myself it's because he's the only person I know on the ship, but deep down I know it's because of the fire I felt when he touched me. The sun makes me sleepy, and I lay my head back against the lounge chair, peering under my sunglasses at the steady stream of travellers going by.

And that's when I see him.

My breath stops.

Him.

A man standing at the bar with precision-cut salt-and-pepper hair and military-straight posture. His height, his build. Oh God, no! He's too far away to tell for sure, but my heart launches to my throat, fighting to burst out of my chest.

It can't be him. It can't be.

But...it could.

I'm not sticking around to find out. I need my own room and a locked door to hide behind. I grab my cover up, throw it on, and walk the other way as fast as I can without drawing his gaze. Through the doors, and down the stairs, not waiting for the elevator.

When I get one floor down I start to run. Down two more floors, out into the corridor as fast as I can go.

And then I career full force into Paul as I turn the corner on my deck.

"Ellen? I came down to say good morning, but..." he says, wrapping his arms around me and then pushing me gently away to search my face. "What's happened? Are you okay?"

I shake my head rapidly, and check behind us up the stairs. Nothing.

"I... I just..." I can feel my pulse racing and I pull away, frantic. I've got to get out of the hall. The elevator dings as it opens, and I jump.

We both jerk to look but it's empty.

"Here, come with me," Paul leads me into the elevator and presses a button. The doors close and he keeps his arms around me, like I'll bolt if he lets go. He's probably right. When we reach deck five, he stands in front of the door, blocking me from view, and when there's no one there, he wraps his arm around my waist, shielding me with his body. I can feel myself shaking.

His room is only a few doors down from the elevator lobby, but the seconds between the lobby and the safety of his room seem like eternity. He locks the door, brings me in to the sofa, and sits me down without saying a word.

I'm a wreck.

I tuck my feet up and wrap my arms around myself. All of the dirty, ugly feelings I thought I had almost forgotten are raging through me again, and I'm having trouble reconciling where I am with the memories of what was.

Paul walks over to his mini bar, flips two glasses over and pours some water. He hands me a glass, turns a chair around and sits on it, watching me like he's waiting for me to self-destruct.

"Do you mind telling me what that was about?" he asks, his voice gentle.

I'm sure I still have the scared rabbit look, because he doesn't press, just sits there calmly, waiting.

When my heart rate slows down, I take a sip of the water, hoping he'll drop it, hoping I can escape these feelings once again and leave them alone. But I don't want to go out there again and face the microcosm of society that might have Frank Fielding in it.

Paul waits and watches.

Paul, who has no connection to the military but a year in college twenty-eight years ago. Paul, who—until I saw the man at the bar—I was searching for.

Paul, to whom I owe nothing, and who owes nothing to me.

Paul, whose eyes are watching, warming my skin with their gaze.

I could tell him.

I could.

So I do.

"I saw someone."

He raises his eyebrows, but says nothing.

"Someone who I thought I knew. Someone...who scares me more than anyone on this earth."

I take a deep, calming breath and another sip of water. Still Paul waits silently.

"A long time ago...that someone..."

I can't tell him.

"That someone..." my voice cracks. Paul moves from his chair to sit beside me.

How is it I'm telling this man, whom I haven't seen for decades, something I never told my husband?

"That someone...raped me. In John's bed."

Paul's arm goes around me—softly, slowly—like I might crack open, like I've said the worst. But the worst isn't there yet.

"And then again, five years later, in a room in the Officer's Mess... with John just down the hall." I have to stop to breathe...in-out, in-out.

My chest, my heart, my lungs, everything that makes up my insides hurts, and still I can't stop there because if I do it's a lie. And I don't want a lie. No more lies. Not here, with this man who looks at me as Ellen.

As Ellen.

Me.

Not someone's wife, not someone's mom, not someone to crush and hurt and walk all over. Just Ellen.

"And then *again*. Five years later…" The tears start and I let them, because there's no other way. I have to tell him. The dam is broken, and the water is pushing through. "John was away and he knew it and he called…called the house where the kids were playing and threatened to destroy John, and I went. I went with him into the woods, *knowing* what he was going to do to me. Is it rape if you don't say no?"

The hurt and the hate bubble over, and I sob outright, all tears and snot and self-disgust. But instead of pushing me away he holds me, Holds me and comforts me…like John never did.

When the storm has calmed, I tell him the bits I remember, the bits I *want* to remember. He calls room service for lunch, and then calls the concierge to enquire about Frank Fielding.

There is no one by that name on board the ship.

He leaves me to go back to his meetings, but not before seeing me to my room and promising to meet me there as soon as he's finished for the day. I spend the day alone, lounging on the balcony and reading a book, ordering room service coffee and snacks, trying to make sense of all of the noise in my head. But there's no sense to be made.

I just told an almost-stranger what I couldn't tell my husband of twenty-five years.

What was supposed to be a relaxing, fun adventure to move on, escape my past, has placed me squarely in front of it, facing backwards. John, Fielding…Paul, they've somehow all ended up on this ship, as real and as present as they could be. I want to forget it all, push it down and put it in the box where I'd kept it for so long. The past doesn't like boxes.

I shower, dry my hair, put on something comfortable, and sit on my tiny balcony with a cool cloth on my eyes. The warm sun and the cold cloth help a little, but I can't shake the confusion of both body and mind.

And the question that's really rolling through my head is will Paul come back? I must seem like a messed-up psychopath. God, my life is a mess!

I start watching the clock at 3:30. He doesn't come.

4:15. No Paul.

There's no reason for him to come back. I'm not even sure I could find his room again. Why would he want to come back? Why am I feeling this way? I should be thinking about John.

4:35. No Paul.

Oh, God. The one good thing that's happened to me in over a year, and he's not coming back. I'm such a stupid, idiotic twit.

I walk from the balcony, to the couch, to the bathroom, back to the couch.

Stop thinking about it. He'll come.

He won't come.

He'll come.

He comes at 5:04.

I jump when the knock comes, and almost spill the water I'm sipping.

"Just a sec!" I yell, check my make up, and then go to the door.

He came. My mercurial emotions switch from depression to elation. I peek through the little peep-hole, and he's standing there, solid and handsome.

Remind me why I dumped him in high school?

I'm still red-eyed, but I'm as ready as I'll ever be to face the world again. Well, ready to face Paul Donovan again at any rate. I firmly stomp on the fear, sadness, and self-loathing.

I'm going to enjoy this trip. I *need* to enjoy this trip. And really, I've been through worse.

"Hi," he says.

"Hi." He walks in to my much tidier room, and slides his hands in his pockets.

"Are you sure you want to go out?" he asks.

I don't, but it will be a useless trip if I hide in my room the whole time.

"No, but I can't hide forever," I say. "It must have been someone else, anyway."

He nods. "Will you do me a favour?" He asks.

"Yeah."

"Will you tell me if you see the guy, whether it's him or not?"

"Okay."

He's not convinced, but we go to the pasta place. I sit facing the door, watching the faces that come through the restaurant as we talk. He has to know I'm doing it, but he's gentleman enough to let me be. Several times he waves at his co-workers as they filter by with their dates—wives or otherwise. I wonder what they think—if he's told them who I am—and I try not to jump each time someone looks this way.

He suggests we go back to his room afterward, so that I can relax my hyper-active defence mechanisms. The two small glasses of wine and the huge dish of pasta have made me less twitchy, but I still can't look at him when there are so many other people around. I want to find my Fielding doppelganger so I can prove myself wrong.

We walk through the pool area, his arm comfortably around my waist, and me trying not to freak out every time I see someone with slicked dark hair. The wine has also made me the tiniest bit dizzy, but not rip-roaring drunk like the first night we met up. We go down one level to his room and he lets me through the door without speaking.

I look around, realizing I hadn't really done so this morning during my panic attack. It's huge, at least three times the size of my little stateroom. A small lamp stands in the corner of the room, casting a warm glow over the large sofa, plush chairs, and polished dining room table. The large-screen TV is blank, but music plays softly from its speakers.

"Gees, Paul, are you paying for this?" I can't help but say, and then once again I want to bite back what I've said. It's none of my business who's fitting the bill. I shouldn't even be in here.

He chuckles, pouring us each a glass of wine at the bar.

"No, the company is covering this one," he says with a sheepish smile. "I would never book something so lavish for just myself."

"No?"

"No." He hands me my glass, eyes dark and mysterious, and gestures at the balcony, which is also at least three times the size of mine. "Shall we sit on the balcony?"

I stand and follow him out. The chairs have plush pillows on them, and the walls are solid, sheltering us from the wind and nosy neighbours. We both walk to the railing and peer out. The sea is black, not a boat or an island to be seen. It feels like we are alone on a huge yacht, sliding through the waves.

He turns to me and leans his elbow on the railing, face thoughtful. "How are you doing?"

Why did John never ask me this question? And why did I never think to tell my own husband the answer before he asked?

It's too late now. John is dead.

"I'm okay," I say before I fall into that hole. "Sorry about this morning."

"For what, being afraid of a monster from your past?"

"No, for freaking out and blubbering like an idiot over someone I *thought* was a monster from my past."

We walk over to the chairs, and sit down. They are pushed together, more like a love seat than two chairs. I wonder if he placed them that way.

"You didn't 'freak out' and you weren't 'blubbering like an idiot.'" He's quiet for a moment, and I feel him watching me as I fiddle with the hem of my shirt.

"Ellen…have you ever told anyone what you told me this morning?"

I can't meet his eyes. "No," I say.

"No one? Not even your husband?"

"No. No one." Bob and Jennifer know little bits, but not the whole story. The years and years of lies and fear have been my secret hell for so long they are a part of me.

Paul's hand flies up to his hair. Well, at least I think it does, because I only feel his movement not see it. I can't look at him.

"Wow," he says.

I *so* don't want to talk about this right now. I want to forget it. Leave it be. Move on. Enjoy the moment, not grind up the past.

He's silent for a few moments, the waves crash below us, the wind blows and I look anywhere but his face.

"Thank you," he says.

This is so unexpected that I look over at him.

"Thank you? For what?" I ask.

"For trusting me enough to tell me."

"Oh."

"Do you want to talk any more about it?"

How can this man be so compassionate to me when I was so mean to him?

"I want to forget about it." I say, once again opting for honesty. "It's history. It happened and I did nothing. I can't go back and change it."

He frowns. "But it wasn't your fault."

I say nothing.

"It wasn't your fault, Ellen. Whatever happened, whether you said no or didn't or went willingly or not. The reaction I saw this morning says it all."

The seconds drag out. I look out at the black sea and he rests his arm around my shoulder. It's more comfort than intimate, but still, I'm hyper-aware of how it feels—the hairs of his arm tickle my neck. His hand rests lightly under my arm.

"Paul?" I say suddenly, turning toward him.

"Yes."

"I don't want to talk about it. But if—when—I do...I'll let you know."

"It's a deal."

Of course then we have nothing to talk about. I take a sip of my wine, he takes a sip of his, his arm still around me, my hair flipping lightly in the sheltered breeze. A seagull flies by, lit by the glare of the ship.

Whether it's the wind, the wine, the shock of the day, or the feel of his arm around me, a shiver runs up my arm.

His hand closes on my side, fingers just brushing my breast.

"You're cold," he says—more of a statement than a question. "Lets go in."

He stands up and takes my hand without asking, taking both wine glasses in his other hand and leading me to the couch.

He refills his glass, and asks if I'd like more. I shake my head. I don't want a repeat display of our first night.

"How 'bout some coffee?" He asks.

"I'd like that."

He orders us coffees and a cheese tray, while I excuse myself to find his washroom. There's a huge tub in it, made for two. The fixtures are shiny brass and the towels are inches thicker than mine. I finish, wash my hands, and stare at myself in the mirror. I'm skinnier than I remember, my collar bones sticking out from above my breasts, and my waist thinner than it has been since the kids were born. My eyes are still puffy, but my hair is long and wavy, and my cheeks are flushed. Maybe it's the wine talking, but I look darned good. Darned good, indeed.

I don't want to talk about Fielding anymore. And I don't want to think about John. I can't deal with the oppressive weight of guilt and shame tonight. John left me alone but Paul is right here, right now, and I want to talk about him. Actually, I don't want to *talk* about Paul, I want to get to know him in other ways. The wine is making me reckless, and here on this ship, I'm so far away from the train wreck that is my life with John, it's like it doesn't even exist. I pucker my lips and adjust my bra and let the moment take me.

When I hear the doorbell ring—the service is fast in first class—I pinch my cheeks for extra colour and walk back out.

He's standing by the couch, flicking the stations on the television— news, Greek TV, sports—but he brings it back to the music channel. Strains of something like Beethoven float through the air.

"Coffee's here," He says.

We sit again, both of us on the couch, and sip our coffee. I don't want coffee. Or cheese. A very, very different want is coursing through my body. I must be truly insane.

The sports channel reminds me of something.

"Do you still play hockey?" I ask. "You were really good in high school." I remember cold nights sitting on a bench in a small town arena, watching Paul score goal after goal. A rush of pride I have no right to feel washes through me.

He smiles. "When I can. Not much call for it in Dallas or London."

"Then how do you keep so fit?" I feel the blush creep across my cheeks. I've just more or less admitted I've been looking.

His smile widens.

Stupid blush. Of course that only makes me blush more.

He reaches out and touches my cheek, but then lets his hand drop. It's all I can do not to grab it and put it back against my face.

"There's a gym at work. I run when I can, and I started rowing last year. Nothing like the Thames at five in the morning!"

That explains the shoulders, I look and he sees me. I didn't think my face could heat more but it does.

"Ellen?" he says.

"Yes?"

"Would you mind if I...can I kiss you?"

He wants to kiss me.

I don't trust my voice... so I just nod my assent.

His hand skims up my side to my cheek, and I lean into it this time, my head tilting slightly and our eyes locked together. His hand is big—bigger than John's was—and it burns my cheek. He slides toward me along the couch and his other hand brushes my hair back, then softly cradles my head.

And then he leans forward and kisses me.

My eyes close, and I let the sensation wash over me. His lips are gentle at first, whisper soft and barely touching. My stomach flip-flops and my hands drift upward, finding their place on his strong shoulders while his hands stroke my chin, my cheek, my neck. Gently, very gently like he's testing the waters, checking for danger zones, but reigning himself back. Like I'm a minefield with Shangri-La in the centre. He wants more; I want more, but I'm in uncharted territory. Although I've kissed this man before, he was a lovesick boy and I was just a child, innocent and yet sure of myself. In control of my tiny, safe world. And with only John to use as reference since, I feel inept here on this man's couch, afraid of doing the wrong thing. Yet parts of my body are very, very sure what they want. I tilt forward and meet his lips, my heart loud in my ears and my breath shallow and quick.

He pulls back—checking my expression, deep brown eyes concerned. The dim light shines on the few grey hairs at his temple.

"Is…is this okay?" he asks, and I can see the boy I dated echoed in the man in front of me.

"Yes," I whisper in reply.

"I don't want to push you." His voice is gruff and deep, and his thumb traces the outline of my lip. "Well…I do. But if it's too soon, I'll stop."

I wonder how many women he's had in his bed since his wife, even before her. He's so sure, so calm about it. I almost ask, but decide I don't want to know. Not right now, not here. Besides, what does it matter? I don't want him to stop…I feel like my dead, broken heart is waking up, and the forgotten parts of my soul are coming to life again. If he can awaken that in me, then it doesn't matter if he's kissed hundreds of women.

"I want you to…" I say, biting my lower lip. "Don't stop. But…"

"But?"

"But I've never…" Oh, God this is embarrassing. "I've never…I've never had…had…"

His eyebrows raise and thankfully he finishes for me.

"You've never had sex with anyone but your husband? Seriously?" And then he blushes—more of a darkening of his skin than a red blotchiness—when he realizes the answer. "Only the one other? Although that wasn't sex, it sounds like."

I wince and then nod.

"No one before John, though?" His hand teases my ear and then slides back into my hair. I'm sure he's thinking about the many steamy nights in a Chevelle with nothing between us but my flimsy underwear… and sometimes barely that.

I shake my head, wishing we could stop this talk and get back to where we were. "John was my first," I say. "You're the only other guy I've even kissed."

"Wow." He sits back like I've shocked him. My scalp feels cold where his hand was. Damn! I should have kept my fat mouth shut. Now he thinks I'm some sort of prude. I groan inwardly at the memory of Michelle calling me just that…so long ago.

"It's just you were so good, back then," he says wistfully. "And I wanted you so bad. Jesus, I thought you would kill me with pent-up teenage lust." He chuckles.

The music from the television switches to something still classical but less exact, like a score from a movie. An oboe rises above the rest of the instruments, lifting through the rush of sea air and memories.

"I'm sorry," I say.

He gives me a rueful smile. "No need to be sorry."

"But I was awful to you back then."

"Back then. Ellen, that was eons ago. Everyone does things in high school they regret."

"I know, but I was so selfish…"

"Teens are selfish. It's what they do. And I was just as bad. I hadn't even considered what would happen to you after I went to college. And I didn't even try to win you back."

In the background the song changes and quietens. He pulls over a big, plush ottoman; biceps flexing, and then rests back against the sofa with his feet up. He tangles my fingers with his and pulls me closer, so that my shoulder lies flush with his.

We both stare at the blank TV screen while his fingertips slide back and forth over my knuckles. Our bodies remember each other's place; we used to do this when we were kids. Only back then it was music videos and sitcoms playing, not Beethoven. Funny how little time it takes to settle together…with all of that water under the bridge.

"Are you sure no one put you up to this? To being here on this ship at the same time as me?" I ask.

He chuckles and uses his free hand to make a criss-cross over his heart and then put three fingers up. "Scout's honour," he says. "Although if someone told me you would be on this trip, I probably would have come anyway, just to see the girl who broke my heart," He teases.

He can't be serious. "Really?"

"Really."

"Huh," I say, not sure how to take this confession. "Don't you think it's weird though?"

"Of course it's weird. But weird things happen all of the time."

"No kidding."

"Do you want me to walk you back to your room? I can if you want."

I don't want.

"Um…do you have more meetings in the morning?" The clock on the television says 12:24. It's really late, and I should let him sleep. I want to let him sleep…but I don't want to let him sleep. I want to stay here. I shouldn't stay here. John…

John is not here. I am *not* going to feel guilt for liking the company of a guy I dated long before I even met John. John is dead.

What in the hell is wrong with me?

Paul shifts so he is facing me and gently brings my hand to his lips. He kisses each knuckle—slowly, carefully—and then raises his eyebrows. "Tomorrow we're in port. No meetings on port days…" He grins mischievously.

"Oh." His lips on my knuckles are pulling strings in my stomach.

I should go.

"So if you want to stay…just a little longer…" he looks up at me from behind long, dark eyelashes.

"Yes…" I encourage.

He pulls my other hand to his lips.

"Maybe we could reacquaint ourselves…" He kisses the knuckle of my thumb. "…A little better…" And then my ring finger. "In that big, lonely bed…"

He turns my hands over and kisses each of my palms, his eyes locked on mine and then he waits for an answer.

The music rises and falls behind us, and I'm so warm, and I remember those eyes and eyes just like them only blue. And smaller hands and these bigger hands and somehow, beneath the surface of everything I feel a shift. Like the sliding of a small wave over a big one, and the block of ice in my chest flows with the waves and I know that the time is right to let it dissolve and give.

"Yes…" I say, and then his mouth is on mine and he lifts the skinny, lighter, different me up and into his strong, gentle arms and carries me across the room to his bed.

The sound of the doorbell chime pulls me from sleep, warm and comfortable and disoriented. I'm lying naked on my stomach in the softest bed I've ever known. The memory of the night lies over me like a fairy tale, a delicious dreamy whisper and I hear Paul speak with someone, the rolling clink of glass on a tray, and then the door closes. Part of me is shocked that I didn't wake when Paul got up—John always woke me with his sleepy clonking about in the morning—and another part of me is shocked that I'm here at all.

I open my eyes as he pads into the room, wrapped in the white fluffy complimentary bathrobe. He smiles at me—all dark, handsome, and messy-haired—and I smile back, trying hard not to feel self conscious, and resisting the urge to pull at the sheets and cover myself to the neck.

"Good morning," he says as he sits on the edge of the bed. His hand softly traces the edge of my shoulder blade. The sun slants in through the window, and I can just see a hint of land. We must have anchored while I was sleeping.

"Good morning.' I say and I close my eyes like a cat being stroked.

His finger slowly runs down the bumps of my spine and then up the length of the long muscle beside it, stopping on the small scar that I know is there and I wish he wouldn't see. He traces it, and to stop the guilt from drowning me, I slowly flip over and wrap the sheet around me, hiding my discomfort in a sleepy sound of pleasure. His fingers trace around as I roll, drawing a slow line along my collarbone.

"Do you feel like some breakfast?" he asks.

His fingers feel so good on my bare skin.

"Mmm-hmm," I purr. I'm not sure who I've turned into...an adult version of fourteen-year-old Ellen, or a guilt-free version of John's Ellen. Or perhaps this Ellen is a mixture of both. But I don't want breakfast, not right now. I want him to do what he did last night...again.

I open my eyes, and tell him just that without saying a word.

An hour later we've had fresh fruit, yogurt, and lukewarm coffee, and we're sitting on the balcony in our robes, enjoying the view. In front of us lies another place I've never seen—the isle of Mykonos. Tourists swarm from the little tender boats along the docks. I take a sip of coffee and smell the salty, slightly rotting smell of the sea.

"Would you like to go and see?" Paul asks.

"See what?"

"The beaches, the shops, the island...we could rent a scooter."

I giggle, and then stop for a moment, wondering at the sound as it comes from my mouth.

"A scooter?"

"Yes, a scooter. Lots of tourists do it. It's a great way to explore the island."

"Oh. Okay." I say, not convinced.

He throws a grape at me. It falls into the folds of my robe, between my breasts.

"Ellen McKinley," Paul chides in a mock tsk-tsk voice. "What happened to that girl I used to know? The one that sat on the back of my motorbike in a thunderstorm?"

I had forgotten all about that.

I dig the grape from between my breasts as he watches and pop it in my mouth with a wicked grin.

Oh. My. God. I can't believe I did that!

"Have you ever been to a topless beach?" Paul asks, echoing my grin.

I almost choke on the grape. I chew frantically and swallow, completely destroying the air of seductiveness.

"No?" I finally squeak.

"Well, that's where we're going," he says, with a note of finality.

"Oh. Okay…I guess I better go get changed."

"I guess you better."

I slip into my clothes from last night, giving Paul a final kiss before I leave. His hand strokes the crease beneath my buttock, and I have to tear myself away from him. He's like a happy drug, and I want to keep going back for more. I slowly let go of the waistband of his boxers and push his bare chest away, wondering if maybe it might be a bit more fun to just stay here in his room.

Of course, as I float down the stairs to my stateroom and sneak toward my stateroom, the pendulum swings again, and I turn the final corner to come face to face with Frank Fielding.

His apparent shock at seeing me there is almost as evident as my horror at seeing him. And then his shock is gone, and he smiles the wide, evil smile that's haunted my dreams. A nightmare smile.

In a strange echo of my last moments with Paul, I shove him—this time it's a hard, frantic shove. He falls backward and then I kick his shin with every ounce of adrenaline coursing through my veins. He grunts as I turn around and run. I run blindly, not looking to see if he has followed. I run up to the buffet, down the next set of stairs to the casino, through it, and up again, grasping for the key in my purse as I go. By the time I reach my floor, I'm sure he hasn't followed. I slide my key into the lock and am through the door in seconds, slamming the bolt home and sliding the chain across with shaking fingers.

God is punishing me. He's standing there in his big place up there in the sky, looking down and shaking his fist. Not even a year my husband has been dead, and I'm in someone else's bed. And now I'm paying for it.

Frank Fucking Fielding is on this ship. Fuck. Fuck-fuck-fuck!

Twenty-five years I played by the rules. I did everything I could for my husband. I loved him for God's sake, until the very end. I would have done *anything* for him. I let the monster that's out there rape me—*rape me*—to save John's career, his life, our family. And what happened? God took him away! He thumbed his nose at me and stole John from me in the darkest of nights and ruined my life in the process. And now, after all of this time, I'm finally seeing a brief but solid light at the end of the tunnel, and Fucking Frank Fielding turns up a gazillion miles from where he should be, walking in the stairwell on the same ship as Paul Donovan and myself?

What the hell do I have to do to break free of this never-ending pit?

I bang my head against the wood panelled wall behind me and slam my fist back into it for good measure. I'm more angry than scared. This is *my* trip. This is supposed to be my salvation—not my damnation.

I am so bloody sick of Frank Fielding! The anger continues to build inside of me, and the spark of happiness goes on the offensive. I *want* to go on this island with Paul. I want to sit on a nude beach with him and laugh. I want to feel the sand between my toes, and I want to drink wine with a man who grew from the boy I once thought I loved. I want to have a *real* adventure, live today for me. I will not let that lecherous asshole ruin my day!

And just like that, I find the strength to keep moving. I shower quickly, a constant stream of swearwords and invective aimed at Frank Fielding rolling off of my tongue. I put on the bikini I found in my suitcase—a gift Maria had hidden there with a note to 'Be brave!'—and my flowing white linen shirt and pants, and then pull my hair back into a loose bun. I brush on a brief hint of makeup, pack a towel and some sunscreen in a bag, and before I'm finished someone is knocking at the door.

The roll of dread, excitement, happiness, fear, and anger that rolls through me almost makes me dizzy, but I walk to the peephole and look, my heart roaring in my ears.

It's Paul.

I unlock all of the locks and throw open the door, so happy to see him—not the alternative—and so glad that I can get off of this boat and hopefully away from the man who has haunted me for years. Paul leans over to kiss me gently, his lips still tasting of toothpaste.

"Ready?" he asks and I nod, not trusting my voice. He takes my hand, and I focus on that, not telling him who I saw, not admitting my fear.

Because if I say it out loud…it will be real.

I'm freakishly aware of the people around us as we load onto the bobbing tender boat and take the short ride to the docks. We're late to disembark—most of the tourists left the ship hours ago—so our tender is almost empty. I scan the faces and see no one I recognize. I'm sure Paul can feel the tension radiating off of me, but I don't tell him why. I don't tell him that it really *is* Fielding. I guess I just want to continue the façade of the fairy tale. The lonely widow meets a handsome prince and sails away to a magical island version of my life…not the victim escapes her horrible life only to run into her own personal nightmare version. Paul rests his arm around my shoulder, and I feel safe here. Not one hundred percent safe, but at least ninety-five.

He helps me off the small boat, and we walk to the little rental hut by the dock. Within a few minutes, we're astride a made-for-two scooter, hair and clothes whipping in the breeze as we head up one hill and wind down another, toward the other side of the island. I feel a bizarre, off-kilter sense of déjà vu—we spent many hours like this as kids. I'm a little flabbier, he's firmer, and we both have streaks of grey and a few extra wrinkles…but it's the same wild, carefree feeling. When we pull up to the beach, the couples and families are spread in front of us, some fully clothed, some in nothing at all. A blonde Adonis walks hand-in-hand with his boyfriend, both buck-naked and completely absorbed in each other. A grizzled eighty-year-old man dangles unashamed as he walks into the surf. Several bright pink and obviously American tourists slather themselves with sunscreen.

My own small-town North American homebody background shows through and I catch myself gawking like an idiot.

Paul is watching me. He chuckles and grabs my hand, walking me to the edge of the beach, up against the rocky point that sticks into the sea.

"It's a bit to take in, but you'll get used to it," he says as I try to focus on spreading my towel beside him. My cheeks are flaming. And then, with a wink, he pulls off his t-shirt, slides off his shorts and his very muscular, um...*everything* is right there in front of my eyes.

Oh.

He leans forward and sets the towel down for me, as I seem to have lost all sense of motor control. His fingers close on my arm, and he pulls me closer, steadying me with his right hand while his left slowly slides the buttons of my shirt from their holes. I'm breathless as the ocean breeze pulls my hair from the loose bun and his fingers brush on my bare skin.

"You, Miss Ellen, have been doing something right," he whispers into my ear.

I smile. It's such blatant flattery, but it's been so long since someone said words like that to me.

"Amazing what rock bottom can do for you," I say, unable to take it. I look down, see that yes, everything of his is still there, and look away to the sand beside us.

He ignores my downcast look and his hand traces the ties that hold my gauzy pants up and releases them too. It's so sensual, so raw, being undressed like this on the beach, with people everywhere. He leans over again and kisses my temple, then whispers in my ear. "Don't sell yourself short."

I'm standing there in front of him in a bikini, something I haven't worn in at least twenty years. It's modest, as far as bikinis go, but risqué to the nth for me. I feel completely bare, and the wind ruffles the little hairs on my arms.

Paul takes a step back and admires me. And I can't help but admire him.

"I wouldn't change a thing," he says.

"You're not too bad yourself," I reply, reaching out to touch his biceps but still not looking down.

He shrugs, and sits down on the spread towels, patting the space beside him. I sit, using every muscle I've got to suck in my small rolls and hold them tight. I'm pasty white, and he's a sun-kissed brown. The small dark hairs on his chest are asking for me to touch them, but I'm feeling so self-conscious that I turn to face the waves instead.

"You've been here before?" I ask.

"Yeah, twice. Once with my ex, and once a few years ago. A friend of mine owns a villa closer to the village. He and his brother rent it out to tourists. I thought it would be a good place to get away."

"Was it?" I ask.

"Not really; too many memories of my ex, and too many couples, of all varieties. And the few singles mostly swing a different way than me."

I nod. The same-sex couples on the beach outnumber the male-female ones.

"I had lots of opportunities to…explore my sexuality, though" He says, his lips quirking up. "Is there anything else here you'd like to see? We've only got a few hours."

"No," I say. "I'm happy here." It's safe, I'm beside a very handsome man who is distracting me from my miserable life, and it's doubtful Fielding will show up.

"Good," he says.

I lie back and close my eyes and he does the same. His fingers weave their way into mine, and they feel like an anchor, tying me to him and yet letting me float. It's a good feeling.

And then I remember the promise I made to Paul. He asked me to tell him if I saw Fielding, and I haven't yet. I can't take another lie. Not to this sweet man who is keeping me tied together.

"I saw him this morning." I say.

He sits up, and looks down at me, his hand holding my fingers tight, not letting me pull away in shame like I want to.

"Him? The guy?"

"Him. I'm positive it's him. I ran face-first into him on the way to my room this morning."

"Shit."

"You can say that again," I say.

A couple splashes in front of us, oblivious to the craziness of my life.

"You're sure, sure?"

"Yes."

"But there was no Fielding on the ship."

"Well it's him. He recognized me. He must be using a different name. I wouldn't put it past him…he's a monster." I shudder, the cool breeze off the water made colder by my memories of a dark night in a park…and other nights in other places.

"What are you going to do?"

"I don't know," I say, because I have no idea. But I like that he's asked me what I'm going to do, not told me what I have to do.

Paul squeezes my hand tight, leans back on his side, resting his weight on his elbow.

"I've only got two more meetings, both of them while we're sailing between here and Santorini. You can stay in my room if you'd like."

He uses his free hand to caress my cheek. My view of the world is Paul, sand, and blue sky. It's hard to think of anything else with his hand on my face. It's hard to focus on dark in all of this light.

"Okay." I say, fully aware of the implications of staying another night in his room.

"Deal," he says, and seals it with a kiss.

We rush back across the island, having both fallen asleep on our towels after a swim in the salty water. Paul practically throws the keys at the rental guy, and we run, laughing and gasping, to reach one of the last tenders just as it departs from the dock. The workers give us stern looks, but it only makes me want to laugh more. Paul's side squeezes tight to mine on the little tender bench, and we scan the faces in the boat, me looking for *Him* and Paul watching for my reaction to those faces.

Paul spirits me up to my small stateroom and orders some room service snacks while I shower. It's odd having him out there, like some sort of bodyguard while I hop in the shower and wash the sand from my skin. No one ever knew about Fielding. So how could they protect me from him? Having Paul in my room while I shower makes me feel safe in ways I have never felt safe—not for twenty-five years. Paul knows. And Fielding has no power over him.

But part of me is afraid this is all too good to be true. The pendulum keeps swinging, and the bad has got to get worse before it gets better.

I wipe the water from my skin, and wrap myself in a towel—no fluffy bathrobes in my room—before sucking everything in and then slowly walking out. But my strutting is for naught as Paul is lying on my bed, fast asleep. He looks so like, and yet so unlike the boy I knew so long ago. His dark hair curls around his ears, and his eyes are shadowed with laugh lines. I can't help but wonder what life would have been like if I'd stayed with him. But then I shake my head. If I'd stayed with Paul there would be no Chris, no David, no Maria. Three amazing human beings would not have existed. I wouldn't change that for the world. Nor would I take away my time with John.

I look out the window, we're still anchored in the bay and the sun is setting over the little harbour and the iconic windmills. A few boats still ferry back and forth from the dock, bringing the stragglers in from their day exploring and transporting supplies for the ship.

The doorbell rings—room service is slower down here on the lower decks. I'd almost forgotten we'd ordered. Paul stirs enough to open his eyes but that's about it. He slumps back down onto the bed and immediately begins to snore.

"Coming!" I yell as I throw on a loose pair of pants and tee-shirt—without underwear—and walk over to let them in.

As I pull the door open, my brain whispers a tiny, quiet warning, but it's too late, the door is wide open before I can act to change anything. And there, in my doorway, stands Frank Fielding.

I'm too shocked to move.

His slicked black hair has more grey in it than I'd realized. His face is lined but still hard. He's wearing khaki shorts and sandals and a white golf shirt, like half of the sixty-something men on this ship.

"Ellen," he says ominously and the chill in his voice is enough to galvanize me into action. I swing the door shut, try to slam it in his face but he kicks his foot forward and the door stops. He shoves it, hard, and pushes his way in, grabbing my arm in the process. "What a surprise to see you here," he growls. We're through the door and the door slams with a bang, but Paul doesn't wake.

All of the loathing of twenty-five years comes bubbling into my chest, and in one tremendous shift of power I knee him in the groin. He hisses in pain like the snake that he is, but doesn't let go. Still no Paul.

I jerk my arm wildly, trying to strike at Fielding's face, but he manages to grab my arm before I connect.

"Get. Out. Of. My. Room." I say, and try to knee him again, but he twitches to the side and punches me in the stomach. The air in the room turns to lead and I can't breathe. I double over in fear and pain and try to catch some air, but he grabs my hand again and pulls me upright.

Paul! Where in the hell is Paul?

"I think not," says Fielding. "I think I'd rather stay with the Widow Michaels tonight. So nice of my darling wife to tell me where I'd find you."

"You bastard!" I gasp, still unable to find the air to breathe in deeply. "How...?"

"Top Secret clearance gives me access to all kinds of things," he hisses as he wrenches my arm around my back. "Like alternate identities."

"You have nothing over me now," I say, gathering steam. "This is a cruise ship, not a military base!"

"Shut up, slut!"

His fist hammers into my kidney and my knees weaken but I can't fall. My shoulder will break if I fall. I stomp on his foot instead.

"You bitch!" he yells but his grip loosens for only a fraction of a second.

He tries to drag me around the corner, and—finally—he comes face to face with Paul.

"Paul..." I whisper with a satisfied half-smile when Fielding freezes. "This is Frank. You can kill him now."

I can't move, Fielding still has my arm, but I watch in movie-calibre slow motion as Paul's arm comes back, gathering force, and then slings forward. I feel the impact, hear bones crunch, hear the asshole grunt as he drops my hand, turns and stumbles away. And before Paul or I can do anything about it, Fielding is out the door.

"Are you alright?" Paul asks, frantically checking me up and down for injury.

"I'm fine," I say.

He grabs my head with both hands and holds my gaze with his big, dark eyes. "*Stay here*," he says. "Lock the door and don't let anyone in until I come back, okay?"

"Okay," I say, stunned.

Paul nods and then follows Fielding, the door slamming behind him, and I'm left alone in my loose pants and t-shirt, wondering what has just happened.

Twenty minutes later, I'm dressed and my hair is drying. My shoulder is sore, my back hurts, and I feel sick from the ache in my stomach, but I'm okay. Paul still hasn't returned. I'm about to call his room, when there's a gentle knock on the door. "Ms. Michaels?" the voice says. "Is everything all right? It's Joselito."

I check the peephole to be sure and then open the door. "Joselito? Everything's fine," I say. He walks in, and the door slides closed.

"I heard a scuffle, and saw two men come running out of your room," I can see him looking around for signs of a fight. "I didn't recognize either. And then the Captain made a staff-only announcement to be on the lookout for a man of the same description…I don't mean to pry, but I was concerned."

I smile at his honest, caring openness. "I'm fine. The man they are looking for tried to force his way into my room. Fortunately Mr. Donovan was here and the man ran off," I say. "Have they found him? The man they are looking for?"

"I'm afraid not. He seems to have vanished. They're searching the ship's registers, but still nothing. He may have taken one of the tenders off the ship."

"Oh."

"Can I bring you anything? Coffee? A glass of wine on the house?"

"No. Thank you Joselito. I'm fine."

He nods. "I'll let you know if they find him. I'm sure the security chief will want to interview you."

"That will be fine," I say.

There's another knock at the door, and I jump.

I look through the peephole again. It's Paul, his face is grim.

When I open the door again, Joselito nods and makes to leave. "Let me know if you need anything, Mrs. Michaels. Just dial 3 on the phone to get me."

When the door closes behind him, Paul holds my arms and searches my eyes. "Are you okay?" he asks. I nod, shocked by the force of his question. He pulls me over to the bed and we both sit. "I lost him before I even made it to the stairwell. Couldn't find him anywhere. He just vanished. But they'll find him."

I shake my head. "No they won't," I say.

"They're searching security cameras and passport photos now. It's only a matter of time."

"You don't know him. He's smart. He'll lay low. He's already using an alias. They didn't even know he was on the ship in the first place! How are they going to find him? And he knows my room number. How did he know I was here? Why is he on this ship, of all ships?" I'm starting to panic again, and I know it, but I can't stop. I look out the window and see that the ship is just now gliding out of the bay. He could still be on the ship, but he could also have slipped away.

"Coming here was his first mistake, Ellie," he says in a calm voice. Calm, not patronizing. "He'll make more, and they'll find him." He pulls me in and once again I wonder at the fact that Paul is on this ship too.

"Look, I talked with the staff, and they're assigning you a new room on the same floor as me. You can stay in mine as much as you want, but there was an empty suite just down the hall from mine. It's an upgrade, free of charge, and he won't know you're there, okay?"

Being on the same floor as Paul would be a bonus, whether I stay in his room or not, and I don't want to be here another minute, knowing Fielding knows where I am. I nod. "Okay."

Paul helps me throw my stuff in a suitcase—most of it's still in there anyway—and carries it to the elevator. We go up to his floor and down the hall, eyes alert, but we only see a tall couple heading out for dinner. No monster-men.

He hands me the key to my new room, and I unlock the door. It's a slightly smaller mirror image of his room: same paintings, same furniture, just smaller, with only a queen-sized bed.

"Is this okay?" he asks.

I shrug. "It's fine. Nicer than my old room."

"And just down the hall from mine…"

"Yes, that's true…"

"So…your place or mine for dine-in?"

I look at him, realizing I haven't thought of that part.

"I'd like to go out." I say.

His eyes widen, almost imperceptibly, but he doesn't voice his surprise. I'm surprised too, but the fact remains that I'm sick of hiding from Fielding. It's time to take control of my own life.

"You're sure?" he asks.

"Yes."

"Well, then let's go out."

"Do you want to choose, or shall I?"

"Let's just go to the regular dining room. I'll feel better with lots of people around, and I haven't been in there yet."

And so an hour later, we're sitting in the ornate dining room, and I'm wishing I'd chosen room service. We're seated with three different couples, all of which are members of Paul's business group. They appear to have known each other for years. The ladies look at me with a mixture of curiosity and contempt as they wonder who I am and how I fit into Paul's equation. I can almost hear their internal conversations. They wear jewellery from expensive stores and dresses with brand names. They speak with cultured accents and are at home in all-expenses-paid, first class staterooms. Paul chats comfortably with them, and I smile, but have little to contribute to the conversation.

It's like I'm back with John, facing down the officers' wives for the first time.

We're listening to one of the overly-loud, somewhat intoxicated ladies—I think her name is Marcella—tell a story, when Paul leans over and whispers in my ear.

"Are you okay?" he buzzes.

I nod, but continue to act interested in Marcella's story.

"We could go," he says.

It's tempting. If we go we'll end up in his big, comfy bed, and I want to end up there. Yes, I do. But leaving would be giving up, giving in. And I'm not going to give up or give in, not to Fielding, not to Marcella or whatever her name is, and not to myself.

I turn to Paul and smile. "Let's stay until dessert is finished."

His eyes are so rich and dark. His hand reaches below the tablecloth and strokes my leg, bare under my black dress.

"You're sure?" he asks.

Remind me why I didn't pick him almost thirty years ago?

I nod. "I'm okay…for now."

Marcella has come to her punch line, and I laugh with the rest although I'm completely distracted by Paul's fingertips on my skin. Unbidden, a memory of John's hand on my leg at another time, another table hits me hard. I squash it down. John is dead. This trip is about me, about me breaking free of him, the military, and my pathetic dependant life.

I don't care if I ever see Paul again after this. He's here now, and he's hot and interested and safe, and I'm not going to let this moment slip away. I owe myself that.

Marcella's friend—Jean? Jeannie?—starts up on a new topic as dessert is served. Just as my chocolate gateau is revealed in front of me, a man with salt and pepper hair and straight posture walks by and I stifle a gasp. Paul looks up, but I know in a second it's not Fielding. I shake my head. Marcella is eyeing me, wondering what's up, but I smile at her as if to say that it was nothing, because it *is* nothing. I need to stop looking. Monster-man is not going to try anything with Paul here beside me. And besides, he has no leverage. John is dead.

The cake is good, and the wine is delicious, but my stomach still hurts and I tire quickly of the business version of the officers' wives— same fake voices, same fake hair, tans, and nails. If there's a kindred spirit in the group, she's not at this table.

Whether he senses it or not, Paul chooses this time to excuse us, stating a promise to walk on the deck in the moonlight. He winks at Marcella, who eyes him suspiciously but says nothing, and we rise to leave. I pull up as much confidence as I can muster, and his arm around my waist gives me more as we walk away.

"Sorry about Marcella," he says. "I've known Marcella and Tony since I moved to London. She's been trying to hook me with one friend or another since the day we met." He chuckles. "It's become her secret goal to send me down the aisle again. Every gala, every dinner party, every event, it's someone different. I can just imagine what's going through her head—seeing me with someone attractive that she didn't personally select."

I smile, blushing at the compliment, but I'm still struck with how different Paul's world is than mine—fancy trips, fancy people, fancy life. They aren't me. And I don't know if they could ever be me. I'm used to cracked sidewalks, broken furnaces, second-hand cars, and people who *think* they are fancy. And even though I've kind of sworn that I won't see this as a long term thing, I can't help but think about how life would be with Paul.

"Penny for your thoughts," Paul says as we walk along the deck.

I try for honesty. I have nothing to lose.

"I was just thinking about what different lives we've led."

"How so?"

"Well you've done everything in the right order, you're obviously successful, you wear expensive clothes, do expensive things…you live in London, for God's sake. And I'm…well…" I falter—I don't want to say I'm no one…but that's what I am.

"You're what?"

"I don't know. I'm not expensive anything."

"And I am?"

"I don't know…are you?"

He's quiet for a bit, our footsteps barely heard over the rushing wind. We're not alone on the deck, but the few people around are very obviously couples, and I feel very safe next to Paul's solidity. I squash my fear of Fielding down firmly. He can't hurt me here. Not with Paul beside me.

"I guess I've learned to be expensive." Paul finally says. "I work hard at what I do and get paid well. Half of what I earn goes to the kids and my ex, but the other half...well, I like nice things, and I can afford them..."

He sounds like he's apologizing for his wealth.

"Paul, it's okay to be that way. I've just never had the opportunity, I guess. David was born when I was nineteen. You don't get rich having kids that early."

Just out from us, a seagull soars over the water, matching the speed of the ship. We stop and look over the railing, his arm still warming my back.

"My friends wear second-hand clothes and drive second-hand cars, Paul. The fact that I'm on this ship at all is a miracle in itself. I would never have even thought to buy myself something so extravagant."

We turn and walk again, back into the corridors and through the busy casino. On the other side, we take the elevators down to his—our—floor and we stop at his room, the first one we come to along the hallway.

"Would you like to come in?" he asks. "I'll understand if you just want to be alone. I'm just down the hall, and you can call me if you need me."

"Do you want me to stay?" I ask before I can stop myself.

He smiles a deep, lustful smile that sends something in my belly into a tailspin.

"I do," he says and pulls me through the door.

The next day, we are anchored in the Caldera in Santorini, and Paul insists I get off of the ship, if only to take the donkey ride up the side of the cliff. It's terrifying. I've never been around large animals of any sort, so just the donkey itself is scary. And then to sit up so high on a creature like that and half-walk, half-trot up the side of a ginormous cliff, with imminent death looming just over a small wall? It's the scariest thing I've ever done. Well, almost.

I try, unsuccessfully, not to look like a screeching idiot. Paul sits comfortably, eyes dancing. When we reach the top, he tells me he started riding in Texas, and has leased a horse for years in London. Of course he has. He's the frigging Marlboro Man. And oddly enough, I can see him as just that—all he needs are the boots and the hat.

How do I get mixed up with these beautiful, perfect men?

"You should meet Captain," he says, as we walk along the narrow streets to a café he knows.

"Captain?"

"My horse."

"I should meet your horse?"

"Yes, you should."

"Paul, if you haven't figured it out, I'm not horse-person material."

The waitress shows us to our spot, a simple table on the tiny patio overlooking the Caldera. It's breathtakingly beautiful: the hills, the white-washed houses, the water, the ship floating quietly.

We order drinks, he a beer and me a fizzy lemon soda.

"I don't think you give yourself enough credit," he says, after taking a long pull of his beer.

I look at him, but say nothing.

"I think that there's a lot more to Ellen McKinley Michaels than you let on."

"No there isn't," I say, because there's not. I'm just me.

"Yes, there is."

"Like what?" I answer. "I've done nothing but raise kids and work at cheap clothing stores my whole life."

"But you have dreams, and now you have time."

We've talked about my desire to go to university some day, become something other than what I am. Paul is encouraging, and the spark that lit so long ago flickers and sputters for just a bit. Maybe someday I'll go. But I'm not ready.

The waitress interrupts us, and we order some typical Greek fare—salads, spanikopita, souvlaki—the stuff tourists are supposed to order at these places. I imagine briefly how sick the residents of this island must be of 'Greek' food. Do they ever just crave a burger?

Paul isn't letting the conversation drop. When the waitress leaves, he looks at me again, his eyes silently assessing.

"Ellen, you've aged maybe ten years in the thirty since I've seen you, although most women would be haggard wrecks with what you've been through…and, God, I have no idea what it is about you, but you get under my skin." He leans forward over the table and his hand takes mine. His hand is warm. "I haven't wanted…anyone…as badly as I want you."

I swallow, throat suddenly dry. The cool breeze off the water feels like the steam from a sauna.

"You're smart, funny, brave…" his hand rubs mine, and his feet find mine underneath the rickety table. "…sexy."

I'm not sure who he's talking about, but it is definitely not me.

"Don't you see that?" he says.

I feel the tears pricking beneath my eyelids, so I look away from him toward the water. No, I don't see that. I'm a lying coward. I'm old. I'm used up. I'm just Ellen, a nobody.

His hand is tight on my hand, like he's holding me with him, willing me to believe what he's telling me, but I don't. A tear, damn it, slips down my cheek. I can't hide it, and I don't move to wipe it away.

"I can't believe no one has made you see that," he says quietly.

I don't trust my voice to answer, so I just watch the water, the cliffs and the houses. They're big and permanent. They don't look at me and find things I don't want to see. They just are.

Another tear slips out and I can't stand the feeling of it cooling my face so I dash it away.

Our food comes, and I don't look at the waitress with my tearstained cheeks. Paul thanks her, in Greek of course—is there anything this guy can't do?—and then sits quietly, waiting for me.

I feel so awkward and guilty and wrong sitting here with this echo from my past telling me these things. I don't want to acknowledge any of it. I want to curl into a little ball and disappear, but he waits patiently across from me as the smell of garlic and grilled souvlaki wafts upward. I want to run away but his hand stays firm, holding me there, staring down my demons.

I wipe away more tears and sniff like a child. Still, he waits.

"You don't know me…" I whisper.

"Maybe not," he says, and I look at him. His face is open, honest. "Maybe I don't know everything about you. But I know a few things. A lot more than some, I think."

For a minute I bristle at the implied criticism of John. It's what Paul means. John didn't know me. Did he? Does loving someone mean you know everything about them? No…loving someone means you accept them for what they are, whether you know everything or not. And John loved me in that way.

"Ellen, I won't change my mind. You are what you are, and I like what you are. And I'm not criticizing John."

It's like he's heard what I was thinking. Why can't I let people think good things about me? My eyes burn, and I want to let the tears come, but instead I close my eyes. I take a deep breath. In. Out. Like I can push away this awful tension as I exhale.

And when I open my eyes again, Paul is still there, watching me, believing in me. "I loved him." I say.

"Of course you did. I loved Francesca. I still love her a little. It's not wrong. But I didn't know we would end up this way, sniping at each other over the phone. And you didn't know John would die. Maybe the same things would have happened with someone else. It's not your fault, Ellen. John didn't die because of something you did. You didn't make his plane go down. It wasn't because of you. It just happened."

The burning behind my eyes gets worse and worse as he looks at me, and I think that I might die right then and there. I think that lightning will strike me down and the sea will swallow me up, and I wish it would hurry up so I could escape this awful, awful feeling inside of me. Because with those words, Paul has shot an arrow right through me and seen my worst demon and unlocked its cage.

Because John's death *was* my fault.

All my fault.

CHAPTER 26
HOUSE #13

May 15, 2008

T HE CLOCK ON MY BEDSIDE table says 4:56 a.m., and John's alarm is screaming, literally screaming in my ears. I thwomp him with my arm, and when he groans, I thwomp him again.

"John, for God's sake, wake up!" I push him hard, angry at him for waking me on this, my day off of work. Sometimes he can be such a jerk. He sits up, and rubs his head, blonde hair flat on the back of his head and sticking up at crazy angles on the top.

The alarm keeps screeching.

"Would you turn the bloody alarm off?" I ask through clenched teeth.

He turns it off but says nothing, and stumbles off to the bathroom. I sigh, rolling over and away from the bathroom light. He's left the door open and it's shining right in my eyes. Typical.

I flip on my stomach, cover my head with my pillow, and try to find the wisps of the wonderful dream I was having…something about oceans and beaches and palm trees—probably a result of the unseasonable warmth of the May air. It's too hot under all of the covers, so I throw them down, arms splayed and bare back open to the air. The wush of John's shower, and the heat of the pillow slowly lull me back to sleep.

But this time it's not a nice dream. It's *Him*, chasing me through a jumbled wood and I'm running, running for my life. Running with the knowledge that if he catches me everyone I love will die. If I don't get away from this monster I can't protect them—John, the kids, everyone.

In the gloom of the dream I trip and fall, and he pins me down, holding me somehow and I can't breathe. The dream morphs, the way that dreams do, and I'm naked beneath him, and his dirty fingernail traces the scar on my back. The scar he left there years ago. He laughs, and the laugh is a promise of worse things to come. I scream and flail, waking up, and my flailing hand connects with something hard—John's face, it turns out. I scream again, pushing and crying and trying to get away because the dream still holds me, and I see both John and Fielding at the same time.

"Babe, it's me! It's okay! It's me, John!" he cries. My eyes are wide, and my heart is rocketing in my chest.

"Jees, Ellen, it's me! It was just a dream!" He's wiping his face and I can see there's blood on his cheek. "The light was just catching a scar on your back, and I hadn't seen it there before, I…I didn't know you were asleep."

I don't say anything because I'm still shaking, still reeling from the revulsion I felt in the dream. I can't seem to disconnect the two—John here, Fielding there.

"When *did* you get that scar? I don't remember it at all."

And then I'm mad. Furious. Of course he doesn't recognize that scar, because he never looked. I saved his ass getting raped and beat to snot and fighting off some psychopathic monster, and he doesn't even see it because he's too busy flying off to his five-star hotels in exotic places. So fucking busy getting promotions, and eating five-course meals at mess dinners, and feeling all important that he never had the time to see the bruises and the scars on his own wife.

"Of course you don't." I say, and I don't care that there's venom in my voice. "You never saw it because you never looked."

"What?" he asks.

"You never looked. You never asked. You don't know what happens in my life John. You have no fucking idea what I go through."

"Gees, Ellen, take it easy," he says, looking hurt and confused.

I will not take it easy. I want him to hurt for not seeing my scars. I want him to burn for everything I've dealt with over the years. I want him to lose for all of the things I've lost, for all of the moments he has missed with children, for all of it.

I fling my hand out in disgust. "Go. Go to your big fancy job,

John. Go put on your nice clean uniform and your shiny boots. I'll be here waiting...like I always do." He holds his cheek, his eye bruising, and I flop down on the bed and roll away from him, making sure the damned scar on my back is well covered, no matter how hot and sticky the morning air is.

Thunder rolls in the distance, and I'm happy to hear it. It suits my mood to a tee.

"Ells, I don't know what I did, but I'm sorry," John says. As if a couple of words would be enough.

He waits for me to say something more, but I'm so angry, so self-righteous that I don't. I lie there in the glare of the bathroom light, tucking my scraped knees beneath me so he won't see them either. And why would he? The scrapes from yesterday are already fading, the blood and dirt washed down the drain.

"Don't wait up...?" he says, his voice hopeful—as if this, our little goodbye ritual, could pull me from my unreasonable fury.

"Go to work, John," I say, not finishing with my part.

And without another word ...he walks out the door.

CHAPTER 27
HOUSE #13

May 14, 2008

THE PHONE RINGS JUST AS I walk through the door from the grocery store. My purse is dangling from one arm, I've got three bags of groceries on the other, the key is still in the door, and the dog is trying to push past me and run into the street. I yank the door closed and throw everything on the floor, picking up the receiver before the answering machine can get it. The clock on the stove says 11:34.

"Hello?" I practically yell into the receiver. A bead of sweat rolls down my back. The weather is so unseasonably hot. It's got to break soon.

There's a click, and then the line goes dead.

"Huh." I say to Buddy, as he sniffs at the steak in the bag. "I guess they didn't want to talk to me."

I throw the steak and the other perishables in the fridge, grab his leash and we head out into the heat for our mandatory, around-the-block-and-through-the-park walk. He's been in the house alone for almost four hours, so I know he needs to go.

The humidity is stifling as we make our way down the sidewalk, Buddy sniffing at every tree, sign, flower, crack in the pavement, and blade of grass. He pulls and pees and pulls and pees, and we head down toward our usual trail with me sweating like a pig. A black car slides by us on the road as Buddy does his business on the sparse grass. The car doesn't slow, and I don't bother to give it more than a passing glance as I pooper-scoop into a bag.

"Buddy, that reeks," I say as I try not gag. I throw the bag in the trash can as we enter the woods. The wind picks up and the trees blow around us, but there are no clouds in the sky to bring relief from the oppressive heat. I search through the leaves above for even a little rain cloud, but there's nothing.

The trees offer a different adventure for Buddy and he trots down the trail, sniffing for squirrels and chipmunks and other treats. But then he stops. It's a different kind of stop—a sudden, haunches-at-the-ready kind of stop.

"Buddy…" I whisper, "What is it?

Buddy growls.

"What do you see?" I say—louder this time—and I search through the trees and bushes for a raccoon, or maybe a coyote. With the wind the way it is, I can't hear anything but crashing branches and rustling leaves. We're in the only part of the trail that is hidden by woods.

I tug on the leash. "Buddy, there's nothing here. Come on, let's go." I'm too far into the park to turn around, so I give a tug and he reluctantly follows.

Two steps later, Frank Fielding emerges from behind a tree, and my heart nearly stops.

"Hello, Ellen," he says.

Buddy growls.

I take a deep breath. What the hell is that monster doing here? My heart is thudding under my ribs, trying to find its rhythm. It's been fifteen years, for God's sake!

Buddy takes a step forward, pulling on the leash. Fielding seems to recognize the intensity of Buddy's stance. A touch of fear hits his eyes.

"Tie your dog to a tree," he says.

I don't move.

Buddy sits, his hackles still raised and his teeth still bared. It's such an odd behavior for my calm, friendly Golden Retriever that it detaches me even more from this bizarre situation. Buddy never growls like this.

"I *said* tie the dog to a tree."

Buddy doesn't look at me, just sits there, eyes locked on Fielding, while I look on like someone watching a TV show. Fielding's hair is greying. He's wearing jeans. Buddy is growling…and he's between Fielding and me.

An angered, ninety-pound dog is blocking Fielding's way.

"No," I say.

"Tie the dog to a tree, *now*." Fielding's face is turns red. His armpits have big sweat rings and his forehead is beaded with moisture.

"I said *no*."

"Ellen, do I need to review what I can do to you if you don't listen to me? What I can do to your husband, who has barely reached the esteemed rank of major after twenty-four years of service? Have you forgotten? I could bring your husband down. Literally."

"Review all you want. The answer is no."

I look at him with a mixture of fear and disgust, then I tug on the leash and turn away.

"Buddy, come." I say.

I take one step, another, and then one more. Buddy almost shrugs, shakes himself, and then trots off in front of me, danger forgotten.

I get ten feet before Fielding reaches me. He grabs for my wrist and pulls, but I yank my arm away and take off running as fast as my adrenalin-powered legs will go. Buddy thinks it's a game, and we both careen through the trees as fast as we can…but Fielding is faster. He slams into me, and I crash down onto the ground, knees grinding in the dirt. They sting, but I scrabble forward and kick back, hitting something soft behind me.

I have just enough time to realize that Buddy's leash is still around my wrist before he turns on Fielding and barks—not a nice bark, a get-your-ass-off-my-human bark.

And then he attacks.

The wind muffles Fielding's scream as Buddy pulls back, sharp teeth ripping skin and muscle. I watch in fascinated horror, sliding away, and then I pull Buddy's leash.

"Buddy, stop!" I say. I don't know why I stop him. I could leave him, let him eat Frank Fielding for a late afternoon snack, but I'm not that kind of person. Fielding shrugs away and I stand and Buddy steps back by my side. Fielding's wrist is bleeding and he's swearing and holding his arm, and I want to laugh. I want to laugh in his cruel, hateful, evil face.

"Good boy," I say as I pat Buddy's head.

"You are going to regret this," Fielding says.

"No, you are. I *dare* you to say anything to anyone, you bastard. If I hear a *word* about this anywhere, I'll march right down to the police, and file my own charges." I think for a quick minute and take a risk. "And I'm not the only one. I know at least two others that will join me in charging you."

Fielding's eyes narrow, but I know I've hit my mark.

"And maybe next time I won't make the dog stop."

He steps forward again as if to hit me, but Buddy stands by my side and growls.

"You will pay for this," he says. "I will make you pay."

And then he turns and fades into the woods.

I don't even feel the scrapes on my knees, the bruises on my wrists. I pat Buddy's head every five steps as I walk home with a surreal sense of well-being.

I fought Fielding and won. I had help, and I may be bleeding, but so is he.

Maybe this will be the last time.

CHAPTER 28
HOUSE #13 (CRUISE)

Early May, 2009

P AUL PAYS, AND WE WALK out of the restaurant and down the never-ending twists and turns of the donkey-poop covered stairs. He holds my hand firmly, but we don't talk. I'm lost in the agony of guilt, and he's lost in his own thoughts, thoughts I can't fathom and don't have the mental stamina to process right now. We take the little tender to the ship, and he walks me right to his room without asking. We go in, and it's as if he knows how to slay my demons. He sets my purse on the table, lifts me up in his strong arms, and carries me to his bed. And then he makes love to me—Ellen—in all of my brokenness and self-loathing, as if I am the only thing that matters in the world.

Like all good things, the last hours of the cruise come too quickly. We spend it in his room, me dreading the return to reality, to John's absence, to another move, to my lost sense of self; and Paul at least saying he dreads going back to his solitary life in London. No one has seen Fielding anywhere. The security people think he got off the ship in Mykonos; and since I don't say anything more, they aren't willing to take it further. I'm dreading the return trip and the possibility that he could find me somewhere, anywhere. Paul offers to come home with me, but I know that I have to do this myself. Besides, he has his meetings in Venice to attend. We order room service for supper and eat it on the balcony, while the sky turns to pink and then fades to deep, dark blue.

"What's your apartment like?" I ask, trying to keep the conversation going.

"It's simple, plain. I've got two bedrooms, mine and one for the girls when they visit. Close enough to the heart of the city to walk to the theatre, but far enough off the beaten track that it's quiet—well, as quiet as it can be in downtown London." He takes a bite of his fresh mozzarella salad, and smiles. "You should come and visit."

"Me?"

"Yes you, Ellen. I don't see any other sexy forty-something's that look twenty-something on this balcony that I'd be inviting to my little love nest."

"Well when you put it that way... But I'll pay for my ticket."

"Absolutely not. I need to spend my money on someone."

I grin. "Okay, you're on."

I wonder if it'll ever happen. This last night has the feel of the last night of summer camp. The quiet acceptance of goodbye—promises made with good intentions, but with the realization that they will most likely be broken.

"What about your new place?" he asks.

"Mine?"

"Yeah, what's your new place like, the one you're moving to?"

"Small. More of a cottage than a house. It's cute though. It has a view of the ocean, and a small garden I can take care of." And it means absolutely nothing to me, I think.

"May I come and see you there?"

"Of course, I'd like that." I'm suddenly shy, trying to imagine handsome, GQ Paul in my teeny little beachside cottage. It's hard to compute. I know, in reality, he won't come to visit. He'll go back to his life, I to mine, and that will be it. Our little game of make-believe lovers will be over. It makes me sad.

"I won't abandon you, Ellen," he says quietly, once again reading my thoughts before I can speak them.

"Paul, how can you not?" I ask. "We live on opposite sides of the world. It's like some bizarre twist of the universe that we even ended up on the same ship. We'll see each other maybe once or twice, and then you'll fade away, maybe a Christmas card or something for a year or two, but that will be it."

He shakes his head. "Not going to happen," he says.

I shrug. I know it will, he knows it will. No use fighting about it. We move on to different topics, and dessert, and then lie together on the lounge chairs, wrapped in a blanket until we both fall asleep.

Sometime in the night, he carries me to his bed, and I smile at him in the watery moonlight.

"Tell me," he says.

"Tell you what?"

"What it was that made you so sad in the café."

"Oh."

The guilt that's been my companion since that unbearably hot morning shoots up and clouds my thoughts.

"It's about John, isn't it?" he asks.

"Yes."

"You feel guilty, somehow. You think it's your fault that he died."

"Yes." The tears well up in my eyes, betraying my guilt like watery beacons.

One spills down my cheek, and Paul reaches over and strokes it away.

"It's not."

I shrug, not trusting my voice to speak.

He says nothing, only watches, wiping away other tears as they fall from my eyes toward the pillow.

I sniff, a wet, ugly sound in this elegant room, but still, he waits.

"That morning…" I say, not to purge my guilt but to fill the empty space.

He watches, and I breathe deeply—in-out, in-out—trying to find the courage to say it.

"That morning…before he left, I was angry. Angry because he woke me from a nightmare, a nightmare with Fielding and all his awful depravity. Angry that he didn't know that I had been attacked by Fielding just the day before…" I wipe my eyes again.

"That morning…John saw the scar on my back for the first time. The one that Fielding left there with his belt…."

The tears are flowing freely now, and it's hard for me to talk without croaking, but I keep going. The words keep erupting from me like little bombs. "When he woke me I hit him—accidentally—because I thought he was Fielding. Then he asked me about the scar and it…undid me.

The fact that for years and years that scar—and others like it—had been there, taunting me, and John—the man I loved with all my heart—didn't see them. My knees were scraped and bloody from just hours before and he didn't see! And I was so angry that I'd done so much to make things work and those little scars were there, and I'd finally fought back and won, and was it too much to ask to have him notice? My own husband? How could he not have seen them? I *needed* him to see them!"

I sniff and breathe, but I can't stop. I sound like a crazy person, but Paul's hand is on my arm, encouraging but not pressuring.

"He couldn't understand why I was so angry, he was so blind to my problems, and when he left I couldn't bear it anymore. I couldn't fake that everything was happy-happy-happy and I was all okay. When he said goodbye—his eye already bruising from my flailing—I turned my back on him. I turned my back on the man I loved and supported and did *everything* for, and he just left…He walked out the door, and I was so angry I didn't say goodbye…and he never…he never came back…"

I can't stop crying. I can't breathe and I can't see, and my body is shaking with effort and grief. Paul slides closer and enfolds me in his arms and just holds me.

"I don't know how that plane went down," I say, my words muffled by his chest, my tears soaking his skin. "The reports say it was the lightning, but the day before Fielding had threatened to take John down if I didn't… and I…I fought him! Buddy attacked, and Fielding was furious. And the *next day*…the very next day, John left and never… never in all of our time together did I let him leave without saying goodbye. And the one time I did… that one time was all it took."

My heart is so sore, and there's so much more to it than that, but it's hard to explain this guilt—the years of lies, the years of cowardice, of not standing up to Fielding, of being too afraid to do what I should have, and then this awful knowledge that threatens to choke me and drown me. I fought both Fielding and John, and where did it get me?

Paul pulls back, and I think that finally I've done it—I'm too broken for this kind, compassionate man—but he puts a hand on either side of my red, tear-soaked face and once again he forces me to look into his eyes. They aren't accusing, they're calm. Solid. Real.

"It's okay," he says.

He wipes my eyes with his thumbs, and I sniff again, trying to stopper the flood. He waits patiently as I sniff and drip and breathe. The hiccupping breaths calm and he waits—watching without judging. And when the storm finally passes, he bends forward and his lips meet mine; and without saying a word, he meets my grief and sorrow with the only medicine that can heal my raw, broken heart.

The night passes and we wake up as the chimes start to call people to disembark. There's no rush—my flight leaves in the evening—so we eat a quiet breakfast, and I walk down the hall to pack the few remaining items into my suitcase. We leave the ship together, and I go with him to his hotel by boat-taxi so he can drop his cases. The wind in our faces is loud and smells of fish. We walk the beautiful streets of Venice together, and then it's time for me to go. I've stopped looking for Fielding, he seems to have disappeared, but it's good to have Paul with me. He's like a bridge between my life here and my life there, and he's big and safe, and he seems to care for me.

Why is it that time slows down when you want it to speed up, and speeds up when you want it to slow down? It seems minutes and I'm standing at the security gate, saying goodbye to him. A quick kiss, a gentle hug, a few whispered promises, and I'm off to my plane, saying goodbye to a happy memory, and heading home to a home that will never be mine.

CHAPTER 30
TRANSITION

Late May, 2009

THIS MOVE IS AGONY. NEVER before has the leaving of one place and the setting up in another been so painful. In some ways, it's a good pain, like the healing of a scab, or the stretching of sore muscles. As much as I hate to say goodbye to life in the cracked-concrete houses of military quarters, I'm happy to be in my own place, a place that I alone picked. But in other ways it's a raw, digging pain that goes deep inside, scratching and pulling at the fragile box I've built around my heart.

I'm leaving John, and all of the life we had together. It's the finality of it. John is gone, John is dead, and the new house has nothing of his smells and none of his memories. All that is left are the photos and the furniture that he once touched.

The kids have gone ahead to the hotel, giving me space, and I walk through our quarters one last time before the move. Buddy's nails click solemnly behind me. The life I had is now packed into boxes and the furniture is wrapped, and I see the empty space that once held John's sandals. I want to be strong and move on, walk away without regret, but the packers have unknowingly destroyed a shrine, a place of memory. I sit on the floor with my back against the wall where I sat once before, looking at the space where the sandals and the mat once sat, at the dirty white tiles, sandy from the in-and-out of strangers as they unfeelingly threw memories in crates. Buddy flops down beside me. His head is warm on my lap, but the tile is cold, just as the house is cold, and I wrap my arms around myself and stare—willing it all to change and return to what was.

It doesn't.

John wore those sandals around the house everyday, took them off when he left, and put them back on when he came home, so I know they were the last thing he touched here on the day he died. If I could have that moment back, the angry, spiteful words, the selfish lack of goodbye, I would hold him, tell him how sorry I am for all of the lies. He would have helped me. He would have left everything for me, probably would have led the charge to find Fielding, but I never gave him the chance. And that hot, dark, stormy morning I was angry at him for not seeing my pain when I'd hidden it all from him. I hurt him emotionally and physically with my own self-loathing, and then he left without a word; and whether it was Fielding, John, lightning, the other pilot, the maintenance crew, or just a tragic, sad accident, I have no doubt that my selfish actions that morning contributed to John's death and the death of his crew.

The empty white space across from me screams its accusations and I listen, but I don't cry today. I will always have this burden. Paul has tried to help me with it, over long telephone conversations across the Atlantic, but it is my own cross, my own chain I must carry.

I'm sorry, too, for falling into Paul's arms so quickly after John's death. I've told few people—only Jennifer and my mother who were both surprisingly positive about it—but I have yet to tell the kids. The guilt, the betrayal of John's trust is too heavy on me yet. Paul has called almost daily, and talking with him keeps me sane, but throws me into a spin of upheaval. His voice lifts me up so high—galvanizes me, supports me—and the dial tone at the end crashes me down again like phone calls with John so long ago. I want Paul here, I don't want him here, I want to be in London, and I want to be in my own space. I'm confused and lost and solid and sure, and each day brings a new jumble of emotion.

I can't sit here forever on the tiles. I have to go. The final steps out this door will be hard, so very hard to take, because I know I'm not coming back. The kids will be here tomorrow, directing traffic, while I head to my new cottage at the beach…alone.

I wait for the tears to come, but they don't. So I pat Buddy's warm head, stand up, brush myself off and breathe deeply, searching for the strength to walk away.

In the end, nothing changes. I open the door and the night breeze hits me, fresh and sweet with spring.

"Goodbye John," I say, hoping for release, but it doesn't come.

And then Buddy and I walk down the stairs, taking it all with us instead of leaving it behind as I close the door.

CHAPTER 31
TRANSITION

Early June, 2009

A THOUSAND CHAIRS FILLED WITH A thousand people. I have to walk by every single one of them to get to my chair. I know, somewhere in my tired heart, that this is a sign of respect for me and for the other widowed women who walk with me. But it's like the military powers that be have cooked up one last torture, one final abuse to heap onto my shoulders and crush me into the pristine cement hangar floor. They are silent, some staring at the floor, some staring at their hands, some staring with sad eyes at me, or my children, or the women beside me who walk in their own private hell. I don't search out their eyes, but I see them anyway as I walk down the aisle formed between row upon row upon row of metal chairs. So many eyes filled with so many memories of men who will not breathe again.

After a full year of exploration and enough money to feed this entire hangar of people for twenty years, the great force that leads our armed forces has raised the bits and pieces of the aircraft that our husbands, fathers, brothers, and sons died in. They found their precious black box, and the investigation into what actually happened continues.

What remained of our loved one's bodies were privately interred yesterday and the days before, in a simpler moment of hell. Perhaps eager to show that they have overcome the beast that is the ocean, they have planned this memorial service to 'bring closure to the Wing and to the Air Force as a whole'.

I don't need closure.

My husband is dead. His eyes closed, my life closed, and my world closed on that day.

For me, this asinine ceremony marks the last time I will bow to the military's will. They have taken all they can from me. My husband, my house, my innocence, and the life I knew. They took it all. Can't they leave me alone? Just when I was starting to feel human again—*bam!*—they cook up another torture to squash me like a bug.

I came today to show that I will not be broken by their taking. Somehow, deep below the thousands of layers I have heaped upon myself to get through the years under their rule, I am still me. Still Ellen. I am opening my own doors now. I am running my own show.

I pull my shoulders back and walk tall with the small procession of women, men, and children to the front row. I walk proud, eyes up, not down. The year has held me down, but my friends and my family have helped to pull me together. And Paul has shown me that I'm not alone.

Had I been downcast like the others, I would not have seen him standing there in the front row, watching. But my pride puts me eye to eye with my nightmare.

He stands there, with his shoulders covered in gold and his chest covered in ribbons, like he belongs in the front row, in a position of honour. All proud and smug like these men meant something to him—like he feels their loss as we do. *Him.* A chill runs up my spine and my breath catches, but I don't stop. I can't stop. I am surrounded by what is left of my family, and if I were to stop they would ask what is wrong. My secrets hold me still.

A wave of hatred so strong and so heavy squeezes my heart and my lungs, and I want to scream. I force that hatred into my eyes, glare the daggers I wish I could throw into his heart, his chest, and his crotch, and then turn from him to the reason I'm here.

John.

His 'just-in-case-I-don't-make-it' picture, with uniform and flags and an easy smile, is blown up to almost life size at the front of the room, watching me. Huge bouquets of lilies stand on either side.

Oh, John. Why did you leave me alone?

You can do it, Els, he seems to say. *I believe in you.*

But...

It's time, Els.

I hear his voice in my head, loud and clear like he's beside me. Does he know, now, what I have done? Can he see the past? Does he know what I lived through for twenty-five years, believing I was saving him when really I was killing myself? And does he know, up in the place people go when they die, that I hate, hate, *hate* everything about it? Does he also know, that my heart has shifted, searching for love and finding lust and friendship in an old flame?

It's time.

Time to what?

I have to walk by Fielding to get to my seat, but I refuse to let my eyes leave John. He anchors me, steadies me, holds away the hatred that threatens to choke me. I don't look away, even when the Master of Ceremonies says we can sit. I know just behind me is Bob Saunders, John's old friend, and not far from Bob is my best-est friend. Jennifer actually flew across the country to be here today. John's parents, my parents, so many people to support the kids and me. Paul wanted to come, but didn't. This is something I need to do with out him.

I don't turn around to find support, even when they read the list of names. I flinch—Oh, God why are they making us relive this again?—when they read John's name, but my tear-filled eyes stay locked on the photo.

And then it hits me.

I have nothing left to lose.

I have nothing left for them to take.

They do not own me. They do not own my house, my job, my life.

I am my own dependent.

Independent.

John seems to smile even harder up there on his pedestal. He seems to nod and smile and say *it's okay, babe, you can do it*. I must be losing it completely, but I don't care.

Someone speaks, says a few words—explains the meaning behind this year-late farce. Someone sings and someone reads, and then the last post plays, lonely and sad and haunting. I cry, not because of John, but because I feel this cord that's been pulling beneath my ribs for as long as I can remember—pulling and crushing and thinning me out—this cord is loosening. I feel it still there, but letting go, and I think that it's changed into something different. A tight strength.

When the moment of silence has passed, and the piper's lament is played, the band strikes up one more time, our signal to file up, say our last goodbyes to the symbolic photos in front and walk away. The huge crowd stands in respect of the widows, the fatherless children, the parents without sons. I glance at Bob behind me.

I don't know if he understands my unspoken question. How could he know? But he nods, in much the same way I felt John, or the photo of John, nod. As if to say, it's time. Close to him, Jennifer smiles her support.

The hatred is still there, burning inside me, but instead of pushing me down, it's holding me up.

I walk up to John in picture form, kiss my fingers and press them to his lips. He smiles at me, encouraging and somehow solid. A small corner of my brain notes that the band has stopped, is changing music. The noise of shuffles, coughs and weeping lingers over my head.

Then I turn around, take seven confident steps forward and slap General Frank Fielding as hard as my independent arm will allow across his evil, twisted, hateful face.

The snap rings out across the crowd in the silence between songs. People gasp from their places by hard metal chairs, look shocked. Some of the women in the second row lean back and screech, eyeing me like I'm a psychopath on the loose. Some of them—just a few—look as if they wish they had done the same thing. Bob Saunders steps through the chairs and comes to stand at my side as Frank Fielding holds his cheek. I dare him to reciprocate, narrowing my eyes and facing him without flinching. I feel, rather than see Jennifer step firmly to my other side.

"You have nothing on me now," I hiss.

There is nothing he can do to me. No threat against John to hold me captive. No more promotions, no more risks of drug charges or court martials or plane crashes. No way to hold my future in his sadistic grip, because my future, for the first time in twenty-six years, relies only on me.

Mrs. Fielding stares at me, holding her husband's arm in dismay. She has no idea why I'm standing here, palm stinging and heart threatening to pound through my chest. She looks at me and looks at him, back and forth like we're a tennis game. Fielding's face is hard and his eyes are black. The band starts to awkwardly play again, but no one is listening.

"Frank?" she asks. "What is going on?"

The entire hangar seems to lean forward in anticipation of his response. What *is* going on?

Two military policemen appear from nowhere—hands resting on their gun belts—and stand on either side of me, ready to take me away. They see me, the sane one, as the danger because I am mourning a uniform, not wearing one. I see Fielding's eyes calculating, and I know that it's my time, my place to act. If I wait, the time will pass, and I'll be just another widowed woman, gone insane in my grief.

"I have witnesses," I say, and stare him down. There's just the briefest glimpse of fear in his eyes, but it's all I need. It buoys me even more, and I grow solid and strong. The power stays with me.

I turn to Bob, who nods, and then I turn to the policemen beside me. "Gentlemen, if you'll come with me, I've got something to tell you. Something you may be interested in."

The fear in Fielding's eyes grows.

"Frank?" Mrs. Fielding says, and I still feel an odd mixture of pity and hatred for her. She has no idea what has happened here. None at all. Her world is about to turn upside down, but after all of this time, mine is finally righting itself.

I smile at him, a cold, hateful, vengeful smile, turn on my heel and walk away—Bob, two military policemen, Jennifer, Beth, and a thousand others behind me—leaving only Frank Fielding and his confused wife standing between the chairs.

When we get outside the building, I stop and turn to look at Bob. The policemen and Beth stand beside us quietly, unsure of what I'm doing. The sky is clear and blue and bright, and the dandelions poke their heads up through the cracks in the cement, celebrating spring.

"Will you support me in this?" I ask. He knows what I mean.

"I've carried this secret for twenty-six years," he says. "I will do whatever it takes, Ellen."

I nod and turn to face Jennifer, who nods as well. I've never told her outright the damage that the monster known as Frank Fielding caused me, but I'm sure she knows.

And then I square my shoulders and face the policemen. My heart is still pounding in my chest. My ears ring with the tension of what I'm about to do.

"I'm sure you're wondering what that was about."

They stare at me, and I can almost hear their thoughts. They think I'm unstable. Loony. Crazy. A deranged widowed dependent.

More people are filing from the building, women coming toward me with smiles and uniforms with grim faces. I'm not ready to see them, yet. I need to get to the point, a point that I've barely even admitted to myself for all of this time.

"I would like to come down to your office and make a formal charge of three counts of rape, sexual assault, or whatever you want to call it, against General Frank Fielding."

Their eyes literally bulge out of their heads. This was not what they were expecting. Bob stands there, steady and still. Beth looks from me to him but there is no trace of shock on her face. I'm pretty sure she already knows this story. I wonder if Bob warned her, long ago, to steer clear of that awful man. And Jennifer grasps my arm, her support evident in the gentle pressure of her fingers.

"I also want to tell you about threats he made to me against my husband, Major John Michaels, and his crew on the day before they died."

"Ma'am," the taller, dark haired one finally blurts out. "These are serious charges. We may need to involve the civilian police force. Are you sure?"

Are you serious? They want to know if I'm sure?

"I don't care *who* you need to involve. That man has to be stopped."

They look at each other and shift their feet. More people come out. One woman, a complete stranger, looks at me with a strange look of hope. I smile at her before I glare back at the military policeman. I really don't want to be here when Fielding comes through that door.

"Uh, okay," he looks me up and down like he's searching for visible signs of violence. He obviously comes up short. I want to kick him for his ignorance.

"I have a witness," I say, eager to get away from here.

"Well, if you'll just follow me in your car, we'll head down to the office where we can talk about this."

"Not just talk," I say.

He nods, but doesn't answer.

As they walk away, Frank Fielding slams open the door of the hangar and surges toward me. His wife hurries to keep up with him. His eyes are locked on me, and his anger is a palpable force as he strides forward, grey-black hair flipping, like an evil gust of wind. I can't help but flinch. For the briefest of moments, I'm nineteen again, and he's standing in front of me, belt in hand. Bob reaches out and grabs my arm, steadying me. Jennifer's grip tightens, and Beth gasps. Fielding ignores them all, and I force myself to stand strong as he barrels ahead until Bob steps forward and puts his hand out, standing in front of me.

The military police join us, one on either side of me, Bob out in front.

"You'll pay for that, Michaels!" he yells, "Out of my way, major!" He shoves Bob's hand aside and tries to push him out of the way. Bob is thirty pounds heavier than he and stands firm, eyeing him like a nasty bug.

"Sir?" the dark haired MP says.

"How?" I yell back at Fielding around Bob's shoulder. "How will I pay? You going to rape me again? Beat me up? Attack me in the woods? *Threaten* my husband?"

His face is so red it's almost purple. His eyes are black pits, and a vein throbs in his temple.

"You wives are all the same," he says, attempting to push between Bob and the MP. "Fucking *sheep*. You *deserve* what you get."

The crowd around us is growing. The kids have gone ahead with John's parents, and I am thankful for that because Fielding is oblivious to the eyes and ears around him. I think he's lost it.

A media guy starts to flash pictures.

"Sir? You may want to…"

Mrs. Fielding looks like she might cry. "Frank?" she says, standing as close as she dares. "What's going on?"

"Major! Move!" Fielding yells, "That's an order!"

Bob, to my everlasting relief, doesn't move.

"Sir, I really think you should settle down." The second MP is standing next to Fielding now, attempting to screen him from the watching eyes of the crowd.

"Frank? Let's go now, okay?" begs his wife.

"Fucking sheep!" He screams. "Sheep! And the only one who misses your useless husband is you!" he says.

He's gone too far. I'm so done with all of his insanity. I close my fists and stand taller, ready to do whatever I can to make this evil man hurt, but the MP's have—by some unspoken signal—moved forward and are holding him by the arms. He shakes one off, then hauls back and turns to punch the other. But the MP—younger, stronger and better trained—catches his fist like it's a child's ball. He twists Fielding's arm behind his back and smashes him down on the ground in one quick, precise movement. Fielding's cheek mashes into the cracked cement, bits of sand stick to his forehead.

"Frank!" Mrs Fielding does start to cry—big, mascara-running tears.

"Sir, I'm going to have to ask you to come with us, down to the office," says dark-haired MP—Sampson. I read on his name tag as he pulls out a laminated card and starts to read Fielding his rights, but Fielding just ignores him.

I look at my nightmare in disgust. Bob steps back, and Jennifer stands beside me, and I watch in revulsion as Fielding sweats and writhes and screams obscenities at the MP's.

And then I turn my back on him. I turn my back and take one step, and then another, away from the crowd and Fielding's anger and his wife's tears. I walk away from his dominance and my fear, from the military and the lies—from the ingrained compulsion to do anything and everything a ranking officer says I have to do. I leave my husband's uniform behind me and I walk to my car and slide in to the driver's seat.

I sigh, rub my eyes and put my key in the ignition. I put the car in gear and prepare to tell my story to loved ones and complete strangers who may or may not believe me.

It's a wonderful, terrifying feeling.

But I'm ready.

CHAPTER 32
SOPHIA BEACH...HOME

June, 2009

I'M DRIVING BACK TO MY cottage after a long, hard week of meetings and interviews and questions. So many questions. Questions from my children, questions from my friends, questions from the police. Questions about pain and loss. I'm talked out and so tired I want to just crawl into a bed and sleep, but I can't do that. I need to be back in my own space. So I buy a latte and tune my radio to a station I can sing along with and drive home to the beach.

I feel the tension draining from my shoulders as I drive away from that place, knowing that Fielding is—at least for the time being—locked in a cell where he belongs as they try to sort out the stampede of women now willing to admit the horrors they went through under his hands. At least twelve women so far, and a few more anonymous callers, with stories of strange, sadistic, scary behaviour. He preyed on the weak— lost, lonely—and often pregnant—women, stalking them in his black sedan and attacking them when they were most vulnerable. They're even reviewing the black box and the fuselage of John's plane for signs of sabotage. I feel stronger knowing I wasn't alone in my fear of him, but I'm sad in that too. How many more women are too afraid to come forward? How many lives have been ruined by his vicious gaze? And will he really pay for his crimes?

As I drive down my little street in the fading light, I see a strange car in my driveway and I swear. A reporter? A cop? The car is grey and nondescript; it could be anyone. I don't want to talk right now, and I certainly don't want to deal with a stranger. For a brief moment, I fear that Fielding has gotten out and is waiting for me here. God knows what he would do. I drive up and cautiously get out of my car, keys between my fingers in defence mode. The car beside me is empty. I walk to the back door and unlock it, flicking on the lights as I go. Buddy barks happily, runs to pee, and then disappears around the front of the house. I call him but he doesn't come and doesn't bark. There's no sign of the mysterious driver.

Fear creeps around my chest, so I relock the door from the inside and walk through the house, searching for signs of someone.

And then, from the kitchen window I see a man sitting on my deck, looking down at the beach. Buddy sits beside him, tail wagging.

"Hello?" I call, loud enough that the person outside could hear me. Who would be sitting on my deck, here? I've only lived here a few weeks. Most of that time I've spent driving to and from the base. No one knows me in this town.

Buddy stands up, barks happily, and flounces to the front door.

The man on my deck turns and I see the flowers in his arms. I don't need to see his face before a smile breaks out over mine—because I know without seeing who it is. I know the wide shoulders, the dark hair, the big hands holding the flowers. It's been only a month since I've seen him, but when I see his grin, a thousand things pop into my head that I want to say. My heart jumps from the pit of my stomach to somewhere flying outside of me. The grinding, oppressive, emotional millstone of the week evaporates, and I'm suddenly light and happy, and my grin echoes his.

He steps to the patio door, flowers in hand, and I can't unlock the door fast enough to get into his arms. I throw it open and vault forward, feeling twenty again, not forty-something. He wraps his arms around me tightly, and I'm crying and laughing and marvelling that he would come so far to see me—only me—because why else would he be in Sophia Beach? He lifts me up like I weigh nothing at all, and then throws the flowers on the table before holding my head in his hands and kissing me soundly and firmly, banishing any doubt that he missed me too.

"You're here," I say, breathless.

"Where else would I be?" he asks.

"London."

"I'd rather be here."

"Really?"

"Really. Are you okay?" he asks.

"Yes…no…I am now," I say. It's been such a crazy time.

"Fielding?"

"In jail, for now."

"Good."

"When did you get here?" I ask.

"This afternoon… I saw the news."

"It's kind of hard to miss. It's everywhere. He was a sick, sick man."

He nods, looking around the cottage. It's filled with soft evening light. Buddy—not as young as he used to be—has already crashed on his bed, watching us with his head on his paws. My new kitten stands from the loveseat, stretches, and waddles over to him. Buddy looks at us with woebegone eyes as she snuggles into the crook of his leg.

I laugh, because I can.

"Can you stay?" I ask, suddenly shy. I want him to stay. I want him here with me, in this safe space.

He grins. "I thought you'd never ask!"

His grin is infectious, and I let it wash over me.

"I brought you something," he says.

"Really? What?" I look around, but all he has brought inside with him are the flowers, and I've already seen them. He holds up one finger, still smiling. "Just a sec."

Buddy sits up and we both watch as Paul walks out to his car. For just a second I worry that he won't come back, but he does, rolling an efficient, expensive looking suitcase.

He slides his hand down into one of the pockets, and pulls out what looks like magazines. He lays them out reverently on the dining table and I step over to look.

They're university calendars. For universities right here, along the Atlantic Coast but also for universities in England, where he lives. I flip through them, colours and words and possibilities laid out before me like dreams.

"They're…universities," I say.

He nods.

"I know you wanted to go. And now...well there's nothing holding you back, is there?"

He's right, of course. There's nothing holding me back.

I turn to him, this small gift going miles, even light-years beyond anything anyone's given me—except maybe the cruise from the kids, where I met him.

"Thank you..." I say, and reach up and kiss him. His lips are soft, like I remember, and his big, strong hands surround my hips and pull me closer, my stomach doing little flip-flops and flutters in response.

He breaks away, leaving me breathless and hungry and wanting, but he smiles again, this time a dangerous, needy smile—not a playful one.

"Got any plans tonight?" he asks.

"No..." I whisper, "No plans at all."

He leans down, and when he kisses me again I let my heart feel what it wants to feel. No lies, no anger, no guilt. No oppressive fear. No one and nothing telling me how to act.

I feel nothing but happiness.

Just pure, independent happiness.

AUTHOR'S NOTE

This story, including the 'Air Force Administrative Regulation' at the beginning of the book, is fictional. Sadly, sexual assault in the military setting is all too real. If you have experienced or witnessed inappropriate, non-consensual or harmful sexual behaviour of any kind, please know that there are resources available to help you.

If you need emergency attention, or are in immediate danger in Canada or the United States, dial 911.

In Canada, the Sexual Misconduct Response Centre is available for members of the Canadian Armed Forces. Call 1-844-750-1648, 7am-8pm, Monday to Friday. You can also contact your local rape crisis centre.

SafeHelpline.org provides online support 24/7 worldwide for members of the American Department of Defense community, and offers a free, confidential hotline service at 1-877-995-5247. Links are also in place for a secure chat service, and online app. Victims/concerned citizens can also text 55-247 within the US to find local resources.

ACKNOWLEDGEMENTS

This story has not been an easy one.

It took nine years to nurture and grow from an idea and a few hasty but emotional paragraphs into a published novel, and another three years to become the book you now hold in your hands. Twelve years of thinking, writing, editing and hoping, editing, promoting, struggling and advocating. As you can imagine, twelve years of work means twelve years of support. There were many, many days where I just had to put it down. Without the support of a long list of amazing people I'm not sure I would have ever gotten up the courage to see it through to a novel form, and without your continued support and encouragement I wouldn't have pushed on to create the Fortunate Frog Fiction edition. I'm sure I'll miss someone, so if you've helped me in any way, please know that I am grateful.

To the military spouses of Greenwood, NS, you may not know it, but a long time ago I started writing words down because of you. You were brave and strong, and made me think of the fears of every military spouse. The first words came from you. And to the hundreds, maybe thousands of military spouses I've met and talked with since that time, your stories and courage kept the spark alive in my mind.

To my original online critique group: Tina Moss, Yelena Casale, Kristi Jenkins and Jen Duffy, thank you for reading my drivel and not telling me how bad it really was.

A second continued thank you to Tina, for pushing me to submit to just *one more* agent after years of rejections…the one agent that counted.

To Frances Black of Literary Counsel, you are amazing! From fantasy YA to a deep, raw adult fiction, you didn't even bat an eye when I sent you *Dependent*—and you encouraged me to keep my dream alive with this new edition. You are the best.

To the many folks who read *Dependent* as it grew into this novel: Tracy, Rachel, Jacquie, and my sister Kathy, thank you for sharing your thoughts. And to the many others who supported the idea of *Dependent* before they read a word. Whether military or civilian, family, friend or fan, your support has been invaluable.

To my parents, who never stopped believing in me. I am blessed to call you Mom and Dad.

To my children, who deal with dust rhinos, boxed food and frazzled mom on a daily basis, thank you for just being you. You are unique, intelligent and amazing. I love you.

To Vicki Morrison, thank you just doesn't seem enough. You knew the worth of *Dependent* before I did, before you even read it. Thank you for pushing me to finish it.

To the people who read the first edition and honoured me with a review, whether good or bad, I thank you. And also to the veterans, serving men and women and military spouses who came to hear me speak, shared their stories and suggested my book to friends, your comments and support helped me to polish further, and to make *Dependent* even better.

And to Tom, who read it first. In a world with so few happy endings, I am always and eternally grateful that you are mine.

www.ingramcontent.com/pod-product-compliance
Lightning Source LLC
Chambersburg PA
CBHW051432170626

46809CB00006B/2429